WE WILL NOT BURN

THE CELESTIAL QUEENS #1

GEORGIA SEREN MILLS

We Will Not Burn
The Celestial Queens #1

Published by Hudson Indie Ink
www.hudsonindieink.com

We Will Not Burn/Georgia Seren Mills– 1st ed.
ISBN-13: 978-1-916562-77-6

For my Grandparents,
John, Jean, Patricia, Alan, Tony, and Shelia.
You are the best people I know.
Thank you for everything.

SkyChangers

Those with the ability to manipulate weather, including the creation of storms, waves, droughts, and sandstorms.

FireBringers

Those with the ability to manipulate fire, energy, and light.

EarthShakers

Those with the ability to manipulate the earth, including the act of cracking, shaking, and moving earth.

MindWonderers

Those with the ability to manipulate the minds of people and inanimate objects, this can be by touch or pure will. They also have the ability to drain others of their abilities.

The Prophecy

Two women, one from the sun and one from the snow, will rise and unite our people. One with the power to control all, and one without, the women will bring about peace… or chaos.

All hail our Celestial Queens.

PART 1

The Strike

They called us frenzied.
They called us uncontrollable.
But we were powerful.
And we wouldn't burn.

PROLOGUE
RAYA

The dawn broke over the horizon in a wave of oranges, reds, and yellows that morning. My mother said it was an omen from the Goddess.

My mother was never wrong.

They came that night. When the sun had finally fallen into its deep slumber and the moon had risen like a phoenix from its ashes. The sky was quiet, and the world paused. It seemed, in that moment, that the entire Earth held its breath.

I heard the screaming before I saw the slaughter.

Tall, faceless, genderless figures cloaked in black, ransacked our village. My mother clamped her hand around my wrist, heaving me away from the massacre. My friends lay beneath my feet, blood dripping from their ever-paling lips. My entire world seemed to slow down. They were too young. Too gentle for such a horrid end.

Why were they doing this?

Fire burned the cottages of our small village and the sound of steel on flesh surrounded us. My mother wept as we ran towards the woods.

And then they took her too.

The sword protruded from her stomach as the cloaked figure ran her through with steel. My mind stilled and I watched my only mother fall to the floor as though she never even existed. I stared at her, willing my own mind to undo the horror that had taken place only moments ago.

A rough hand grabbed my upper arm and dragged me away from her, weakening the ever-present tether that connected every mother to her child.

I was shoved into the back of a carriage like luggage, left to wonder what would become of me as I sat alone. The sound of chaos surrounding me finally began to die out and I thought of my mother, her glassy eyes burned into my memory. Then, I thought of the hundreds of people that were slaughtered that evening and the entire bloodlines lost forever.

They took everything from us.

My heart ached in my chest, breaking softly.

I would never be the same again.

1

RAYA

A SUNBURNT SKY

TWELVE YEARS LATER

"The sky was flooded with ash. The smell of death coated the inside of my mouth. There was no hope."

- OPAL BLOSE, REGIMENT ONE OF THE SAGE GUARD. THE DAY OF THE FOOTHILL'S AMBUSH.

The sprawling fields stretched far beyond my gaze as we crested the hill. I stared out at the open land, wondering how long it would be before I saw it again. An orchestra of sweetly singing birds filled the sky as the evening sun danced playfully along each blade of grass. Grass that tickled my bare feet as I waded through it, grateful for a moment of peace in this life full of chaos. The wind gently lifted the edge of my white dress and my body, too, became one with the elements. I was wind and fire and earth all at once.

"Finally," Alias almost whispered from behind me, as if he had waited years, rather than days, to be here.

We stared in silence at the place we discovered when we were only children, the only place we called home.

"I'll miss it," Alias said. "Will you?"

"Of course I will," I said looking back at him. "But we'll see it again soon enough," I added, attempting to calm our combined nerves.

Alias glanced over at me before taking off into a run, sprinting through the tall, dry grass like the careless child he once was. His laughter touched my bones softly and I followed him moments later. I ran slowly, though, fanning my arms out, wishing to touch every blade of grass I could reach.

The golden light bounced off Alias's cropped, black hair as we laid on a small patch of short grass, staring at the sky, wishing we could float away with the clouds.

"No matter what happens tomorrow, I will always find my way back you." Alias spoke quietly, his strong voice sounding so much older than only nineteen.

"I'm not worried," I said. "They'll have to draft us together." I smiled, but no matter how much gusto I pushed into my voice, even *I* could not truly believe what I was saying.

Alias and I had different skills, we were different people. There was an extremely high chance that we would be separated. I rested my head on the grass and closed my eyes, sending up prayers to a Goddess I did not fully remember.

As the night drew to a close, the sudden thought that everything would change tomorrow dawned on me. Matron Clara was probably already done packing our scarce belongings.

Come tomorrow, we would be drafted and sent to The Foothills to train. Everything would be different. No more escaping the barracks or games. No more hiding from Matron or the younger children that followed us everywhere we went.

I reached out a hand and clamped it over Alias's.

"We'll be fine, Raya, we always are." His words usually soothed me, but today they didn't.

The walk to Matron's barracks was too short and too quiet, as though we knew words were too much for a moment like this. By the time we reached the chipped red paint on the front door, it felt like there was already too much distance between us. Matron stood in the kitchen, listening out for the little ones sneaking out of bed. I turned to Alias.

"So, I'll see you in the morning?" I asked with a smile.

"Yes, in the morning." He smiled back before heading towards the boys' rooms, dragging his feet along the floor as his moved.

My eyes lingered on the decaying home around me, the domed ceilings with old carvings of forgotten Sorcerers and Gods littered everywhere.

We had spent our entire youth in this building. It was one of the less fortunate training barracks, one often overlooked by the Sage Guard. The Sage Guard that I would soon be a member of.

I tiptoed around the nursery Alias and I used to hide in, watching over the youngest members of our 'family'. I slid my finger over the dusty picture frames, laughing quietly at the drawings Matron had framed years ago. My eyes lingered on the picture Alias drew of us, over a decade ago, in the grass. Matron Clara was kind when so many other members of the Guard were not.

She was always more of a mother to us, instead of a trainer like the rest of them. Images of my life before Matron Clara whizzed through my mind. Fire, burning, my mother, but they flew away before I had a chance to cling to them, to understand them.

Tomorrow, our lives would be decided. Tomorrow, we

became real members of society. I swallowed against the dryness in my throat.

I snuck into the girls room, almost tripping over the numerous cots littering the space, and sunk into my small bed with a sigh.

Everything would be fine.

I had been training for this my entire life. We were left in the ferocious woods for days at only twelve years old, using our wits and skills to survive. We were handed a sword before a pencil. Taught to hit a target before being taught how to spell our names—that came after.

The Sage Guard were certain that we must only become scholars after we have bested every weapon and won every fight.

I was the first in the barrack to learn to write my name.

By the time the sun had awoken I was sure I had only slept for two hours, and when I saw Alias's face, it looked like he got the same.

Matron Clara was in a panic, I could never have truly imagined her a solider in the Sage Guard as she flew up and down the stairs, attempting to get everyone over the age of nineteen dressed in their best clothing and next to the door before mid-morning.

I stifled a laugh as Alias trudged towards me in his yellowing, oversized tunic, and brown trousers. He stuck his tongue out in return.

"Ah! None of that when the Guard arrives," Matron snapped. "I want all of you on your best behavior."

Alias fell into line beside me and adjusted his collar. He

looked, His eyes on mine, and he sighed. There was something new behind his gaze. Something troubling him.

"What is it?" I asked.

"Nothing." His eyes roamed over my face wistfully "I'm just trying memorizing your face." He smiled, and I brushed him off.

Alias was my best friend, but he wasn't cold, wasn't calculating like me. I often thought he lacked the guts to become a member of Regiment One. I prayed to every Goddess that I was wrong.

"Don't say that, Alias, we'll be drafted together and then we will spend so much time together that you'll get sick of the sight of me." I nudged his arm before my gaze suddenly snapped to the four carriages trudging up our cobbled driveway. I could feel Alias's gaze hot on my cheek.

A nervous chitter was soon silenced by an even more nervous Matron Clara, as a women clad in black armor and a sage sash ascended the stairs. She was followed by many similarly dressed soldiers, and I sucked in a breath as they swooshed past Alias and me.

"Matron Clara." She spoke clearly and with a slight accent. "I see you've had a large number of children turning nineteen this year." She walked up and down the line of us. Assessing each of us.

Matron bowed slightly; we followed suit. "Yes, Captain Jala, seven in total."

"Anything I should take into account?" Captain Jala asked.

"Crass," she pointed to the boy to my left without hesitation, "is excellent with a bow, he hit the bulls' eye before his ninth birthday." She beamed with pride. Captain Jala nodded.

Crass was assigned a position, no longer a trainee in the barracks; he was a member of the Sage Guard, Regiment Nine. Four more trainees were assigned before Matron turned to Alias.

"Alias, he is a fighter and a great hunter. He is talented with poison and explosives."

Alias winced, I knew how he hated his role, how he hated himself for the lives he had taken to keep our training facility safe.

"Raya." She turned to me, beaming. Clara knew me.

I did not resent my skills like Alias; I was not ashamed.

"I dare say she is the best child I've trained. Fluent in every weapon but strongest in throwing knifes and daggers." Clara rattled off my various skills. "Although…" Her words brought me back from my daydreams. I knew what was coming. I knew what she was going to say. "She is barren."

The words stung me like a slap to the face and Alias grabbed my hand.

"An injury from before she arrived. Our healer is sure of it." The clinical way in which the Guard spoke of my inability to bare children made my skin crawl.

"She and Alias, they are inseparable, have been since they arrived."

I stared at Matron, seeking comfort in her words. Captain Jala stared at us both for a moment.

"Alright, Alias, let's see if you are as good as your Matron says," Captain Jala teased. "Regiment One." Alias's hand tightened around mine. Regiment One. The highest rank for a trainee.

"And, Raya." Jala turned to me and my heart began to pound. Taking a deep breath, Jala looked back to Matron. "An empty womb is not a curse, for a solider it can actually be a blessing." I nodded, clamping down my jaw. "Regiment One."

As the words left her mouth, I felt Alias's arms around my shoulders as he squeezed me into a hug.

"No funny business, you two, let us not forget that this is war."

Captain Jala's voice was stern as she abruptly turned on her heel, walking to the carriages without another word.

War. War that we would be heading toward in mere moments.

Matron almost looked sad as she handed us the bags of possessions we arrived with.

"Be safe, children, and *Sage Guard save our motherland,"* she almost whispered, and the children surrounding her mimicked the chant.

The carriages were worn but sturdy as Alias and I climbed into the one assigned for our regiment; twenty sets of eyes stared back at us. Our barrack must have been the last in their journey. Two jet black horses stood in front of it, ready to pull. The carriage itself wore a thick layer of black paint, the only color a strip of sage green that wrapped around it as a banner of pride. Or warning.

The house became smaller as we rode further and further away, and I finally felt free from the bounds of childhood. I was the master of my own destiny now. Goddess help me.

I stared out the carriage window, watching a foreign world slip by. Monasteries dedicated to saints and sinners flew by, cobbled streets filled with carts, markets selling spices, and lanterns were all covered in flags of burnt oranges, reds, and yellows. The eternal sunset. It was the Festival of Sacrifice, when families would offer up their children over the age of nineteen to join the Sage Guard, to fight in the second Great War. The tradition dated back hundreds of years, ever since the first Great War began and the sky was drenched in fire, like a burnt sun.

Alias squeezed my thigh as the great mountains came into view, the brown and red peaks shot up through the clouds. The other carriage carrying the other children from our "home" veered off. They would all live together at the Sage Guard's biggest compound. Only Regiments One and Two continued their training alone. A small pain dug around inside my heart; would I ever see my family again?

"Listen up!" Captain Jala boomed, catching our attention. "Do not forget that we will be entering Zetka soon and that the Foothills are extremely close to the border… Do not be stupid."

A snicker sounded from a man behind us, Captain Jala threw a deadly stare in his direction.

"You will not move without my say so, understand?" Her stern voice was laced with iron. Her long, almost white, blonde hair hung at her hips and her dark brown eyes seemed to make contact with all of us at once. She was tall and lean like a wraith, her body seemed to move like a dancer.

As we crossed the border into Zetka, Alias slipped his arm around my shoulders, more for his comfort rather than mine.

"Alright?" I asked, looking up at him.

"Yep," he said without tearing his gaze from the world passing around us.

But his eyes betrayed his every emotion.

Alias thrived on control and, here, in this carriage, in this war-torn country, he had none.

Crossing the border was like crossing into a different world, not a different region. The lands were barren, as though everything and anything was afraid to grow. It felt like the whole region was holding its breath, even the sun seemed dimmer.

The carriages were silent and swords drawn, despite the

fact that the foothills were right on the edge of Zetka, it was imperative that we remained on our guard at all times.

Alias squeezed me slightly closer to him. I should've felt safe next to him, protected by seasoned soldiers and their weapons.

But I didn't. It felt wrong.

It felt as though we were riding straight into a trap…

By the time the iron gates of the Foothills came into view, my body was sore from constant tensing. The thick, battle-worn and impenetrable gates swung open with a shriek as we entered the barren gardens of the compound. It was icy and lonely.

A cobbled courtyard greeted us first, and without a word of warning a large, stone, castle-like building stood ahead of us. Gardens of deep green fanned out around it, meeting stone walls tall enough to protect this place from centuries of war. The short spires were clearly used as look-out towers and the gardens were littered with groups of trainees doing exercise drills.

This was the Foothills training barracks. The magnificent training barracks we had been taught to dream of our entire life.

Our carriage stopped abruptly outside something marked "L".

Bathing chambers.

Once unloaded we were ushered inside immediately and pushed into the large building. The room was empty, with the exception of many iron tubs filled halfway with lukewarm water. Any sound from our almost silent group bounced from wall to wall, creating a cacophony of echoes. Our instructions were clear and Captain Jala's departing words sharp.

"Clean and redress in Regiment One uniform."

The newly joined members of Regiment One stared at

each other and the shared tubs. Our training in our home barracks had readied us for anything, nakedness was not something we shied away from.

"Well, this is cozy," the snickering boy from our carriage called to me, nudging me with his elbow. He whipped his tunic up over his head and threw at me. The fabric hit my neck. The other members of Regiment One covered their mouths to hide their laughter.

In three seconds, I was face to face with him and, in another, my fist connected with his jaw. Blood sprayed from his mouth.

I dropped his tunic at his feet. The laughter died quickly, snuffed out like a flame.

"What the f—" the boy started, his voice clogged with the blood from his bleeding nose.

"Raya," Alias scolded me. "You don't need to fight everyone."

I huffed a breath. He knew me too well. How many times had one of our arguments ended in broken bones on both sides?

I supposed that was the byproduct of training children to be lethal.

Regret leached through my bones almost instantaneously.

"I didn't mean—" I began.

"I know." He scrubbed his hands over his face. "It's not the same as it was before, I'm nervous that you'll get yourself hurt," he whispered. We stood in silence for a moment, each of us not sure what to say to the other. I wouldn't change and nor would he.

"Although he definitely deserved it." He smiled, breaking the silence and nudging me with his elbow.

Once calmed, the entire room took a quick dip in the tubs.

The walk back to the main building was freezing and

quiet. I wondered if this was what our life would become now, public bathing and lewd comments, I cringed visibly.

"What's wrong? Group bathing not your thing?" Alias teased, and I smiled back. Rolling my eyes, I allowed myself to laugh.

Group bathing was the least of our problems.

2

JOY
THE SEA IS A LONELY HOME

"Kai, Goddess of sea and protector of Dayra, please send us a bountiful summer and blessed, calm waters."

- A PRAYER FOR THE OCEAN, MOSTLY USED BY THE PEOPLE OF DAYRA.

The reddish-brown vessel, littered with green and orange barnacles, swayed gently in Port Dayra. I floated beside our ship for a moment longer, dwelling in the silent bliss that the water gifted me. Feeling it's reassuring push at my back, forever keeping me safe and warm.

"Joy!" Jameson called in a singsong voice.

I screwed my eyes shut, trying to ignore him until he sung again, his voice louder and shriller. I pulled myself beneath the waves, silence engulfing me softly. Floating gently, my hair a crown above my head, I thought of tonight's celebrations. Huffing a breath as I broke through the surface, I launched into a hasty breaststroke toward the rope ladder. Each time I swam toward the boat, I felt as though I was swimming back to the real world and unwelcome nausea swept through me.

I heave my sodden body up the rope ladder reluctantly, wringing the salt water from my hair when I reached the top.

"That 'drowned rat' look is really working for you, Joy. You almost have me weak at the knees," Jameson drawled from the opposite deck, his long body folded into a broken and lop-sided armchair.

"Really?" I asked sarcastically, before peeling of my sodden shirt and hanging it over another broken piece of furniture that, perhaps in its last (and less destructive) home, might have been a chair. I rolled my eyes.

"Don't forget," Jameson called after me as I left the deck, the sun bouncing off his short blonde hair, "We're docking for Kai'd tonight. Remember, it's a celebration, Joy, maybe put on a dress? Or just your nice work boots?"

I cringed but nodded over at him before disappearing into the cabin. I had forgotten that tonight was Kai'd. This evening, the whole island would come alive for the celebration of Kai, Goddess of the Sea.

There was no point in arguing the demand that every boat must dock during the celebration; it was Dayra's oldest rule, claiming that "we must give the ocean a day of peace and tranquility".

I shivered at the thought, making my way through the cluttered mess that was once was my room. When the twins joined our crew last month, there was no use in demanding space, or privacy. I often longed for the days when the beaten old ship belonged only to me and my parents. We spent hours, sometimes days, floating in the ocean. No plans, no people, and no distractions. Only us. Like we were the only people left on the planet.

But there was no use wishing for things that were

impossible, there was no use dreaming about my own space when everyone aboard our ship shared a room, if not a bed, with someone else. I peeled my soaked underwear and t-shirt off until I stood completely nude, reaching for the sheer orange dress that I hid in the back of my closet, only to be worn once a year on Kai'd.

I huffed a sigh, throwing the dress on my makeshift bed and heading to the basin to wash away the salt and grime of hours at sea. It felt as though I was scrubbing away a layer of my skin. Scrubbing away the protection that the ocean gave me, I felt vulnerable for a long moment and took a breath, straightening my back. I looked through a crack in the planks, it was already way past midday. All boats needed to be docked before the sun began to set.

I washed my body roughly and combed my hair, wrapping my curls up in a satin scarf for protection. The scratchy material of my sunset orange dress ended just before my knees. It sat in two layers, one a tight, stretchy layer that started with two thin straps and wrapped snuggly around my body and the other, a sheer, lighter layer with bellowing sleeves that was placed over the top.

"Wow, Joy," Kassy said from the doorframe, her voice thick with awe.

"You look beautiful," Lacy finished her sister's sentence for her.

The twins were the youngest members of our crew, they joined a few weeks after their fifteenth birthday, although they acted much younger. They travelled from Zetka when their parents had been killed in battle. They were striking, not only because of their beauty but also their pale skin. Our crew had picked up orphans, strays, or defectives from every corner of the continents, but we had never seen skin so icy and pale. I looked down at my own creamy brown skin and then glanced back to the twins. My face split into a grin.

"Thank you! But look at you two." I struggled with the compliment. surely, they were too old for matching dresses.

"Did you find them in the Gally?" I asked, pointing to the gingham printed dresses gingerly. If Jameson struggled to tell them apart before, he would have no hope now.

"Yes! They're great, aren't they?" Lacy said, her north continent accent sharpening her T's and R's.

"Here," Lacy said, passing me a turquoise flower, "Everyone gets a flower today." She grinned before both girls skipped down the hall and onto the upper deck.

I crumpled my face into a sour grin as they left… What had happened to make them so childlike and immature? I dreaded to find out.

"…Seven, eight." I looked up from where my hand rested on Romy's head. At twenty-four, he was short and round, but moved faster than any of us, scuttling like a crab. He looked up through his cropped ginger curls at me. "I only count eight," I called over to Jameson.

"Joy! I'm right here, for Kai'd sake! You don't need to count my head anymore," Jameson argued as he trudged over to me. I smiled smugly before bopping his head with my hand.

"Nine!" I shouted sarcastically. "The family are all here!" My smile lasted only a moment before I headed for the gangplank.

Jameson, Lolita, and I had created the counting game when we first decided to set sail from the Southern continent to the Northern. Lolita, the eldest of all three of us insisted it was the only way to make sure we would all stay together and safe. Not long after, the count went from three to four to five and so on. I smiled down at my scruffy work boots as I recalled those first days when we felt like the world was our own. I looked back at Jameson, throwing him a smile to soften his ego before turning to my left, to where Lolita usually stood.

A small part of my insides turned to ashes.

I took a breath.

No matter how much time had passed, I would not ever stop turning to my left.

I could almost feel her there, see her. The soft, low hum of her voice, the fiery red of her hair, and the way the waves cascaded down her back. The way she smiled. The way she always knew what to say. The way she held me when the sea was rough, and then again when we were much older, giggling and touching with shaky hands.

I closed my eyes and slowly breathed in the scent of the ocean.

3

RAYA
FIGHT OR FLIGHT

"The fire burned for hours and yet touched nothing but the enemies surrounding us."

- AN ANONYMOUS ACCOUNT FROM THE SAGE GUARD. THE DAY OF THE FOOTHILL'S AMBUSH.

Covered in snow and ice, the Foothills could never be our home. It would never be a place to feel truly safe or calm. I supposed that is why they trained us here, to create warriors that did not balk from fear. Despite my first impression of the magnificent building, I realized the realities were much colder.

Snow frosted the grass into stiff peaks that jabbed my palms, and running on icy cobble stones brought on blisters and bruises. During the day, my body ached painfully from our grueling exercises and at night, my mind longed for restful sleep.

But it was too quiet.

Sharing a home with up to twenty other children all at once, with most of them being younger, did not make for a quiet, peaceful home. When living at Matron's, Alias and I would take trips to the tall grass of our field and wish for peace and quiet. Now all I wished for was company instead of silent nights and endless space.

When I finally dropped into sleep my mind conjured up nightmares. They were fuzzy and out of focus, as though someone had dipped them in water. They were all, in many ways, showing me the same thing.

Everyone around me was dead or dying, I couldn't breathe for the scent of blood. The Earth was cloaked in darkness and the sun dared not to rise. My feet would not move, and my body was slack. I felt my insides roar and scream, louder than they ever had before. Louder than they did on that Gods forsaken day all those years ago.

But I could do nothing, for I did not know how.

"If he speaks another word to me," Alias leaned over and whispered to me during breakfast, "I'll be forced to kill him." The sound of Alias's voice pulled me from my daydreams and into the real world.

But the darkness still lingered.

"Are you quite alright, Raya?" he asked, nudging my shoulder with his hand. I forced a smile.

"Yes, fine. Just not getting much sleep," I said, yawning for emphasis. "Anyway, who are you going to kill?" I asked with a smile.

"Opal. You know the asshole you punched in the face?" Alias raised a brow.

"Hmm," I fake pondered for a moment, "No, sorry, I have no idea what you're talking about." The side of his mouth curled up.

"Why are you going to kill him?" I asked, pushing my porridge around the bowl.

"He stabbed me," Alias said calmly, as if describing a pony he had seen in the forest.

"What?!" I choked on my porridge.

"Yep, stabbed me! Right here!" Alias laughed as he lifted his shirt to show me his abdomen. An angry, red scratch sat in the middle of his stomach. I looked at it carefully, it was a nasty scratch, caused by hand-to-hand combat, probably a dagger, but it was a scratch, not a stab wound.

"So, you're planning on killing him… because he nicked you with his dagger?" My tone was light and mocking. He began to argue but after looking down at himself, he stopped.

"Yes, I am going to kill him because he nicked me with his dagger." He smiled as he spoke and I couldn't help but mirror his expression.

"I suppose you've gotta do what you've gotta do, kill him." I shrugged. "I'll help," I joked, laughing into my bland porridge.

"Anyway, how was training yesterday?" Alias asked, looking up from his dry toast.

I paused briefly, wondering if he had already heard and wanted to hear me admit it. I huffed a sigh.

"It was fine, you know training. We run, we fight, we conquer the world…" I trailed off, shoving a mouthful of porridge into my mouth.

"Yes, same for me too. Although I thought I heard something about a tall girl breaking a red-head's wrist?" he teased.

"I did not break it!" I said defensively. Alias stared at me with a grin. "Well, not on purpose!" I sighed dramatically and looked up at Alias.

"The only truthful thing about that statement is that I am tall. And she was a red-head," I said. Alias rolled his eyes.

"Who knew you were so lethal?" Alias asked.

"Maybe you were just slowing me down," I joked. "To be honest, I'm glad to be rid of you!"

"Glad to be rid of me?" Alias countered softly. "I was getting bored of handing you your ass every day on the sparring mat." He winked, and I faked a shocked expression.

"In your dreams, Alias," I muttered, using my spoon as a catapult to fling porridge at him but he ducked, and a pregnant pause sat between us.

"You could never be rid of me, Raya. I'm not going anywhere," Alias whispered softly. I smiled but it didn't quite reach my eyes. The sound of one hundred other people eating and talking poured in from around us, enveloping us.

"Matron did not raise us to be weak." My words were hard. "The red-head and I were sparring, and I broke her wrist," I said nonchalantly. "I've done worse to you." I stood up from the table and ruffled his hair roughly, knowing exactly how long it had taken him to style it.

Alias smiled fondly, before stuffing burnt toast into his mouth.

"Hey," a female voice called from behind me as I wondered slowly to my shared room a few moments later.

I turned and sucked in a breath; it was the red-head from the fight. My eyes darted to the small array of bandages on her wrist.

"Hey," I replied. "Look, I am sorry about your wrist," I

began, tucking my hair behind my ears. She looked confused for a moment as though she had forgotten all about it.

"Oh, don't worry about that, accidents happen, right?" She smiled brightly and I nodded awkwardly.

It was not an accident. She bit me during our fight. Bit me! Did she really think I would let her get away with it?

"I was actually wanting to ask you a question." Her voice cut through my thoughts, and I raised an eyebrow. "About your friend… Alias?"

My mind paused for a moment. Questions? About Alias?

"Ask away," I muttered, looked down at my standard issue trousers and boots.

"Are you two…? Well, are the two of you… a couple?" the girl stammered and ended with a smile. I choked on a laugh.

The thought had never crossed my mind. Alias was my best friend. I couldn't imagine him as anything more.

But then I thought of our fields of wildflowers and our home with Matron Clara. I thought of the way he always made me smile. I thought of how I dreamed my life would be, and he was always there, his strong arms and lovely face. I wasn't sure how I felt because I had never let myself so much as daydream about it. We were family, the only family each other had. I could not risk that. I would not risk that.

"No. Alias and I are not… together. But he is my best friend, he is my family," I responded, finally able to find the words.

"Okay." She narrowed her eyes slightly, as if not quite believing me. "Thanks." A few tense seconds passed slowly. "It's not me who's asking, by the way, Alias is great to look at and all but… he's not really my type." The girl smiled and walked away.

"As you know," Captain Jala's voice boomed across the crowded room, "Next week you will be sent on your first mission across the battle lines."

I glanced across the room and locked eyes with Alias, he smiled uneasily. We had been training relentlessly for three months. My tall body now lean and corded with muscle.

"These tasks may be supply runs to our safe houses in the battle field, weapon distribution, or intel collection. Each group of six will be provided with a seasoned leader and the necessary tech for the job."

My palms began to sweat as Jala's words slithered from my ears, into my brain, then down my back.

"You will all be tested on your ability to work as a team in the field. These missions will be dangerous, and it is likely you may be harmed if you are not careful."

I glanced at Alias again and he pulled an exaggerated fearsome face, making me smile.

"But this is war, and you are soldiers. We have trained you for this." Her words were curt and lacked empathy. She strode from the podium and out of the door.

A small, plump man waddled to the podium once she was gone, pulling a list from his clipboard.

"Group one… intel," he began, and I realized that these were our groups for the missions.

Fear overtook me in one sharp sweep and my knees began to shake. Anxiety reared its ugly head within me, and panic spread around my chest. The night I lost my mother flashed behind my closed eyes. Alias would be sent out on mission, into Goddess knows where. He could be captured, killed by the savage Sorcerers. I couldn't stand to lose anyone else, not after I had lost so much already.

"Pullman, Gracie, Lucy, Gen, Adria, Fordo." The squat man took a deep breath. "Group two… supply run." He took a large, bored intake of breath once more. "Alias…" My ears pricked up at the sound of my best friend's name.

"Opal, Lea, Kida, Lexa, Raya."

Relief pressed down on me so fiercely I thought I might pass out. I could almost feel Alias's excitement from across the room. The rest of the groups and names were rattled off in a series of minutes, but I couldn't hear them. Despite Alias being on the mission with me, the anxiety would not stop running through my veins.

I could not be any less then exceptional on this supply run. I could not lose Alias on this supply run. There was no telling what was going to happen out in the field.

The plump man excused us, and I ran from the building into the icy fresh air. The grassy land around us had become my safe heaven. The place I was so keen to be rid of had somehow become the only safe place in a land of such destruction. All of a sudden, my lungs were no longer big enough for me to inhale the air I needed.

"I know that face." Alias sauntered up to me with a smile.

His smile soon dropped as I turned to face him.

"Raya, are you alright?"

"I… don't know I-I'm having… trouble breathing," I gasped between short breaths. The empty land surrounding the Foothills became smaller and my back began to sweat. I keeled over, resting my hands on my knees.

"Make it stop," I whispered into the cool air.

"Raya, we're prepared for this. I am here and you are too. Imagine everything else is simply melting away. This feeling, it doesn't control you," Alias began the same speech he always gave me when I felt this way.

His words were calming but they did not stop my legs and

arms from shaking, rattling as though something inside them begged to break free. I was a trained warrior, prepared to kill and fight until my last breath with flinching. I had bested everyone in Matron's barrack, won countless fights here already, but the thought of Alias leaving on a supply run had the ability to break me? It didn't make sense. I breathed quickly at first but then slower as the seconds turned to minutes and my palms stopped sweating. On shaking legs, I stood to my full height and sighed. Alias swiped the sweat-soaked hair from my forehead and smiled softly.

"There, easy," he joked, and I choked on a laugh.

"Uh huh, so easy," I said as he rested his arm over my shoulders and guided us toward our rooms.

Safely tucked beneath Alias's arm, I sent a quick prayer to Astrid, the Goddess of Strength, and decided the darkening clouds above were not an omen of our oncoming mission.

My mother would have disagreed.

"Again," our captain barked after each pull up.

My muscles screamed at me, feeling as though my body might split in half. Sweat stung my eyes and soaked into my hair. The training was grueling and brutal.

We woke before the sun and finished long after it had returned to its slumber. I had expected this, but I had not been prepared.

I heaved my body up to the bar again, ignoring the captain as he reached up and tugged on my foot, my breathing heaved and my blood boiled.

"Stay there, Orphan, if you drop you'll be doing pull ups until you die." His grip, although soft, felt as though it was breaking every bone in my body, and my heart hammered so hard I thought it was going to explode. He removed his grip with a smug smile and moved. "Alright, troops, rest," his voice boomed, and the entire group fell to the floor at the same moment.

My muscles echoed the pain over and over again. I was getting stronger, there was no doubt about it, however, my mind was becoming more uneasy, food made me nauseous, and hunger made me want to die.

Sleep was welcomed but always plagued with hideous nightmares. Most nights I ran and ran and ran around the track, narrowly avoiding the snow, until my body couldn't physically run any longer, and only then did I have deep, dreamless sleep.

The days seemed to ebb and flow and merge into each other. Every day the same, come rain or in shine.

I stood in the training center one morning, my eyes fighting exhaustion when the captain strode in confidently, a spring in his step.

"Pair up." His voice was loud and ugly. "Now!"

I edged toward the nearest person, a boy around my height with almost white hair. People did not make friends here; we could have done all of our training together but, to me, he was a complete stranger.

I dipped my head in a nod, and he repeated the gesture. Today we were fighting; it was supposed to be training but everyone here was playing against each other.

My life here was a competition.

And I was losing.

My body was so tired, and it felt so weak. Nightmares clung to my skin like the sun and each day chipped away at my hope for a better life. I found myself longing for Matron's overbaked pies and the smell of burning bread. Matron was born to protect the weak and the ones who could not protect themselves.

She was a terrible cook, but we forgave her for it because she loved us when our parents could not

4

JOY

ALL GUTS, NO GLORY

"Even the ongoing party on the streets outside seemed to quieten when she entered the tavern."

-A DIARY ENTRY FROM ROMY MAS, MEMBER OF JOY AND JAMESON'S CREW.

The streets were packed, from the overflowing color-explosion that were the fruit stands to the hobbling, happy customers from Lucki's Tavern. We clumped together within the crowd, sweaty bodies rubbing up against us.

"Alright, be home by sun-up," Jameson stated loudly to the crew. "And don't do anything I wouldn't do," he said with a wink and our family disbursed.

Romy and the twins disappeared into the glimmer of bright orange and blue fabrics, while Lila and Tuppen scuttled to the nearby pleasure house. Jameson and I exchanged a look before bursting out into a fit of laughter. We be-lined for our favorite place ashore, Laylani's pub, grabbing sticks of smoked meats and sweet mangos drizzled with lime on the way.

"Joy! Jameson! It's been too long!" Laylani barked from across the pub as we pushed the half-broken doors open. She bounded over to greet us, narrowly missing various stumbling customers on her way. She was tall and curvy, just like me, with broad hips and sparkling blue eyes. Her deep red hair reminded me sweetly of Lolita. I couldn't help but smile.

"Laylani, you are looking as radiant as ever," Jameson drawled.

"You would've thought this one might have given up by now," she spoke in my direction, gesturing to Jameson with a tilt of her head.

"Oh, he is a very persistent person," I said with a smile.

"And very handsome?" Jameson looked at me with pleading eyes.

"Plus," I leaded forward slightly and whispered loudly, "he's extremely handsome, don't you think?" I said with a smile, Laylani choked on a laugh and Jameson smacked my arm lightly. "What? Oh, did you want more subtlety?" I gave a faux-gasp and gestured to the brown bottle gathering dust on Laylani's bar. We strolled further inside and slumped onto crooked stools.

"Hey," I said to Jameson while Laylani poured the drinks. "Do you remember the last time we were here?" I rested my arm over his shoulder, stretching slightly to reach.

"Yeah, I remember." He gave a small smile and kissed my cheek.

It had been the night of Lolita's final goodbye. We lit candles on the ship and laid flowers in the ocean. A cool, salty breeze slowly wrapped around us as we laid Lolita's body to rest in the place she loved most in the world. The memory washed over me.

"I thought we'd have more time, my love," I whispered into her hair, my tears landing on her ever-cooling cheeks. "I

miss you; I miss your laugh, I miss the way you make me smile, I miss the way you loved me, and I miss the way you saw the world." I heaved in a deep, shuddering breath. "But I know we will see each other again one day, so I'll miss you and I will keep missing you until we meet again." I let the tears fall against my cheeks, Jameson rested a hand on my shoulder. "I wish you could've stayed." My voice was quiet and calm. "It's time for you to go home now." I pushed her gently into the lapping waves and whispered quietly into the night.

We had come to Laylani's pub after the ceremony. None of us wishing to climb aboard our home without Lolita. We slept on the armchairs and sofas dotted around the tavern, all of us cuddled and squashed together trying to keep warm in the winter months. Part of me knew Lolita was there with us, lulling us into a dreamless night sleep.

"In a strange way it was kind of nice, don't you think? Having all our family together to celebrate someone we loved." Jameson tucked a strand of hair behind my ear. I nodded, fighting the stinging in my eyes.

"Yes, it was nice." I smiled as Laylani slammed the shots in front of us and raised her own glass.

"To Lolita, the life and soul of the party," she cheered, throwing me a smile.

Stumbling outside to gaze at the fireworks, Jameson and I marveled at the celebration that raged on the streets. Paintings of Kai'd and turquoise banners hung from every building. Children drank sweet, blue drinks beside their parents, and teenagers swayed to the vibrant music surrounding us. A priest stood still on the steps of a monastery reciting the prayers of Kai'd to passersby. His hands stretched to the sky and then the sea, praying for blessed tides and ample bounty.

Jameson and I were never religious people, however, praying to the Goddess of the Ocean was something we had done ever since we were children.

I grabbed his hand in mine and whispered the prayer along with the priest. A small smile tucked itself into Jameson's mouth as he began chanting with me. The fireworks littered the sky above us and the prayer wrapped itself around our hearts. I felt full and content for the first time since losing Lolita. I squeezed Jameson's hand when the fireworks ended and cheering erupted from every corner of our island.

"Thank you," I whispered for only his ears.

"Always, Joy. It's me and you, remember? Always," he whispered back and slung his arm over my shoulder, leading us back inside.

The pub seemed to have double the number of customers than before we left. We squeezed between a tall, lean man and a muscular woman, muttering apologies before reaching our seats.

"What the hell's going on, Laylani?" I shouted over the hundreds of voices competing to be heard.

"What do you mean?" she shouted back. I gave her a dumbfounded look, motioning to the masses of people in the small pub.

"It's packed!" I said, and it was like the room itself started to stretch.

"Don't you remember?" She shook her head. "After the fireworks?" She attempted to prompt me. "For Kai'd sake, Joy, the Gias competition!" she shrieked with a laugh as the familiar scene unraveled around me.

Tables were folded away and chairs pushed to the walls.

Two tables stood side by side in the center of the room. Six small ceramic squares sat on each table and the pub quietened in anticipation. Laylani hoisted herself up onto the bar.

"Alright, everyone, you know the rules," she began, "Six rounds and the winner stays on," she shouted.

"And what's the prize for winning?" Jameson asked, knowing full well what it was.

"A year of free drinking!" Laylani cheered, and the bar echoed her call. "Who's up first?" she called, and the game began.

Despite the number of times, especially on Kai'd, that I had spent in Laylani's pub, I had never quite understood the game of Gias. It involved moving the squares and lining them with the black painted patterns facing upwards. If it weren't for the drinking and inevitable fighting, it would bore me to death.

A tall woman, introducing herself as Sam, won the first round and then continued to win the next three. Three middle aged men attempted to beat her but failed. She had a scar from her brow to her lip and dark-black hair cropped at her jaw.

"She's a bit…" Jameson muttered, not taking his eyes away from her.

"Terrifying?" I finished for him, watching the way she threw the dice carelessly… and then threw a table in frustration.

"Round five!" Laylani boomed, and the towering women sauntered around the tables with pride.

"Who's next?" she growled, and the crowd seemed to sink beneath her gaze.

"I'll give it a go," a voice chirped from beside me.

The crowd quietened as a cloaked women wandered into the circle as though she had all the time in the world. This stranger exuded confidence and self-assurance. The room became impossibly quiet, the only sound was her boots against the wooden floorboards. She lifted her hood with the grace of a dancer, her long auburn curls falling around her shoulder blades. She was undeniably and completely beautiful. Her skin was warm and dark, many shades darker than mine. She was of similar build to me, much like many of the women hailing from the southern continent, with swishing hips and high cheek bones.

"Who is that?" Jameson whispered to me as the two competitors stood face to face.

All of a sudden my words became lodged in my throat. I coughed loudly and the stranger turned to me. Goosebumps covered my skin as our eyes met and heat rushed to my cheeks. She smiled and turned away.

"I have no idea," I whispered back, and the game began.

I watched as the ceramic squares were moved with precision by both competitors, and realization dawned on the towering women; this would not be an easy game. The game slammed onwards, and the crowd began cheering.

Who was this strange woman? And what would happen if she won?

5

RAYA

A ROAD WE DARE NOT TREAD

"They left early; I don't remember what time. Everything was normal, nothing was out of place."

- CAPTAIN JALA

We woke before the sky. Donning layers of clothing and weapons, Captain Jala strode from one end of the Barracks to another. I watched her lean body cut through the howling wind, already blowing a gale. I reached for my laces, using all my strength to avoid looking for Alias. Where was he? This was the most important morning of our short military careers. My body felt jittery, it had all morning, as though butterflies were flapping inside my skin, pushing around, trying to get out. I swallowed.

Where is Alias? And as if the gods themselves heard my question, Alias plopped down on the bed next to me.

"Morning, darlin'," he whispered, a smile tucked into the corner of his mouth.

"Where the hell have you been? We're moving out in five," I scorned him sharply.

"Don't worry! I'm here, aren't I?" His tone suddenly became defensive and I eyed him slowly.

"Are you alright?" I asked pensively.

"I'm nervous, Raya," he whispered, resting his hand on mine.

I nodded and smiled. It seemed as though the entire room was feeling as nervous as Alias and I. A buzz of anticipation seemed to suffocate us as I stared at the clock.

When Captain Jala gave us the signal to move out, my heart leapt into my mouth. We had been training for three months and yet I felt like it was still my first day here. I swallowed against my dry mouth, this was really happening. Alias nodded and looped his crossbow over his head. I followed suit and, as one, we began filing out of the building and into the icy courtyard. The world around us was cloaked in night, ominous and cruel.

"You know the rules and you know what to do," Captain Jala spoke over the wind before nodding, turning on her heel and marching back into the building. Was that supposed to be inspiring?

"She's not coming?" Alias whispered to me.

"I guess not."

The group shuffled slowly on the thick ice that sat on the edge of our compound, trying not to slip. Suddenly I felt completely unqualified to be here, every single fighting stance and healing treatment flew from my brain. The cloud of anticipation seemed to follow our group to the edge of the Foothill's compound. We paused. Once we stepped over that edge and into the thick snow, our mission would truly begin. The six of us, and our seasoned leader, Captain Luka, stood at the edge of the compound, no one daring to make the first move.

"C'mon, soldiers," our leader whispered loudly, "It's just snow."

We looked over at one and other, daring each other to go first. Without evening thinking I kicked a leg out and crunched into the soft snow. A deep exhale was heard from every member of our team. Opal Blose was the first to pipe up. "It looks like we've all underestimated you, Rachel." He smirked.

"It's Raya," I corrected him. "Asshole," I muttered before marching after our leader. I stared at the group Alias and I would be working with; a mix of skin colors, eye shapes, heights, and builds.

On paper, our plan was simple. In a safe house, located around a day's walk away, lay Sargent Whels. He was injured in battle, his soldiers managed to transport him to the safe house before being shot down by hidden enemies.

The ever-persistent war sat comfortably on the border that connected the Southern and the Northern Continents. It had been said that Northern soldiers and Southern soldiers had be fighting for land for the last hundred years. But that cannot be the whole truth, can it? A hundred years of war, hundreds and thousands of casualties, all for land? I shook my head and focused on the task at hand.

Assuming Sargent Whels was still alive, we were to stabilize him once we arrived at the safe house, and bring him back. Easy. Two days, maybe three, and we should be back in our icy home. I wrapped my military jacket further around myself, thankful that I decided on three layers rather than the advised two.

Just as the sun began to rise on the empty plain, our leader suggested a break. We weren't to sit in order to keep our muscles from getting cold. So, we stood in an awkward circle and ate various types of hard cheese and nuts. I stared at my shoes.

Something rustled in a lonely tree and that familiar fluttering feeling spread across my skin, but this time it was more intense, almost painful. I winced, stretching out my arm to rest on a tall tree stump. It felt as though something ached against my skin, almost impossible to describe.

I heaved an icy breath and the pain receded slowly, but I felt hollow. A squirrel jumped from behind the tree, a pile of nuts in its paws. The group was silent, all their eyes trained on the now still tree.

"Squirrel," I muttered.

"What?" Opal mused.

"The rustling," I pointed at the tree. "It was a squirrel." I shook my head and heaved my backpack across my shoulders.

We began walking again in a tense silence, snow crunching beneath out feet, our labored breathing the only sound. I heard Alias before I saw him creep up next to me, his familiar gait etched into my memory.

"Are you alright?" Alias whispered as we trudged deep into a white forest, branches snapping underneath our feet.

"Fine," I muttered. The feeling from earlier had lingered on my skin and a headache pounded between my eyes. Alias reached for my arm.

"Raya, what is it?" he asked sternly, and I knew he didn't believe me.

I couldn't tell him about this, though, there was nothing to tell. My skin felt tingly, and my head hurt, that was it. So why couldn't I just tell him? Why couldn't I be honest?

"It's nothing really, I'm just tired." I smiled at him, and he nodded.

“I’m sure we’ll be there soon,” Alias reassured me. “I can protect you,” he said with pride and suddenly, I felt irritated by his constant need to shield me. I could protect myself. I was just as strong and as fast as he.

I was just as lethal.

This time, when the tingles emerged from deep within me, I didn’t mind it. They seemed to agree. I smiled and nodded at Alias.

“Yes, I’m sure we will be.”

Eventually, the sun set completely and the night sky shrouded us. I couldn’t even see my own hand in front of my face. Surely, we would set up camp soon, it was not safe to be out here without our vision. We daren’t light torches this close to the border, so we stumbled and tripped our way through the never-ending forest, praying to every God that would listen, that we would be at the safe house soon.

The night was cold and the darkness of the forest unwavering. Despite our asking and attempt at convincing, our leader, Captain Luka, kept us moving.

“It’s not safe to be in the forest longer than necessary. If we camp here, there is more chance of us freezing to death or being eaten by a wolf.” The leader’s voice was clipped and harsh. The other So we marched on, our toes numb and our spiriting crumbling.

Several hours and twisted ankles later, morning broke as we stumbled from the forest, the sun burning our irises. My legs were jelly and my eyes begged to be shut. Alias was further behind me, barely able to stay vertical. I stared at our ragtag group, some resting on nearby rocks and others throwing up. Twenty-four hours of constant physical exertion will do that to you.

“Okay, soldiers, just a few more miles.” Our leader spoke for the first time in hours. I sagged in defeat.

"We need rest," I said, my voice sounding weary.

"There is no time for rest, a man's life is at stake."

"If we keep going, six more lives are going to be at stake," I argued, my voice stronger than anticipated.

Captain Luka looked from me to the group, each of them barely awake.

"Twenty minutes," he barked and perched on a nearby rock.

We stood in a huddle, holding each other up, scarfing down bread and water.

"That was… impressive," Alias whispered, slyly passing me two squares of chocolate, my eyebrows raised.

"Where did you get this?" My voice was hushed but I couldn't help the excitement that filled me. Chocolate! I hadn't seen chocolate in years, never mind eaten it. I popped a piece into my mouth with a sigh and leaned my head on Alias's shoulder.

My body rested but my mind would not. Thoughts of this mission swirled around my brain, like, how could this mission be planned or practiced if we're going to save a man's life? How could they know he was wounded when handing out assignments?

I glanced at Alias beside me, practically asleep standing up, his face beautifully rested and soft. The sun was slowly taking its place in the sky. Soon I'd be able to feel my toes. Finally, my mind rested, and I nibbled on the other piece of chocolate, perfectly content for a moment.

"Let's go," Captain Luka shouted, waking us suddenly. "C'mon, up! I've let you rest long enough," he said sternly before whispering, "Pathetic," in our direction.

Alias straighten slowly with a frown and I smiled.

"Why are *you* smiling?" he asked, raising an eyebrow.

"Did you hear him?" I asked. "He said that he 'let us rest

long enough,' because we're 'pathetic,' but look," I pointed to him, noticing Alias follow my gaze. "His hair is all messy and his uniform rumpled!" I laughed but Alias still stared.

"He clearly almost fell asleep! Could you imagine? He forces us to stay awake but can't keep his open eyes open?" I said, brushing the dirt and snow from my trousers. "It's the little things in life," I murmured with a smile.

"Right," Alias said, ruffling my hair quickly.

"Let's go, soldiers," the captain shouted. "Safe house is only nine miles out." He heaved his backpack over his shoulder and set off trudging through the snow ahead.

The first three miles may as well have been three hundred, my legs burned and blisters formed on my feet. My body begged me to stop, begged for rest or water or anything other than this constant trudge through the snow. I arched my back in effort to stretch when laughter sounded next to my right ear. I turned suddenly. Nothing.

Nothing but the wind and my own mind driving me insane. But the laughed sounded again, this time in my other ear.

"We know what you are," one voice whispered, its voice dark and old.

"She is only fooling herself," the other voice giggled like a schoolgirl.

"You're lying to everyone."

"Even your precious Alias."

"Oh, how I'd love to rip him—"

"Enough!" I yelled and the entire group turned to stare.

"We're still six miles out, Raya," Alias's hushed voice made flushes of embarrassment spread across my cheeks and neck. I nodded.

6

JOY

LET THE GAMES BEGIN

"They kicked the door down! I hope they do not expect me to pay for that myself!"

- LAYLANI GLASS, OWNER OF LUCKI'S TAVERN.

Laylani threw the victor's hand in the air and the crowd roared so loudly the pub began to shake. She had won, the stranger from the crowd had won. Sam slammed her fist into the table and stormed out of the door, several smaller, crying women following her. Jameson and I cheered so loudly, my throat began to ache. We jumped and threw our hands in the air. This felt like a victory, and we needed a victory. I jumped on Jameson's back and he whirled me in a circle and through the crowd, towards Laylani and the stranger.

"Alright, alright," Laylani shouted to the wild crowd. "We need to know our winner's name, don't we?" she asked, and the crowd cheered again. She turned to the stranger and leaned in close. Laylani smiled and held her hand in the air, the pub silenced almost immediately.

"Our champion, the woman who is drinking in my pub, free of charge, is… Dahlia!"

The crowd echoed her until Dahlia's name was being chanted throughout the entire pub. I smiled to myself, chuckling as the brown beams above us began swaying ever so slightly, as though they, too, were cheering along with us.

I glanced up and Dahlia was looking straight at me. Even though her curly hair covered most of her face, I felt like I saw right into her mind. She smiled a shy smile but one of joy. I sucked in a breath and mouthed without thinking, "congratulations." She smiled and mouthed, "thank you."

Laylani bounded over to me with two shot glasses balanced between her hands.

"I like her," she said, glancing back at Dahlia leaning on the bar and then to me. "She asked me what your name was." Laylani wiggled an eyebrow as I gulped down my drink.

"What did you tell her?" I asked as nonchalantly as possible. She remained quiet. "Laylani?!"

"Alright," she said with a smirk. "I told her your name was Joy."

"And?" I asked.

"And what? She asked me your name and I told her." She shrugged her shoulders, and I rolled my eyes. "Do you have a little crush?" she teased and I scoffed, feeling the blood rush to my cheeks.

"I don't even know her; we've never even had a conversation!" I protested.

"Mmhhm," Laylani hummed. "When I told her your name… she wrote it down," she said with a wink, before pouring me another drink and slinking off into the crowd.

Wrote it down? How hard is it to remember a three-letter

name. I feigned being angry, attempting to murder the butterflies in my stomach.

I stood alone, watching Laylani flirt with drunk customers as Jameson danced with a girl on the makeshift dance floor. I sighed, staring up at the framed oil paintings dotted alone the walls, at one of the women. She was a pirate, a true pirate, like the ones who wore the hats and walked the plank and fought enemies. We didn't really do that anymore; it was too hot for hats and Jameson used our plank as more of a ledge to dive off. We still fought though, I was adamant that each of our crew knew how to fight, with fists and swords.

"She's beautiful" a voice sounded behind me; it was soft but sharp like a velvet-wrapped sword. She stepped beside me with a smile.

"She was more than beautiful," I said quietly, and Dahlia nodded.

"Yes, she was a pioneer, the first female pirate…" she said with a smile. "But she was beautiful nonetheless." Dahlia turned to look at me, her hair brushing against my shoulder.

"I've been told that you're a pirate," she said with a smile, her skin creasing around her eyes. I laughed, turning to face her.

"I am no pirate," I said. "I just like the ocean."

"And I am no Gias player, but I still won the competition," she said taking a sip of her drink, I mirrored the action. "Would you like to dance with me?" she asked softly, trying, and failing, to tuck a curly lock behind her ear.

I smiled, about to accept but suddenly Lolita appeared in my mind. Was I being unfaithful for being attracted to another women? Would Lolita want me to move on and be happy? Did I want to move on?

"I can see your mind working behind your eyes," Dahlia said quietly. "It's just a dance, Joy, feel free to say no, I won't be offended." The sound of my name on her tongue was new and exciting and my breath seemed to quicken.

"I never told you my name," I teased her.

"I know," she said, holding out her hand, and without overthinking it, I took it.

There was something odd about Dahlia, she played Gia and strutted as though she was a street rat, like the rest of us, like she'd been running about the cobbled streets for her entire life and yet when she danced, she was… regal. I walked onto the crooked wooden floor, expecting her to stumble her way through a halfhearted waltz like I was, but instead her body slackened and then solidified as though she was preparing for battle. She glided along the floor, twirling me and avoiding my clumsy feet without a single thought.

"Who are you?" I whispered into her shoulder, and she shuddered with laughter.

We spun around the floor, dancing to song after song and at one point we switched partners, and I was suddenly wrapped in Jameson's long arms.

"Having fun?" Jameson teased over the music.

"Surprisingly, yes," I answered, my face aching from laughing.

"That smile," he said. "It's my favorite." He planted a kiss on my cheek and I held him closer. "The power of Kai'd," he whispered into my ear before spinning me back into Dahlia's arms.

"The power of Kai'd indeed," I whispered to myself.

The night seemed like something from a fairytale, I never dreamed life could be this good since I lost Lolita. Kai was looking down on our island. My thoughts seemed to melt and reform over and over again. It was okay for things not to mean anything, and it was okay for things to mean something too. For a moment, I was happy and carefree, I did not mind the feeling.

The smash of metal against metal woke me from my trance. Two palace guards stood at the threshold of Lucki's Tavern. At once I glanced over at Jameson, he stared back at me, beginning to make his way toward me with furrowed brows.

The music stopped suddenly, flat notes scratching our ears. The crowd shouted in angst and my hand shot out to grip Jameson's.

Three people stood in the doorway, their faces hidden, and their bodies cloaked in black. They reached up their hands in sync and swords materialized from the air. A gasp overtook the crowd and people began to scatter as the beings marched into the room, knocking aside tables, chairs, and people.

It took me a moment to realize that they were stalking toward us. Jameson, Dahlia, and I stood, frozen to the spot. I pushed against my feet, begging them to move but they did not budge. A tear slipped down Dahlia's face.

Jameson stood, his legs shaking, his face twisted into something I had not seen before, more than the confusion or fear that I was feeling. Something different, almost… recognition. The candles seemed to dim before snuffing out completely, and darkness buried us softly.

"It's going to be okay," I whispered, more to himself than to Jameson. I squeezed my eyes shut.

But then the candles flickered back to life and the room came into focus. I breathed in deep, looking over at Jameson.

But he was not there.

I was not holding his hand.

I was holding Dahlia's.

I dropped her hand instantly, hastily looking around the

room for Jameson. I raced around, searching every nook and cranny. But I knew he wasn't there. I knew I wouldn't find him. My mind and my body seemed out of sync. My body wouldn't stop searching even though my mind begged it to give up.

"Jameson!" I cried out, and I felt a hand against my shoulder. My heart burst as I turned, only to find Laylani. Fat tears began pouring from my eyes.

"What happened? Did they take him away?" I turned to Laylani and tugged on her blouse. "They did, didn't they? Why did they take him? Where did they take him?" A thousand questions burst into my mind, but one statement followed my every thought.

I was all alone again.

Why would they take my Jameson? Had he done something? Had he forgotten to pay up after another losing card game?

I crumbled to the floor, unbothered by the hundreds of eyes staring at me.

"Everyone, out," Laylani shouted. "Show's over."

I cried until I couldn't cry any longer, until my body became dry, and I worried that suddenly I would begin to cry tears of sand. As the patrons left, I thought of my crew. They had already lost so much; they could not lose someone else.

"I'm going to find him," I said to no one in particular. "I'm going to find him and bring him home." The confidence in my voice did not waver but hundreds of questions swirled through my mind like smoke. Why did they take him? What could they possibly want with an orphaned ship captain? I had known Jameson for the last ten years and he had never mentioned anything about this. Was it a fluke? Or was he keeping secrets from me? I sighed, standing hastily, aiming for the door.

"Where will you go?" Dahlia's voice rang out quietly. I swung my head in her direction.

"They can't have gone far."

"You will not find them here, not on this island." Her voice was steady and strong.

"What are you talking about?" I stalked toward her. "Do you know where he is?"

"I-I didn't think," she stuttered softly. "I didn't think they would look for me here."

"Who?" I got dangerously close to her now. "Who took him?"

"Hunters. They hunt the continents for… for certain people." She ran her fingers through her hair. "I had been safe here, I thought they couldn't get to me but… I was wrong." She attempted to walk toward me, but I took a step back.

"Why did they take him instead of you?" My voice was deadly and calm.

"I don't know… When you reached your hand out towards Jameson, I took it instead, I didn't think—" I slammed her body toward the wall, my forearm against her neck as I unsheathed my dagger and held it against the soft skin of her throat.

"You sacrificed Jameson to save yourself?" I roared, pushing the dagger slightly, enough to draw blood.

"It's not like that," she struggled against my grip. "I didn't mean to, I can't… I couldn't go back." I pushed the blade again.

"Wait! Wait!" She screeched. "I know where his is! I can take you."

I pulled the blade back ever so slightly.

"Tell me!" I demanded.

"We both know that as soon as I tell you, I am a dead woman." Her voice regained some of its strength.

I seethed, knowing that as soon as she spoke, I would have driven the dagger into her windpipe.

"I'll take you," she whispered, rubbing her throat as my pressure lifted. I tightened my grip on the dagger, striding for the door before I turned back.

"He better be alive when I find him." I threw the dagger with all my strength, and it landed mere inches from Dahlia's face. "Or a dagger to your throat will be the least of your worries."

7

RAYA

DROWNING

"I'm sorry."

- RAYA

The safe house appeared just as the sun soared at its highest. Beads of sweat mixed with dirt dripped down my forehead and back, and even Opal Blose had finally stopped talking. I couldn't find the energy to be relieved. I was losing my mind; the voices had been quiet ever since my outburst. I knew that it wasn't real, but I couldn't shake the feeling of wrongness that seemed to follow me.

I stared at the safe house, attempting to clear my mind; the house was huge, more of a royal mansion. Pale, stone columns stood proudly at the front of the building, their strong structure keeping the building up right. Though clearly eroded from time, the house stood regal and beautiful, with green vines snaking up the wall and large, brown, wooden doors marking its entrance. We stood in silence just before Captain Luka motioned for us to crouch.

"Okay, we believe, from the letter we received from the guards, Sargent Whels is on the ground floor in the second dining room."

"Who needs a *second* dining room?" Alias whispered to me, and I smiled weakly.

"...We move quickly and quietly. Alias, you'll go with Opal to retrieve Sargent Whels, the rest of us will sweep the house. I want us in and out of there in minutes." And with that he rose, checking the long sword at his side and the crossbow over his shoulder.

"See you after?" Alias said as Opal beckoned him towards him.

An odd feeling whirled in the pit of my stomach but I nodded my head. Of course, I would see him after, what other choice was there?

"See you after," I said, giving him a quick hug before jogging towards the rest of my team.

We stalked slowly and quietly towards the house until we stood outside, each of us with our backs flat against the wall. Soon Alias slipped inside, Opal on his tail. Silence pushed against my skin, adrenaline pumping through my veins.

A minute passed, then two, then five, then ten. Alias should be back by now. I looked up at the blue sky, frowning at the clouds blocking the sun. I stared at the door, willing Alias to run through it, Sargent Whels in hand.

"Captain." Alias's crisp voice rung over earpieces; I sighed in relief.

"What's taking so long, Alias?"

"He's not here... Sargent Whels, he's not here."

Silence followed his voice. I stared at Luka, his complexion ashen and stark. And suddenly I was no longer staring at him, I was staring at the white stone behind him. At the red splashed up the wall. His unseeing eyes stared at me from the frozen ground, with an arrow perfectly seated in-between his eyebrows.

The ground beneath me moved as I was dragged into the house, my name on Lexa's lips. Inside the house was chaos, soldiers friendly and foreign fought, some falling, never to get up again. I locked eyes with an attacker, his bow already raised, but I rolled away, pulling out a showing knife, hitting him between the eyes. Another arrow aimed for me but this time I was slower, the sharp steel grazing against my thigh.

Lexa pulled an arrow from a fallen enemy and sunk it into the next. I grabbed her arm, and we charged up the stairs, swords drawn and arrows firing sporadically, almost aimlessly. I slipped on the stairs when Lexa's grip on me loosened as she fell, an arrow lodged in her chest. Her face was a mask of surprise and sadness. I reached for her, but I was not fast enough.

"I'm sorry," I whispered, knowing she was already dead. Our team seemed to be falling, one after the other. I tripped over Opal, alive but hanging on by a thread, as I staggered to the second dining room.

I couldn't see Alias, and the noise of metal on metal prevented my shouts from being heard. Blood coated the fraying carpets as bodies fell.

And suddenly I was nine years old again.

The dead solider at my feet was not a stranger, she was my mother.

The world began to blur and spin, I couldn't let this happen again. I couldn't lose everything again. I blocked a blow from our cloaked enemies and disarmed him in moments, shifting though the crowd of chaos, hoping to find Alias. A heavy sword came down hard narrowly missing my shoulder, the vibrations throwing me forward, onto a dead body.

No not a dead body, it was Alias. He was broken and unconscious, but he was alive. The attacker raced towards us, his sword arced high in the air and his long, dark hair flowing wildly behind him. I couldn't lose Alias, he was my only family, my only person. I looked around at the chaos surrounding me and my blood began to boil.

This was not right.

This was never right.

My mother's glassy eyes, the sword through her chest, tripping over my friends' bodies, Alias's lifeless shape.

My blood began to sing and lightning coursed through my veins, begging for release.

My enemy was mere paces away. I couldn't not defend us. I had to make a choice. I would not sit here and watch everything I cared about burn to nothing but ash and memories. A sharp tug began to ball in the pit of my stomach, the butterfly wings beat against my skin, and my vision became crisp.

The smell of fresh cut grass and my mother's perfume filled my nostrils.

And suddenly everything slowed, almost stopping. My hair rose around me, as though gravity did not exist. Alias's eyes cracked open as he regained consciousness, the instinct to shrink into myself clawed against me, but I could not be afraid, not this time. I dug into the foreign entity inside myself, feeling the pleasure-pain rip through my body.

And I did the only thing I could.

I let go, a scream ripping through the world.

And the world dissolved into fire and lightning and heat.

Silence pounded against my ears.

I was no longer hurt or tired, I was alive and buzzing with power as the floor cracked beneath us.

"Raya…" Alias whispered.

My hair slowly floated back down to my shoulders and my glow faded. I tilted my head back and breathed deeply, I had never known content like it. It was like I had told a secret I had been holding in for a hundred years. I opened my eyes slowly, gasping at the destruction around me. The floor to ceiling windows surrounding the dining room were smashed, the harsh winter air blowing through the room. I looked at the attackers surrounding us. They were all dead. My entire body was covered in scorch marks.

"We need to go," I said, attempting to stand on shaky knees.

"Raya, stop." Alias's loud voice echoed through the room. "What was that? What is going on? I don't unders—" he said, beginning to push the beam off his legs.

"I don't understand either," I said quietly. "All I know is that we were going to die and now we aren't." I finally met his eyes. "We need to leave, now."

"And go where? Back to the Foothills? They're going to want some sort of explanation of how the two of us killed…" he paused and looked around the room, "Sixteen soldiers!"

He was calling me a murderer.

"I saved your life!" I yelled. "Without me, you would've been dead by now!" Tears of frustration filled my eyes.

"Raya, stop talking," he said holding up a hand.

"Are you seri—" I began before he clasped his hand over my mouth.

"Do you hear that?" he whispered as the faint sound of horse hooves hitting frozen earth filled the room.

"Maybe it's help from the Foothills?" I said hopefully.

"How could they have gotten the message so quickly?" Alias said shaking his head. "More attackers?" he suggested.

We moved towards the broken windows, daring to peek

outside. A single carriage raced towards us with a foreign banner flowing in the wind.

"We need to run," I said quickly.

"Where? There is nothing but flat lands for miles." His voice barely a whisper. "We need to surrender, then maybe they won't kill us."

"Maybe they won't kill us?" I mocked him. "That's the best outcome here?" I argued quietly.

"Do you have a better idea?" he said and I paused, my gaze flicking from Alias to the dead bodies around me. I shook my head.

"Everything is going to be fine," he said, shuffling towards the staircase.

I wished he wasn't such a terrible liar.

The safe house reminded me of Matron's training barracks. It was big and old, but it felt hollow. Alias walked in front of me, and I saw his hands reach for a weapon whenever I got a too close. He was afraid of me. The thought alone was like dunking my hand in boiling water, but part of me liked the burn.

Movement caught my eye as Opal Blose hobbled towards us. He was alive, barely, blood dripping down his temple and one eye gone completely. Alias motioned for him to follow. Were we the only ones left?

We took the stairs slowly, cringing when the they creaked loudly. Alias looked back at us as we approached the front door. A bolt of nervous energy ripped through me; my palms began to sweat. The sound outside stopped abruptly, making the only noise our combined, shallow breathing. Alias turned to look at me and nodded once.

"Everything is going to be fine," he whispered. I nodded back weakly. Opal coughed quietly, blood on his lips.

"We need to do this," I whispered at Alias's hesitation. "Or he's not going to make it," I gestured to Opal.

Alias nodded and reached for the door handle, twisting it slowly. My heart hammered in my chest. *Everything is going to be fine*, I repeated Alias's words over in my head.

I didn't see what was behind the door; I heard Alias scream my name and Opal attempt to fight but my world exploded into a blinding bright white all over again, but this time it wasn't mine.

And this time I wasn't sure who would survive.

8

JOY

DO I KNOW YOU?

"She deserves to know who I am."

- DAHLIA'S PRIVATE LETTERS.

The sun crested the mountains and the moon disappeared. There was rarely a time that Kia wasn't bathed in light. The sun burned my retinas as Jameson and I returned to the ship in the early hours of the morning. Almost everyone had already returned home, for the first time ever, Jameson and I were late. The boat swayed calmly as it always did, the ocean more inviting than I'd ever seen it.

I slumped onto the tattered armchair, letting the open air and sun warm my skin. I closed my eyes, memories of last night littered my mind, Jameson and I drinking, dancing, both of us not ready to return to reality. I looked down at my orange dress and cringed, I had been wearing this for almost twenty-four hours. I stood but my head began to spin and the colors around me burst and shrunk.

"Are you alright, Joy?" Jameson called out, noticing my frozen posture. I nodded, turned on my heel and began to run.

But I stayed in the same place, running in almost slow motion as Jameson watched, his mouth moving but no words coming out.

"Joy!" he called as I sprinted and suddenly fell to the ship floor and hit my head.

I woke with a jolt, my body bathed in sunlight and morning dew. Swiping at my damp cheeks, I sat hastily and winced, my back ached from sleep on the deck and my head felt heavy. For a moment I had forgotten Jameson had been taken, I had forgotten about the horror of the night before. A sigh sounded beside me as Dahlia awoke slowly, her body slowly uncurling from the fetal position she spent the night in. We had spent the previous evening planning. Supplies, maps, crew, possible dangers, and navigation. We planned into the early hours of the morning, until our heads began to droop, and our eyes closed softly.

A tremor snaked down my spine.

Today we would set sail for the Northern Continent. Dahlia did not enclose any details other than; we were heading north. The lack of control slowly began to eat at me, I was the captain of this ship, this was my home. It was horrifically hard to tell the crew they could not join us on our search. It was too dangerous, too risky. I couldn't survive another loss.

"Jameson is our family too," Romy's voice was harsh and bitter. "I don't care if you are the captain of the ship!"

"Romy, please, I need to know that you will keep the others safe," I said weakly.

"Joy, if you do this," he stepped closer to me. "I will never forgive you!" he shouted.

The twins were crying behind him, their almost white

skin ashen and grey. I looked back at Dahlia, her head down, tying a knot at the base sails. But I knew she was listening. Heat crawled up my neck and onto my cheeks. I reached for Romy, but he flinched away, turning towards the cabin door. His fists curled and uncurled over and over.

"Bring him home, Joy," he whispered. Relief washed over me softly and I took and deep breath.

"I will, Romy." He turned back towards me. "I promise."

We took large strides towards each other, embracing in the middle. I wrapped myself around him softly. Despite him being my elder I had spent the last nine years watching over him. He was the fourth member of our family, back when Lolita, Jameson, and I were sailing around the world, without any worries or fears. I could almost hear the laughter and feel the cold water of the northern continent. I sighed in Romy's arms.

"Take care of them, Romy," I said as we parted, looking over at the rest of my crew. He nodded.

Lila, Tuppen, Kassy, and Lacy stood in a small semi-circle. I wished with my entire heart that Lolita was here to help me say goodbye. I prayed to Kai'd, begging her to deliver me safely back to my family. I hugged each of them, squeezing them tight.

It would keep me strong.

I would stay strong for them.

I would bring back Jameson and we would sail away.

Setting the world on fire as we go.

The sun was on its assent into the sky when I wound in the anchor and opened the sails. The sound was like coming home. Like welcoming me back to a place I had almost forgotten. We hadn't set sail since we lost Lolita. I hadn't seemed right to do it without her. Our boat creaked and ached, moving forward for the first time in months.

"Are you ready captain?" Dahlia's voice was entirely too bright and jolly. I rolled my eyes.

"Do not mistake your presence on this ship for trust or want," I stalked towards her. "You are here as a map and nothing else."

Her face fell ever so slightly but recovered quickly.

"The journey is going to seem much longer if you refuse to talk to me, Joy!" she shouted.

Anger wrapped around me. How did she not understand? I was in this mess because of her! I was alone again because of her. For a moment, I wished for my father's patience and my mother's guidance. I had not seen their faces in almost ten years, but I remembered them completely.

My father's dark skin covered with even darker tattoos. His eyes an unearthly golden yellow much like my own. My mother was beautiful. Her creamy brown skin marred with scars from a past she refused to talk about. Her hair sat in dreadlocks, brushing the bottom of her back, she would intertwine shells and stones within the strands, making her look like a mermaid from deep in the ocean.

My mother and father had a love that belonged in novels. I always dreamt of having that kind of love and I did. Lolita loved me just like my father had loved my mother. We belonged in a novel; we deserved more time than we were given.

We were robbed.

Just like my parents were.

Dahlia coughed behind me, shaking me from my thoughts.

"Are you ready?" Dahlia asked and I nodded.

I stared at the soft blue of the horizon, closing my eyes, and imagining it was Lolita and I going to save Jameson.

Not some traitor I could never trust.

The boat heaved forward, jerking us around before settling softly on the waves. Sighing, I let myself worry one more time, before folding my concerns away and slipping them into my pocket. I needed to focus.

I would bring my Jameson home.

Anyone that got in my way, would meet the end of a sword.

9

RAYA
SHOOT TO KILL

"This is the only way, Raya. You know I'm right."

- ALIAS.

Iced water surrounded me. Drowning me softly. Again, and again. The water leaving me just before my consciousness slipped away.

"How long have you known?" A female voice sounded around me, or above me. I wasn't sure. My head lolled to the side, a firm grip in my hair the only thing keeping me vertical.

"How long have you known?" The sounds around me suddenly became crisp and the voice belonged to Captain Jala. I snapped back into reality. What was happening?

"Captain Jala?" My voice was hoarse, and water clogged.

"Awake now?" she sneered.

"How long have you known?" Her voice was laced with venom.

"Known what?"

"How long have you known you are a Sorcerer?" Her words struck me like slaps. She dunked my head back into the iced water.

A jeer from the corner of the room piqued my interest. My entire regiment stood in the empty, hollow room watching me be tortured.

Alias stood awkwardly, his eyes not meeting mine, wincing as Jala tugged my hair harder.

"A Sorcerer?" My voice clung to the silence.

"Don't play dumb with me, girl." Jala cracked the handle of her sword to my temple, drawing blood.

"Captain," Alias whispered through gritted teeth. Jala ignored him.

Another crack to my temple pushed me into oblivion.

I woke again, the setting sun shining through the small window. My mouth dryer than sand, I reached out for some water, only to find out my hands and feet were chained. Alias was no longer with me, either he walked out, or he had been dragged away.

"Alias tells me that he did not know." Captain Jala stalked the chair I was sitting on. We were in the same room as before… sans the ice water.

"Did not know what?" Anger burned in my stomach, hot and heavy.

"He did not know you were one of *them,*" she spat. I rolled my eyes.

"Sorcerers are extinct, Jala."

She stiffened at my dropping her title.

"That is not true, girl. Sorcerers live among us. Do not insult me further, we saw the lightning from miles away and it was not from the heavens," she snarled. "You are one of them, filth." She slapped me across the face with the back of her hand.

She paced back and forth, her eyes burning like the skin on my cheek.

"I should kill you on the spot," she spat. "A liar in my barracks, a *Sorcerer* in Regiment One?" She spoke as though the word burned her tongue.

I stared at her through my eyelashes. Had Alias told her what had happened at the safe house? Why hadn't he defended me?

He knew I was not a… that I could not be a… Sorcerer. Could I?

Captain Jala pulled my chair forward, so it balanced on its front legs. Her arm the only thing keeping me from slamming into the concrete floor.

"But that would be a waste, don't you think?"

I grimaced at her, stars floating in my vision. She pushed the chair back down to four legs, the wood rocking back and forth before stilling. Jala lifted a cup to my lips, but I clamped my shut.

Did she think me stupid?

She rolled her eyes. "I see you have not forgotten your training." She smirked and took a sip from the glass first.

How could I forget my training? How could I forget when Jala had poisoned our food, making us seize and writhe until we were half dead, before administering the antidote. It was punishment she said, we should've known to check our food before we ate it.

I recalled the vomit that soaked my clothes.

Opening my mouth, I swallowed the water in one gulp.

"If you want to survive," Jala bent so that we were eye level, "I suggest you listen carefully because I will not repeat myself." She refilled the water glass.

"There is a place, a place that is protected so fiercely that none that have tried to infiltrate it have survived. It is home to the last surviving Sorcerers." She grimaced as my breathing hitched.

"The war in Zetka is escalating, the Southern Continent is now recruiting Sorcerers. Our soldiers are perishing faster than ever before. We need a way to learn their secrets, a way to have the upper hand on the battlefield." She smirked. "And now we have one."

"What do you mean?" I asked, knowing full well what she meant.

"You are now of their people." She paced around the chair. "The Sorcerers are a danger to everyone; they refuse to comply with our laws. Their power is untamable. They are a threat to our peaceful existence."

"*Peaceful existence*?" I mocked. "We are fighting a war that has been going on for hundreds of years. Perhaps instead of trying to tame the Sorcerers, you should be asking for their help?" My voice did not falter, did not break.

Captain Jala stared at me.

"I had hoped you would accept the mission without any backlash, but I suppose not," she hummed in disappointment. "Infiltrate, gain their trust, learn their secrets, and report back." Her smile was like a snake. "Or I'll kill you. And him," she pointed at Alias as he was pushed through the door.

Purple bruises bloomed on his face, cuts and gashes littered his skin. Fat chains hung from his wrists, and I swallowed against my dry throat.

"Let him go," I demanded.

"I will, just as soon as you agree." She smiled.

Blood seeped into Alias's clothing, his eye almost swollen shut. One life in exchange for Goddess knows how many.

Thousands of memories funneled through my mind. Alias

and I had grown up together, been each other's family when there was no one else. I couldn't let him die.

I pulled against the chains on my wrists.

"Alias?" I called out, he gave a small smile, his teeth coated in blood.

"Raya," he rasped softly. His voice trickled over me, like a feather trailing my skin. I closed my eyes; would I risk the lives of many for Alias? Jala knew my weakness, my only weakness. The man I had grown up with, my only family.

Guilt clawed up my throat, talons sinking into my skin.

"Okay." My voice was barely audible. "I'll do it."

A wide smile spread across her face.

"You have six moon cycles." Jala raised her hand and Alias's cuffs were unlocked. "They have heard about your…" She couldn't bring herself to talk about what had happened in the safehouse. "They want to meet you, they've sent word. They claim that since you are one of *them*," she tutted, "You belong with the rest of your *people*."

I swallowed against the dryness in my mouth and nodded.

"There is a location in which we will deliver you. You will learn their way of life, but do not fall for their kindness," she sneered as I scoffed. "They are vicious creatures, unable to feel remorse or love. Their very nature is an untamable violence. Do not trust them."

I nodded, then she explained that they would most likely check me for weapons before slipping a hand into my boots to retrieve the daggers there, ripping the part of my trousers that covered my thigh, to reveal the knife sewn into the seams.

"You are skilled, Raya," she winced. "Probably one of the best I've ever trained." She ran a finger down my cheek. "Such a shame that you are one of them." She pushed her nail into my skin, hard enough to draw blood before er hips swished and she left the room, long white hair bouncing as she whispered, "What a waste."

Another man, presumably a guard, took her place in front of me.

"In order to protect their location, the Sorcerers," he bit out the word, "need you to arrive… incapacitated." I raised an eyebrow.

"Incap—" I began to ask but pressure hit my skull and stars exploded in my eyes.

And then it all went dark.

10

RAYA

WELCOME TO THE JUNGLE

"...Broken rib, scratches, cuts, and bruises. Oddly, she was covered in scorch marks."

- ELIJAH'S MEDICAL JOURNAL.

I woke alone, my skin feeling dull and rough against the foreign sheets beneath me. My body remained rigid, afraid to move even an inch. Memories from the previous day and night swirled together like dye in water. I remembered Alias falling, his life so close to being taken. I remembered the rapid fluttering beating against my skin and the feeling of eruption, of blinding lightning and fire and power. I remember Jala's taunts, the ice water and the choice between my people and my person.

Then nothing but darkness until my body was hauled from the ground to a carriage, to this room where I had remained ever since.

I had no idea how or when I arrived in this foreign place. Where was Alias? His screams lingered in my mind, branded onto my soul. His cries of anguish and loss will live inside me forever. Had Jala kept him safe as she promised? Would he come for me? Another question lingered, louder than all the others. Was he afraid of me?

The stiff sheets struggled against my weak body as I sat up, stars swam in my vision and my head ached softly. The room was dark, dawn had yet to break over the horizon. But my world no longer contained the blues, greys, and whites of the foothills.

Everything seemed creamy and warm, wrapped in deep purples, oranges, golds, pinks, and red. A soft breeze blew in from the open window, grazing my skin softly. I sighed, tilting my head to the sides and stretching my arms, pushing the rising panic down into my stomach. Everything was fine, everything would be okay.

I looked over, noticing the matches and lantern resting there. Had someone been here? Whilst I was sleeping? Striking it hesitantly I lit a match, the lantern, and then various lonesome candles around the spacious but cozy room. Large floor to ceiling bookshelves crowded together in one corner and a rocking chair sat in another. The bed was big, big enough for three people comfortably. I glared at my reflection in the round mirror above the dressing table. The skin beneath my eyes was dark and limp, I looked half dead.

I felt it too.

I swept around the rest of the room. Simple but clean bathing chambers, and a gilded armoire stuffed with dresses, trousers, and tunics.

Six moon cycles would pass quickly, no doubt Jala would try to have me killed after my work, but I could get away. Deliver what she wanted and grab Alias. We could travel to the Southern Continent and be pirates or performers.

I checked myself, my clothes heaped in a bloody pile, and the draws for my weapons. Nothing.

Pulling out my mud and gore-stained boots from beneath the bed, I felt around the edge until the small outline of a dagger met my fingertips. Ripping the leather, I pulled out the knife, tossing it in my hands a few times until I became accustomed to the weight.

I slumped back onto the bed, knowing that the only way I was going to get out of here, was on my own.

I needed a reason for someone to come into the room, a reason for someone to start talking. Noticing the crystal jewelry box, a plan formed. Knocking over the box with one hand, I sliced the dagger down my forearm with the other. Sliding the weapon under my pillow to safe keeping.

Playing the part of the fumbling fool, I muttered a curse to myself before reaching down to collect the pieces. Extravagantly wincing as I embedded a few larger shards of glass into my arm to make it look as though it had shattered against me.

A small screech fell from my lips as blood, much more than I had anticipated, began spilling alarmingly fast until suddenly my entire forearm was covered in blood. How had this happened? I had only embedded a few chunks into my arm. I had been careful not to slice anything important. Had the dagger slipped? I rolled my eyes at my own stupidity.

Footsteps thudded outside my chambers, and I stood up swiftly, wincing at the movement. Knuckles rapped on the wooden door and only moments later it swung open. I stood frozen, suddenly aware that only a thin satin nightgown separated air and my body.

Who had dressed me? How much time had passed since my conversation with Jala?

A man stood at the threshold, he wore fitted trousers and

tunic, much like the uniform I had worn only days before. His clothes were worn, like another layer of skin. A royal guard, I guessed. He ducked into the room, his large frame bigger than my own, despite my being the tallest girl in Regiment One. His dark hair swished against the tops of his shoulders as he turned his head towards me, his brown skin glistening slightly with sweat. Bushy eyebrows raised above green eyes at my silence.

"You're bleeding..." he said, his voice soft and deep. I nodded.

"The jewelry box," I managed to stutter quickly. He nodded, looking down at his own hands awkwardly. Silence engulfed us and I stared at the floor. Was he going to say something or just stand there.

"Are you going to help me?" I demanded, but more silence followed. It scratched against my skin. The man continued to stare at me, cold, emerald eyes meeting mine.

"Are you listening?" I blurted quickly, unable to keep the words inside me anymore. He paused, assessing me quietly. Remembering my part to play, I whimpered softly.

"Why am I here?" I whispered, forcing a single tear to roll down my cheek.

"How would I know?" he answered, he gaze lingering on my rumpled bedsheets.

"You're the first person I've seen since..." I paused, wringing my fingers. "I don't know what... I don't understand... where am I?" I hated myself for begging a man like an insolent child. I was a member of the Sage Guard. Or at least I used to be.

He raised his eyebrows yet again. "What is your name?"

I sighed inwardly.

"Raya," I muttered.

"And your last name?" he asked, looking bored. I bit my

lower lip and fiddled with the hem of my nightgown. A pang of pain stuck my core.

"I don't have one. It's just Raya."

The man rolled his eyes.

"Okay, Raya, I don't know why you are here and, to be honest, I don't really care. Ezra asked me to stand at your door and make sure no one entered or exited. I was told to keep you safe. Nothing more." I scoffed, rolling my eyes. Was he some sort of idiot?

"I don't need protecting," I argued, and the stranger eyed my blood-soaked sleeve.

"Clearly." He turned to leave. "I'll have someone come and stitch you up." He strode for the door but stopped. "Try not to break anything else."

And with that he swung the door open and slammed it shut, leaving me once again in the cold. The world around me seemed to ebb and flow, suddenly I wasn't aware if this was reality or a horrific dream I was having while my body lay slowly dying at the threshold of the safe house.

An awful feeling seeped into my bones, rising to my skull.

Where *was* Alias? Surely, he had not let Captain Jala trade me for secrets. My breaths came in short bursts, never fully filling my lungs. Suddenly my limbs felt heavy and all I could see was the blood dripping down my arm.

Drip.

Drip.

Drip.

My training tried to push through my thoughts.

You're losing blood, Raya. Hold pressure to the wound.

But I couldn't

My skin began to ache, just like it had in the safe house.

Just like it had when my only friend became afraid of me. Just like it had when I became a murderer.

"No," I demanded my body to listen to me, falling to my knees, I whispered into the room, "I cannot do this again." It felt as though a thousand tiny needles were pricking my skin, I was certain that my body was slowly shutting down. All my fight was gone, left in pieces like a corpse on a battlefield. What was happening? Was my body giving up on me? I had only a few cuts on my arm, this could not be because of blood loss, could it? A scream pierced my ears, my vision blurring as tears threatened to spill.

"Enough please, it hurts," I almost whispered to the dawn. I laid flat on the floor, the aching subsiding ever so slightly. A headache began to form in between my eyes and my body felt limp. I breathed deeply, my body melting into the floor beneath me. Everything paused. My mind stilled softly.

I could not imagine a life of days like this.

I wept silently for all that I had lost. I wept for my mother, our village, my childhood, for Alias, for Opal, for our entire squad and I wept for myself.

A broken girl from a broken family with a broken heart.

My training attempted to save me again.

Stop weeping, Raya, you've survived worse. GET. UP.

I ignored the voice.

Death did not seem so scary in that moment. The headache deepened and I let it, drawing pleasure from the pain.

Pain reminded me that I was a human.

But I did not feel human, and I was no longer myself. The old Raya had died in the safe house, just like Lexa had. I stared at the ceiling. A soft tap sounded on my door.

"Hello?" I said, my voice barely audible. The door

opened just a crack and a small elderly man poked his head around the corner.

"I was told there was an incident with glass?" he said, his too-big glasses slipping down his nose. I nodded, unable to get up off the floor.

"I—" I began and he nodded.

"I understand, pet, each of us has been in your position once," he said, moving slowly toward me and guilt suddenly pierced my heart. He had not been in my position before; I have done this to myself.

"Please do not fret, I am here to help. I promise." He gently knelt next to me, holding out a hand. I took it and he slowly hoisted me to seating position.

"I am afraid I cannot lift you onto the bed." He smiled sadly as though we shared a secret, it was only then that I realized he was missing an arm. "One moment," he said before scurrying back the way he came. I rested against the bed, dropping casually in and out of consciousness. The kind man reemerged with the giant brute from earlier. He was so rude, I thought to myself.

"I assure you that you are not the only person who feels the same," the elderly man said with a smile.

I must've insulted him to his face. If I had more energy I might've cringed. He threw a disgusted look my way. Tension seemed to stretch the seconds into minutes and then the minutes to hours. An uncomfortable atmosphere settled around us, like fog stripping away my eyesight. I stared up at the ceiling, the off-white and peeling paint staring back at me until my eyes fluttered shut.

"Khol, just lift her to the bed, and then you can return to sulking," the elderly man sighed. "I'm Elijah," the man said to me. "A friend." He smiled, and I returned the gesture, once again staring at the ceiling whilst Elijah began to root through his brown satchel. My breaths began coming in short and my eyes rolled back in my head. How much blood had I lost?

A lovely silence filled my head, and I realized I was dying. It scared me because I was not afraid to die. If anything, I was almost ready. Cool air brushed against my cheeks.

"*My darling, stay with me.*" I bolted forward, vomit burning my throat.

"Raya?" Khol said but I could not hear him.

"My love, we need you to stay." Tears prickled my eyes as my mother's voice filled my mind. "*I am so proud of you.*"

"Mama?" I whispered, tears dampening my nightgown.

"My darling, do not cry. I am here."

I whimpered softly.

"You do not need to do this; you do not need to share the secrets of these people. Of our people." Her sweet voice tickled my spine like a warm hand.

"Our people," I said louder than before, tears uncontrollably streaming down my face. "Mama, you're here?" I sobbed.

"I am always here." I could almost feel her hand against my cheek.

"Don't go," I whispered, dipping back into unconsciousness.

I woke only moment later, already feeling emptiness. Elijah remained unfazed, still rooting through his brown bag but Khol stared, his face stunned and tinged with sadness.

"Khol, will you lift her to the bed, please?" Elijah looked up, sighing at, still-on-the-floor, me.

"But, Elijah, she—" he began to protest.

"Lift her onto the bed, Khol, please." Elijah smiled but I could not see. I was clinging onto my mother's ever quietening voice. I yearned for her. The pain of loss burned through me, ripping me apart bit by bit, slowly destroying me. My mother was gone, and I would never see her again, I would never return home to her again. Reluctantly, Khol lifted me, watching the tears silently slip down my cheeks.

"She's bleeding," he said without looking back. "Elijah, she is bleeding," he said again, this time louder and sternly. Elijah rummaged around in a little brown satchel.

"Yes, I know that," he said with a sigh.

Khol bent low, our faces close, and cautiously laid me down on the dreamily soft bed. I began to cry louder, feeling the gaping hole my mother's death created growing larger and larger. I couldn't breathe. I didn't want to breathe. Khol stared down at me, but I was too upset to be embarrassed or annoyed or anything other than completely miserable.

"That will be all, Khol, thank you," Elijah said before laying various vials and tools on the bed. Once Khol had vanished it felt as though the air had been returned to the room.

"Right, let's fix you up," Elijah said, and I smiled weakly, a heavy silent settled over us as my tears began to slow. "I'm so sorry, Raya," he stated and I nodded, for there was nothing else to say. No other words were needed, he was sorry and so was I.

Finally, my breathing began to slow as Elijah plied me with medicine and stitched up my cuts. I stared at the ceiling again, slipping, slowly and helplessly, into unconsciousness.

11

JOY

IF THOU SHALT NOT SUCCEED... GIVE UP?

"Our journey has begun, and we should be with you in a matter of weeks. You should have never doubted me."

- DAHLIA'S LETTERS FROM THE BOAT.

Sailing within the Southern continent was like drifting through a small globe of paradise. The crystal waters remained mostly calm, as if too lazy to create storms or threats. We floated softly, the warm waters lapping against the boat gently. I stood at the railing watching the sun rise. I hadn't slept in what felt days, I couldn't relax. There was a stranger on my boat. I stared at Dahlia as she slept, paced, and played cards around me. Stifling a cringe I looked up at the waking blue sky.

It was possible to sail across the world on a ship of this size with only one crew member, but I needed a map and that map happened to be Dahlia.

She knew I didn't want her there. She was a reminder of what I had lost and quite honestly, she was unwelcome.

But she knew how to sail, and fast. My mind wondered to Jameson again. Was he even still alive? Had he been murdered by the sick bastards that kidnapped him? My blood began to boil again, all my anger focused on the figure bobbing towards me.

"Awake again?" Dahlia's voice was filled with concern. "You look terrible." I rolled my eyes. Doubt flushed through me.

I should not have trusted her.

Not with something this precious.

But I had no choice. She had made that clear.

"You think I can sleep?" My voice was clipped and harsh. "My best friend is probably encaged in goddess knows what, with goddess knows who." My voice remained an angry whisper. "So forgive me, Dahlia, if my appearance is not up to your standards."

I walked away from her, my legs aching. I knew my emotions were heightened because I had not slept, I knew that my patience was wearing thin, I knew that I needed to sleep and be strong for Jameson.

But every time I closed my eyes, I saw his face from across Laylani's bar. The confusion and fear. I knew it was fear for me, fear for my life. I sunk to my knees and curled into a ball once inside my small bed chambers. The ship no longer felt like home, it felt like a foreign land that I no longer recognized. Looking over at the bed I couldn't help the thoughts of Lolita. Sleeping softly, her red hair covering her face and bare shoulders like another bed sheet. The sunny mornings when we would just hold each other for hours, our naked bodies pressed against each other, unbothered about time passing around us, basking in the normalcy of being in love.

Cold seeped into my body. She wasn't here anymore, and

I would forever be broken without her. Loneliness followed me with every step to the bed. Time bent around me, I did not know how long I laid still, staring at the ceiling, before sleep dragged me away.

Lolita stood within the flames; her body untouched by the heat. Another girl stood beside her; she was almost glowing. Her brown hair splayed around her head like a halo, like she was underwater. Another figure walked towards them, his hand reaching for Lolita. It wasn't a stranger, it was Jameson. Their hands almost touched… they were almost together.

I opened my eyes softly, the remnants of my dream clinging to my skin like an unwanted embrace. I had been plagued with the same visions for the last four nights. My head was no longer my own, I found myself standing at the helm of the ship, staring at the horizon, attempting to understand the reoccurring dream.

Was it Lolita? Or was Jameson trying to reach me? Who was the other woman? She was clearly not from the southern continent, her pale skin stood in contrast to Lolita dark black skin. The stranger's pale skin mirrored Jameson's. Where they from the same region? It was clear that she too was a descendant of the Northern Continent, unlike Lolita and I who hailed from the Southern Continent.

I wanted to believe that the dream was magical. That it was a message from Kai'd that we were heading in the right direction, but magic had not been seen in decades. I had never even seen it but a part of me always hoped it was real. That part of me became smaller and smaller as I got older and older. It was hard to believe that something existed if you had never laid eyes on it.

But a slither of the childlike belief still lived on inside me, it had to.

Without hope I had nothing.

I watched the sky awaken and bloom into its climactic crescendo. I have seen nothing but sky and sea for almost a week. Every day I worried that I would be too late to save Jameson, every day I imagined returning home without him.

Heavy footsteps sounded hastily behind me, Dahlia's eyes were wild and bloodshot as she reached for my arm. I couldn't help tugging my arm away, my eyes searching her quickly.

"Joy! What are you doing?" Dahlia's voice was a high screech. I spun around search for imminent danger, my eyebrows drawn together.

"Did you not hear my shouts?" Her body trembled and shook. "We need to get inside. NOW." She grabbed for my arm again, hauling me toward the inner cabin.

But it was too late.

My body was thrown into the air, flying across the deck until my back hit an empty barrel. Pain shot along my back, all the way into my spine.

Stars exploded in my vision. I cracked an eye open, my sight blurry.

Dahlia lay a few feet away from me, unmoving.

A laugh sounded from across the ship's deck. At the sound my head flew up, dizziness ripping through me.

Our ship had been hit… by another ship. A part of our ship was completely shattered. I analyzed it quickly… enough damage to stop our journey or even sink us.

The clouds seemed to darken, and the sky stilled. Blood trickled down my cheek, stinging like a slap. My body remained on the floor, attempting to ready itself for any possible situation.

Wood snapped and splintered on the side of the boat. The bow of the foreign ship dug into ours, I felt the movement then. We were being pushed, the sails of the opposite ship were flying high, the wind propelling them into us.

Heavy boots stomped against the floor of the ship; slow steps walked toward me. I kept my breathing even, if I was lucky, he would believe me unconscious.

How I loved the element of surprise.

If I moved too quickly, they would kill me but if I moved too slowly… they would kill me.

"What do we have here?" A whisper crawled up my spine, making me cringe. A small sword slowly dragged across my face, drawing a thin line of blood.

I slowly moved my foot, checking the hidden dagger remained there.

A hand touched my shoulder, pushing down the strap of my dress.

"Do you like that?" The disgusting whisper spoke again, and a jeer sounded from the adjacent ship. In one swift movement I reach for my weapon, twirled away from his touch, and plunged the dagger into his lower stomach, dragging it up to his sternum as I stood.

"Did you like that?" I whispered.

A bubble of blood choked from his mouth as he tried to cry out for help. His body slumped to the floor heavily, and I wiped the dagger against my linen dress, a smear of red marking me as a murderer.

I had been called worse.

"Come on, sweet girl," a voice drawled from the other ship. Another man sat on the bow of his ship, his feet dangling down. He was different from the other men, he was tall and lean. In other circumstances you might have called him handsome.

"Give us the girl and you'll never see us again." A smirk lifted the corner of his mouth. "Promise," he said, jumping down onto the deck of my ship with a heavy thwack. His eyes dragged over the bleeding dead body at my feet and he grinned.

"This is definitely not Florence's work." He bent to inspect the body, using his two index fingers to pull the sagging face into a smile. "She did not teach you?" he asked although it was more of a statement. "But she's here." He twirled around, his unhinged mind whirling. "Come out come out wherever you are," he sung into the horizon.

The stranger danced toward me, grabbing my hand, twirling me and dipping me low. I struggled against his grip, ripping my hand away.

"Flooooorrrreeeencccce," he sung again. "Come out or I'll gut her... you know I will." I was not sure who he thought was on this ship. I looked over to Dahlia, but she was gone.

She had left me alone with this stranger.

Why was I surprised?

I did not know these waters that well, perhaps he was looking for a different ship? Does someone owe him a debt? Perhaps this is an extremely odd romantic relationship. I pulled a sword from the barrel full of them. The metal sung softly.

"Oh," the stranger said flirtatiously, "you are becoming more and more interesting."

I gave him a mock bow, never breaking eye contact.

"What can I say? I am a woman of mystery." I stepped closer to him, my sword scraping along the floor. "But I am afraid..." I rose my eyebrows....

"Captain Harlow." The man lifted his hat and swept it across the floor as he bowed deeply.

"I am afraid, Captain Harlow, there is no Florence on this

ship." The sword scratched the wood as I wiped the dripping blood from my cheek. He jumped and scurried toward me hastily.

"Ah! But that is what you think! She is deceptive, you see… not to be trusted." I rolled my eyes; I had known many deceptive people in my days.

"Then I suppose we've come to a standstill. You want a Florence, but I do not have one, what now?" I had missed my own strength; I had missed my own wit and ability to fight.

"Perhaps I could take you instead?" Captain Harlow eyed me.

"Oh, I'd rather you didn't." We circled each other slowly.

"I think you'd fit in nicely with my crew." He looked down at the body and nudged it with his feet. "And your ship does not look as though it'll last much longer… not to mention the man you just killed." He jumped closer to me, sword in hand.

I fell into my fighting stance and looked over at the splintered wood and the small puddle of water welling against it. Could we make it to land?

"No, the next island is miles away," he winked. "If that's what you were thinking… I suppose it's join my crew or die." Movement in the corner of my eye caught my attention, the Captain turned toward it.

"I'm bored." He clasped my wrist, twisted, and pulled my back flat against his chest, a small dagger at my throat.

"Florence, come out or I'll slit her throat, I've played your games long enough." He pushed the dagger into my throat, drawing blood.

"Stop, please, I do not know a Florence."

"That is where you are wrong, sweet girl," Captain Harlow whispered in my ear. He dragged the dagger, and a scream escaped my throat.

"Enough, Harlow." Dahlia sat on the bow of his ship, her legs dangling just like Harlow's had moments ago. Air rushed to my lungs as I was released.

"Oh, Florence, it's good to see you, sweet girl."

"Oh, Harlow, I wish I could say the same."

12

RAYA

GET DRESSED

"It was as though the sun beams were on fire, I begged them to burn me too."

- RAYA'S JOURNAL.

The sun was already setting when I finally pulled myself from a dreamless slumber, creases from the bedsheets imprinted on my face. I felt almost normal, my cuts stitched and my headache now only a very dull thump in the back of my head. I hastily reached for the glass of water beside my bed and drained it immediately. I sat up slowly, attempting to flatten my wild hair.

The room was the same as when I woke hours ago, if it wasn't for the stitches and blood stains, I might've thought Elijah and Khol were a dream. The sun painted colors of burned orange and deep red throughout my room and I felt the urge to reach out and touch them.

The weight of Jala's words lived within me, floating along my bloodstream, never letting me forget my duty to the

Sage Guard. I stood softly, my legs much stronger than before, and headed to the bathing room. I relieved myself, splashing cold water on my face and cleaning my teeth before staring at myself in the cracked mirror. A scorch mark starting at my chin, passing through my nose, and ending at my eyebrow sat faintly across my face. I traced my finger across the white lines hesitantly, almost expecting it to be hot beneath my fingertips.

Looking down at my hand I noticed the healing scorch marks running from my fingers, all the way up my arm and beneath my night gown. Without having to check, I knew the marks were covering my body. The thought did not repulse or scare me. Delight surged through me.

I had never felt more like myself.

A timid knock sounded on the door, breaking me from my gazing.

"Hello?" A small voice spoke from behind the thick wood.

I walked over soundlessly and twisted the handle. My months of training with the Sage Guard humming beneath my skin. Unexpectedly, a girl of similar age to me stood at the door's threshold, piles of different fabrics balanced in her arms. Her black hair slipped over her shoulders and her eyes, small and narrow, were a bright emerald green.

"Ezra sent me," she said by way of greeting, her eyes never quite meeting mine. "Fresh clothes," she said as she placed the fabrics down. "Dinner is served in an hour." A blush spread across her pale cheeks.

"Have you met Khol yet?" she asked. I nodded.

"I hope you're feeling better." She bowed her head. "I am Nai."

"Raya," I said softly. "You're from the Eastern Continent?" I asked. She nodded.

"My friend Alias, his mother was too," I said, fondly remembering Alias's pale skin and the soft slant of his eyes. "It's very nice to meet you, Nai," I said with a nod of gratitude.

She returned the gesture, leaving the room soundlessly. I stood silently for a moment; my heart began to thump in my chest. I missed my friend terribly, the thought of him being harmed in any way caused panic to slip into my heart. I calmed myself quickly, distracting myself with the fine clothing in front of me.

The fabrics slipped through my hands softly, like sand in an hourglass. I had not expected fresh clothing or hospitality of any kind. The Sorcerers were cold, unfeeling, and I would not forget it.

A knock sounded at my door again and I grabbed the small dagger from underneath my pillow, hiding it beneath my dress.

"It's Khol," he said hesitantly, assumably wondering if I remembered who he was. I paused.

"Come in," I said, trying to hide the irritation in my voice, and the door opened slowly. He walked in, his presence filling the room.

"Ezra sent me to ask if you are feeling well?" he asked, never dropping his warrior pose. I stared at him for a moment, almost not believing his words.

"Who is Ezra?" I moved closer to him. "Or will you answer with some ominous statement that gives me no indication where I am or when I'll be freed from this bed chamber?" His face seemed to slacken.

"Set free? You are not being held captive, Raya," he spoke sternly.

"Then why will no one give me any answers? I've been kept in this room for, only the Goddess knows how long, with nothing but my own thoughts?" I slumped onto my bed.

"You need to get dressed," Khol said bluntly.

"Have you not been hearing anything I've been saying?"

"Yes, take your clothes into the bathing room, dress, and I'll tell you everything," he spoke plainly, and I opened my mouth to object but stopped as he shoved the clothes into my arms. I stomped to the bathing chamber and stripped to my nightgown hastily.

"I—" Khol began, his voice travelling through the crack in the door "We found you, unconscious, at the edge of Zetka."

Memories of the safe house, the raid, and the death flooded my mind.

"We heard about the… blast you created, villagers reported seeing lightening and unfathomable heat. We hadn't seen anything like it since… In a while." He took a breath as I stepped into the forest-green gown. I scoffed at the dress, because obviously I couldn't wear regular clothes.

"The Sage Guard," he scoffed at the words, causing my teeth clamped together. "They were all too happy to give you up, you know how they feel about *our kind.*" I flinched.

Our kind.

"When Ezra and I found you, you were half dead. Beaten to a pulp and almost frozen to death." My memory swam blindly, trying to avoid the torture I had encountered.

"I'm sorry they did that to you."

A gap yawned open within me at the sincerity of his words. My eyes stung with unshed tears. Khol cleared the emotion from his throat and spoke again, almost as if he was attempting to right himself.

"There were marks from carriages and foot soldiers, but it

was empty when we arrived. You were just lying there. To be honest, we thought you were dead." He spoke about my life as though it had no meaning at all.

"And the man with me?" I had hoped Alias would have waited, even from afar, to make sure I was safe.

"Raya, when we found you," he paused. "You were alone."

I paused mid-dressing, my gown unbuttoned and my hair still wild. Swallowing back another tear I nodded to myself.

"Alone," I whispered to myself.

"Yes, alone," Khol repeated back.

Sadness drifted through me like a bad idea. How had I lost so much in such a short space of time? I wished that I could turn back time. Or punish Jala for taking me away from everything I'd even known. Tears rolled down my cheeks even as I scolded myself for crying.

Soldiers did not cry.

In the corner of my eye, I saw my hair begin to lift from my shoulders. The memory of Jala's disgust and the pain she inflicted came roaring to life.

How dare she?! My skin pulsed softly. I turned to the mirror, staring at my reflection. The glass in front of me cracked, showing a thousand different images. All of them showing Khol now suddenly behind me, his arms on the basin either side of me. Caging me against his hard torso.

My chest heaved, each breath brushing my back against his chest.

"Raya, you need to calm down." He leaned down, bridging the height gap between us, but I couldn't calm down, I didn't know how. I closed my eyes, the power pulsed.

"Raya, do not let it control you."

Fat tears dropped onto the tile beneath our feet.

The mirror cracked again, falling into the sink with a crash.

"Raya," Khol warned.

And then white-hot pain shot through my entire body, my eyes flying open. Khol had simply placed his hand on my shoulder. My hair dropped faster than it had risen, and the power slithered back down to the pit of my stomach.

"You are an embarrassment, learn some control," he spat, quickly stepping away from me. Coldness leeched into where his warmth had pressed against me a moment ago. I turned to him, finally facing his brutally beautiful face.

"No one has ever taught me control," I whispered through gritted teeth. We stood in a heated silence for a moment, heat pulsing of us. "How did you do that?" I asked, my curiosity getting the better of me.

"What?"

"Make me stop."

He paused for a moment and rolled his eyes.

"You really have no idea about any of this, do you?" He scoffed. "I am a MindWonderer, when I touched you, I took away your power and fed it to my own." He looked down at my half-dressed state.

"Turn," he demanded, and I did. He buttoned my dress, his warm fingers brushing against my cold skin.

I shivered, walking away as soon as he finished. I swept the mess that was my hair up, pinning it with the emerald hair pin Nai had delivered earlier. I marched past him, stepping into my army grade boots, the only thing I had left from the Foothills. Khol stared at me grimly, looking from his polished black boots to my old, dirty ones.

"Lead the way, prince," I said with a smug smile, and we headed for the door. My body oozed false confidence. I didn't know where I was and where I was going.

But what I did now… I was being taken to the leader of the Sorcerer's.

My work was about to begin.

13

JOY

POWERFUL LIES

"She owed a debt and it needed to be paid. Simple."

- CAPTAIN HARLOW

I stared at Dahlia, my gaze flitting from her to the captain. They spoke like old friends, old friends who kept their swords raised.

Old friends oozing with malice.

Their history felt long and thick, I wondered how long it would take me to wade through it. To understand who the people in front of me were and how they had become the perfect balance of friends and enemies. The sun had reached its apex and the sea swayed slowly, I reached for a rag to clear away the blood.

Their gazes snapped to mine at the movement.

"Steady," I said softly as they glared at me. "I am merely hoping to clean the blood away." I looked down at the body paling on the deck. "We should also do something about him, he's starting to smell."

"Throw him overboard for all I care," Captain Harlow picked his teeth and grimaced. "He was just a means to an end… but don't tell the rest of my crew." He shrugged with a smile. Dahlia gave a humorless laugh.

"And you wonder why you are always alone." She stalked toward me and grabbed one of the dead man's arms, motioning me to take the other. We heaved him overboard, his splash disturbing the ocean's peace.

"You throw us away once you no longer have use for us." Dahlia's words were strained, tainted with hate and longing. Suddenly I was painfully aware that I knew nothing about Dahlia or Florence or whoever the hell she was.

"And yet you wonder why I left you," Dahlia gestured around us wildly. "Why everyone leaves you." The captain's constant smirk disappeared and he stepped back as though wounded.

"You left because you could not face the truth, Florence." He stepped closer to her, resting his hand against her cheek. "Do not fool yourself in thinking otherwise."

I couldn't help the cringe that snaked up my spine, the idea of his hand on her cheek made my stomach churn. Turning away, I focused on the horizon, on the delicious heat from the sun's rays.

But something caught my eye.

My eyebrows crumpled, my heart beating out of my chest. I squinted, concentrating on the dark, green blob resting on the deep, blue skyline.

On the land taking shape.

Sweat pooled on the bottom of my back.

Were we here? Had we finally found Jameson?

"Enough." I turned to Harlow and Dahlia, interrupting their hushed conversation. "Dahlia, is that it? Are we here?"

I looked again at the island. It was achingly familiar, the crystal waters, the lush wildlife and… the mountain?

Dayra's mountain? We weren't just in the Southern Continent; we were back at Dayra. I fought back tears of frustration.

"What have you done?" My long legs ate up the floor as I strode to Dahlia. "Did you steer us off course while I slept?"

She reared back, her face smeared with hurt.

"This isn't me," her voice was clear and strong. "I didn't do this." Her eyes pleaded with mine. "You have to trust me."

I scoffed.

"Trust you?" My laugh was harsh and cold. Harlow stalked to the edge of the boat; his eyebrows crumpled.

"Do you smell that?" he whispered.

"Is it so hard to believe that one day you could trust me?" Dahlia's voice rose.

"You are the reason I have lost everything!" I gestured to the slowly sinking boat. My slowly sinking home.

"Stop!" Captain Harlow's voice was almost a shout. Blood rushed to my head, my anger laying just beneath my skin. "Stop with this nonsense quarrelling." His gaze lingered on Dahlia.

"Do. You. Smell. That?" He spoke clearly, his usual jest lost from his voice.

As the words left his mouth the scent of coffee, the ocean's breeze, and Lolita's lavender perfume wafted up my nose. Dahlia's gaze landed on me, her pupils dilating.

"Magic," she whispered.

A cool breeze tickled my neck. Magic. The seductive goddess. The golden temptress.

"Magic?" My own voice turned into a whisper. Lolita's perfume lingered in my nose; she was all I could smell. She was everywhere. My stomach rumbled hoping for a mug of coffee. Sighing I breathed in again, feeling almost high from the scent.

"Try not to get wrapped up in it," Dahlia's voice was breathless. "It loves chaos." I looked back at Dayra to find it was no longer the island I knew, the sky was no longer blue, thunder rumbled, and dark blue smothered the world.

"They used magic as protection," Harlow whispered. "That is why you saw Dayra and I saw…" His voice faded toward the end.

"You said there was no land for miles!" I turned to him as harsh sheets of rain began to fall. "Where is this weather coming from?" I yelled over the thrashing.

"They must have a SkyChanger on the shore," Captain Harlow stalked toward his ship.

"More than one for a storm this size."

Harlow nodded to Dahlia.

"C'mon, you must board my ship." He almost looked sympathetic. "You will drown if you do not."

My hair stuck to my head, the rain beating against my body relentlessly. The fabric of my dress became heavy as I slowly walked toward his outstretched hand. I knew nothing of the world I was stepping into. I looked back one last time. My parents jumping into my mind.

"It's ours?" My voice high was and naive.

"Yes! It's all ours, my love, no more inns or tents." My father lifted me into his arms.

My mother stood behind us with boxes in her hands.

"Welcome home, baby." She planted a kiss on my forehead. "Now we'll be together forever." She stepped up onto the gangway, looking back with a smile. I sighed, relief washing through me.

Home.

"Joy? We must go now." Dahlia's soft voice wrapped around me like an embrace.

"Harlow has his crew tying ropes to your ship, they will drag it to land. It can be fixed, Joy, I promise." She rested her hand against my cheek. Pulling away, I stared at her.

"You shouldn't make promises you can't keep, Florence." I stepped up onto the ship's bow, my voice emphasizing her name.

Stumbling down, clutching Captain Harlow's hand, my feet landed on the ship's deck, spots of water and blood dripping onto the wood. Lifting my head, Harlow's face was mere inches from mine.

"You truly are becoming more and more interesting."

14

RAYA
SING ME TO SLEEP

"Raya's stitches are healing perfectly... however, is it her mental state that I worry about."

- ELIJAH'S MEDICAL JOURNALS.

I followed Khol's tense body down the corridor. At first, I thought we were in a palace, the grand rooms and ancient inscribing reminded me of that of the Foothills but the further we walked, the more it became obvious that we were not in a castle.

We were in a temple.

It was not clear who or what the temple was worshipping but marble carvings of naked goddesses and ancient prayers I could barely translate littered every nook, corner, and wall. I slowed, staring at a painting covering an entire wall. It was a woman, tall and fair-skinned, she held a ball of light in one hand and a flicker of fire in the other. Her hair floated around her head as though she had stopped gravity herself. A shiver crept up my spine as I thought of my own hair rising back at the safe house.

"Raya," Khol snapped, breaking my concentration, I jogged over to him, turning to take a last look at the painting. The smell of fresh cut grass and my mother's perfume enveloped me again.

"Do you smell that?" I whispered.

Khol stopped outside wooden double doors, so tall I had to crane my neck to see the top of them.

"I smell freshly brewed coffee and…" his voice trailed off at the end, his brows furrowed. I cleared my throat nervously.

"It's magic," he muttered. "Some say it smells of love." He cleared his throat. "Get used to it, there's plenty of magic here."

I nodded, taking in the new information.

Movement in the corner of my eye stole my attention, Khol was wringing his hands. I smiled smugly.

"What do you have to be nervous about?" I asked, he didn't even look in my direction.

"I'm the one who has been dressed up like a doll and taken to a 'grand hall'…" I gasped dramatically and said mockingly. "Am I going to be sacrificed?" Khol rolled his eyes.

"They wouldn't dare," he said, and my smile fell. "I am not nervous for myself, I'm nervous for what is to come." He pushed the doors open as though they weighed nothing and strode into the room.

The domed ceiling looked as though it was made of solid gold, a lone table stood in the middle of the room. The smell of meat, cheese, and fresh bread filled my nostrils and my stomached growled loudly. A women sat at the head of the table, glasses perched on the edge of her nose as she read from a large scroll. Her dark hair was littered with grey strands and her tanned skin marked with scars, and a snake tattoo wrapped around her bicep. She lifted her head when Khol cleared his throat.

"Khol darling, come on, sit down." She stood, walking over to us with the grace of a dancer. "Your father is just taking Ottie to bed, he won't be long," she said softly before turning to me. "You must be Raya," she said, completely unfazed by my presence. "I am Ezra, I'm glad the dress fits. I thought you'd feel comfortable in green." She smiled before moving back to her seat, gesturing for us to do the same.

I felt my insides curl as I began to sit, what was going on? Why was everyone acting as though it was completely normal for us all to be eating together? And what was going on with Ezra and Khol? I sighed.

"Are you hungry?" she asked, breaking a bread roll with her hands.

"Ezra, she wants answers, not bread," Khol said. "And so do I."

"Khol, I wish you would not call me Ezra, I am your mother, show some respect," she sighed.

"Raya can tell you why she's here." She turned back to her bread.

"Ezra," I said, the name feeling foreign in my mouth. "I do not know why I am here." Did they know what had happened at the safe house?

"Yes, Raya, we know what happened at the safe house." My eyes shot to meet Ezra's. Khol rolled his eyes.

I huffed a sigh as the fresh cut grass wafted near me. I was already getting sick of the smell. Ezra set her knife and fork down.

"Clearly, Khol has not been so open with his knowledge." She threw an irritated look towards her son.

"You are gifted, Raya, that is why you are here. That is

why the Sage Guard were bound to let you live with your people. Just like me and Khol and almost everyone here." Her words sunk into my skin.

"Do all Sorcerers live here?"

"Most but not all, Sorcerer's on the Southern Continent have their own Temple, we liaise with them often." She flicked a non-existent piece of fluff from her shoulder.

"It is safe here, Raya," Khol chimed in. "That is why we live here. Out there," he thumbed toward The Temple walls, "we are hunted and tortured." He stared at my body as if he could see the scars beneath my clothes.

"And if I want to leave?" I said, back ramrod straight. Khol pulled out a chair for me and I sat, reaching for a bread roll.

"I'm afraid I can't let you leave, not yet." Ezra's voice was sweet and deadly.

"I thought this wasn't a prison?" I turned to Khol, who stopped with a forkful of meat halfway to his mouth.

"The Temple is not a prison, it's a sanctuary for *our* kind."

I bristled at her words.

"If you wish to leave, you may. But not until you have control, I will not risk my family," she said sternly.

"What do I have to do with your family?"

"If they find out about you, they will find our Temple and we'll all be dead before the sun has set." Ezra finally made eye contact with me. "You can leave when you gain control and you are no longer a threat." The double doors swung open again, and a tall, red headed man swept into the room.

"She is finally asleep," he stated before joining us at the table, planting a swift kiss on Ezra's cheek. He was gracefully handsome, much like an older version of Khol. The same smattering of scars covered his arms and a curved tattoo sat around his right eye. Happiness oozed from him. He grabbed a Turkey leg and dug in, completely ignoring my presents. Ezra cleared her throat.

"You must be Raina," the man choked around the food in his mouth.

"Raya," Khol and I corrected simultaneously. The man hummed a response before silence enveloped us.

"And his is my father, Jonas," Khol spoke through gritted teeth.

"Ah yes, Jonas, sorry. You'll have to accuse my manners. It has been quite the day." Jonas smiled sweetly.

Khol had kept quite the secret. He was the son of The Temple's leader, and he was my way to freedom.

I sat on my bed, my arms wrapped around my legs. Suddenly my big room seemed very small. Perhaps I should've eaten more at lunch, I didn't have the energy to remove my dress or sleep, and my traitor stomach's rumble filled the room. At some point I began to cry, I wasn't sure when I started but I couldn't stop. I sat there, curled in a ball until I fell into a fitful sleep, dreaming of my life at the orphanage, dreaming of Matron's burned pies.

A soft knock woke me, my eyes almost swollen shut from crying. The sun had only just begun to set.

"Raya?" a soft whispered filled the room. "It's Elijah, may I come in?" he asked poking his head around the corner, and I nodded. He crept in softly, a plate of food in his hand and his brown satchel on his shoulder.

"You slept through dinner," he said, setting the plate down and helping me sit up. I reached for the plate, but the food tasted like ash in my mouth.

"May I look at your stitches?" he asked gently, and I nodded again. Elijah inspected them softly, nodded, whispering to himself, and writing in a small brown note pad.

"You are healing brilliantly."

I smiled weakly and he perched on the armchair beside my bed as I forced the food down.

"Ezra is a good woman," he said with a smile. "She is not keeping you here to punish you, she wishes to help you." He rolled up his sleeve and showed me the stump where his arm used to be. "She has helped me a great deal, I've lived here for the last twenty years as a healer." He stood from his chair and brushed of his spotless trousers, and I watched him thoughtfully as he walked to the window and paused. "There are people in this world who wish to hurt people like us. Those people claim to be protecting the world, but they have wiped out hundreds of bloodlines and families." He looked to me, letting all of his sorrow and anguish lay upon his face. "They have told the world that our kind is extinct and it's better to keep it that way. If you leave without learning how to control your power, you will draw attention to us and then none of us will be safe." A small smile graced his face as he pushed his glasses up.

"Do you understand?" he asked and I nodded.

"What is your gift?" I asked and he grinned.

"Shall I show you?" He closed his eyes, smile splitting his face and… disappeared, only to reappear seconds later the other side of the room. I gasped.

"I am a jumper, a form of MindWondering," he said. I blinked, and he was back in the chair.

"Why are you a healer?" I asked suddenly filled with energy.

"My jumping is helpful in battle, but we do not need to fight anymore," he sighed. "And I wish to help people, because no one helped me."

We sat in comfortable silence for a moment, it felt like Elijah and I had known each other for years. Soft guilt tried to pierce my heart for what I had to do. Elijah had known loss, just like I had. He had no other place to turn, just like me. I reached out and grabbed his hand.

"Thank you," I whispered, I finally had some of the answers I craved.

"Can I ask you a question?" I blurted, catching Elijah as he turned to leave. He nodded with a kind smile. "Before…" Words evaded me.

"Your… awakening?" Elijah finished for me.

"Yes, before my awakening, I heard these voices in my mind. Strange voices that I hadn't heard before or recognized." I prayed Elijah didn't think me strange for asking such questions. "I was hoping you knew what they were?" I finished with a grim smile.

He stopped for a moment, really soaking up the words and thinking deeply before he began pacing.

"It could be rogue Sorcerers," his voice cut through the silence, making me jump.

"Probably MindWonderers by the sound of it, trying to mess with your mind." He rolled his eyes, as though he was scorning small children.

"But why?" My curiosity bubbled within me.

"Perhaps they sensed the strength in your power? Perhaps they were spying for the Sage Guard? I can't be sure."

"They knew my name, and the name of my… friend," I spoke softly, his words catching up with me. "There are Sorcerers that work for the Sage Guard?"

"MindWonderers can reach into your mind, take knowledge without you even noticing." He chuckled, possibly at my naivety. "And yes, those Sorcerers help the Guard hunt us, that is why we stay within the walls of The Temple, because it is safe here."

I sucked in a breath, nodding solemnly.

"What is it?" Elijah asked, watching me thoughtfully. I wanted to tell him that I was shocked, that I could have spent my life hunting Sorcerers, hunting him. But I wasn't ready to part with that information, not yet.

"I thought the voices…" I hated how weak I sounded, "I thought they would have meant something or been useful in some way." I shrugged, hoping to seem as unbothered as possible.

"I suppose they were not useless," Elijah smiled. "They guided you toward your power, toward The Temple." He squeezed my shoulder.

"I'm pretty sure it was the house I blew up and the dozen soldiers I obliterated that led me here." My voice was flat.

This time Elijah shrugged. "Semantics."

He hopped of the edge of the bed.

"You can open the doors," Elijah said as he walked toward the door.

The setting sun called out to me so I slipped off the bed, opened the doors, and stepped out onto the balcony. Closing my eyes, I smiled at the sweet breeze sweeping my hair over my shoulders. The sun rays seemed to engulf me, wrapping me in their light. If the balcony was not beneath my feet, I would have thought I was flying. I called to the feeling deep down in my stomach. The feeling I dared not touch for the last nineteen years, the feeling that had caused me to lose everything. I felt my hair leave my shoulders, I felt the halo above me, and my smile widened. Ecstasy rolled over me, but I kept it tampered down. The sky was clear, not a cloud in sight. I called forward a bit more.

And just like that, the serene sky was gone, and lightning struck the balcony, missing me by only inches. In my surprise I let go of my tightly gripped power and fire blossomed in my hands. Panicked and dazed I pulled and pulled the power back down, but it did not listen.

Suddenly a thought dawned on me.

I was not in control.

Take a breath I heard my mother's voice, almost like she was standing right behind me. And I did. The light struck again, scaring me. The smell of my mother's perfume became sickly sweet around me.

Take a breath. And I did.

The fire warmed my palm intensely but did not burn my skin. My hair remained in the air, but the halo was gone.

Take a breath. And I did.

The dark began to lighten. Sweat trickled down my back and my body ached with tiredness.

I could not keep doing this. The fire went out just as my knees buckled under my weight. I fell and stayed on the balcony.

It seemed a good a place as any to sleep.

15

JOY

HOOK, LINE AND SINKER

"I need more time... She needs more time."

- FLORENCE'S PRIVATE LETTERS.

Bodies roamed Harlow's ship, some tall, some short, fat, thin, brown, white, black. It was as though every single person had come from a different corner of the world, like this was their meeting point. Smoke bloomed from one corner and spiced meats cooked in another. It was a living, breathing organism; everyone had a role. A tall black women balanced on the rim on the ship, a dagger between her teeth and a rope in her hands, she reached up, tying knots and fixing sails. A muscular man with buttery brown skin and cropped black hair, stood with his arms crossed. He grinned widely, clapping Harlow on the back as Florence hopped down onto the ship.

"Thought we'd 'av to send a rescue party." He eyed me and Florence, giving us a mock bow. "Welcome home, Flo," he said with a grin.

"I am not home, Ewan." She turned to Harlow. "This is merely a means to an end." She smiled smugly.

"What of Markus?" Ewan rose his eyebrows with a smile.

"Gutted like a fish," Harlow's throwaway words lingered on the deck of the ship. "And then he fell overboard."

Ewan laughed loudly, clapping Harlow on the back before sauntering toward the ship's held, resting his hands on the steering wheel. The rain had stopped only moments ago but the dark cloud remained.

"What happened to… the, the SkyMaker?" I said softly.

"The SkyChanger," he emphasized the word, irritated. "Settle down, we sent them a signal." My broken ship bobbed behind us as we dragged it toward the island.

"Jameson is not here, is he?" I asked Florence, avoiding eye contact. She shook her head, dragging a hand through her sodden hair. Staring at her I noticed that the entire ship we stood on was dry.

Bone dry.

Cold water dripped down my back.

"He is… magic, isn't he?" I motioned toward Captain Harlow, standing watch over his crew like a shepherd watching his lambs.

"He is… something." Florence smiled shyly, staring at the approaching island as we got closer to it. "We should be there before sundown." Her hand twitched as though she wished to reach for something. "Once the ship is fixed, we will set sail again, I promise." She smiled again, turning to leave.

"Thank you, Florence." I spoke before my mind could register what I was doing.

"That's nice." She spoke again and I raised an eyebrow. "I always wondered how my name would sound in your mouth."

The sky was a swirl of burnt orange, like ink dropped in water. It felt as though the island was close enough to touch. Leaning against the edge of the ship my mind filled itself with images of the storm, the ship, the magic and the SkyChangers. I had never seen magic, my entire life I had thought it was a myth or a legend from a time long ago.

I thought it extinct.

But now, as I stood on a ship, clad in linen trousers and shirt, my damp hair drying into a crazy afro, I had no idea how I got here.

"Do you need help with that?" The tall women from earlier stood behind me, her dagger now safely tucked into her boot.

"Sorry?" I choked on my words, looking down at my outfit.

"Your hair," she gestured to her own black hair, braided into beautiful swirls. "It'll only get hotter on the island."

I touched my hair, course from the rainwater and dry sun. Embarrassment flooded through my veins.

"I can braid it if you like?" She stepped closer, my head only just reaching her shoulders. I nodded enthusiastically.

"I'm Braisha." She smiled brightly.

Just as the sun began to steady its descent down to its slumber, my hair was pinned in several beautiful box braids, coconut oil smeared thickly on my scalp and the tips of my hair.

"They're beautiful, thank you so much." I stared at my reflection in the cracked mirror, in that moment I realized how much I looked like my mother. I forced back the tears in my eyes. She had not had chance to teach me to braid my own hair.

I had not been this content in years. I touched my hair and scalp softly. Braisha held out an orange silk scarf.

"To protect your scalp from the sun," she said with a smile. I opened my mouth to say thank you, but Captain Harlow interrupted me.

"Ready the sails, man the boundaries, Land ahead." He smirked, looking at the figures awaiting our arrival on the beach. "Oh how lovely. A welcome party."

Sand and salt scratched against wood as the ship was heaved upon the shore, sailors ankle deep in bright blue waters, damp ropes heavy in their hands. Jameson would have loved this, the camaraderie, everyone working together for the same goal. It took until sundown to haul my broken ship onto the sand, I watched the agonizingly slow process, aching to be part of it, but I had already been shrugged off, separated from the group.

"Don't interrupt the process, Killer." Harlow had loved branding me with a new nickname. "You'll only slow them down."

Three strangers, presumably native islanders, stood watching our process. They did not move throughout the entire night, one of them lighting a torch, fire flowing from their hands. We occupied only a small portion of the sprawling beach, craning our necks more often than not, hoping to view the island beyond the tall clusters of trees.

"We will not dock here long," Captain Harlow spoke softly, interrupting my lonesome thoughts. "And I will not leave without Florence," he said nonchalantly.

"Without Florence I am stranded, I need her." My voice was strong and demanding. "You only want her for some petty revenge."

"Why I need Florence is none of your business." He stepped closer to me, our faces mere inches away. "I had her and she fled, do not think I will make the same mistake twice." His shoulder cropped hair swished as he spun on his heel. Blood rushed to my cheeks and my fists clenched.

I focused on the soft sand in-between my toes, on the salty breeze, on the setting sun. Two women of a similar age to me stood on the sand a few feet away from me, the taller one with her short blonde hair tucked into a red head scarf and the other with long blonde hair flowing down her back. Their pale skin was bronzed by the sun rays; their cheeks scattered with freckles. They were attempting to pitch a tent, their voices rising as their struggle continued.

"Jodes! Listen to me! We need the wood to cross over." The taller one stood with a hand on her hip.

"No! When Dad taught me, he said they go parallel!" the other shouted back.

"How do they balance if they are parallel?"

"Erin! You. Are. Not. Listening. To. Me!"

I walked over cautiously, thankful for my headscarf as the sun continued to burn.

"She's right," they both turned to me "They need to cross over."

The taller one, Erin I guessed, stared at me.

"You're Joy." She stepped closer to me and I looked down at her ankle, at the 444 tattooed there, I nodded.

"Captain Harlow is not happy with you." Jodie stood up from beside the tent, her cropped t-shirt showing an identical 444 tattoo above her hip. Did all of Harlow's crew share this particular tattoo or just the two of them?

"Is Captain Harlow ever happy?" I ask, bending down to look at their handy work. Jodie knelt beside me, grinning.

"You'll have to excuse my sister… she likes us to stay under the radar and with you here…" Her voice trailed off.

"I understand." I began to cross the wood. "I mean only to help you, I promise."

Erin stood, watching me closely. I understood her unease, I was a stranger and she wanted to protect her sister. I would have done the exact same with Jameson.

"You know Florence, right?" Erin's voice rang out over the crashing shore and screeching gulls. I looked up slowly, careful over my choice of words.

"She's helping me find someone." I returned to the wood.

"She's a good woman."

"I suppose. I am still yet to see that side of her," I muttered to myself.

"Who are you looking for?" Jodie looked up from the collapsing stack of wood. I paused, unsure whether to share my most precious secrets with strangers.

"He is…" I paused, looking at the sisters. "I suppose you could say he is my brother." I swallowed back against the sudden flow of emotion that filled me.

"You'll need a new boat," Jodie said, pointing to my broken one. I nodded solely.

"Do you have a crew?" Jodie asked softly.

"Jodie," Erin warned quietly, oozing maturity despite the women being a similar age.

"What?" Jodie raised an eyebrow. "I'm just asking."

"You are never just asking." Erin rolled her eyes.

"Perhaps this is what we have been waiting for." Jodie stood, clasping her sister's hand. "A chance to do father proud." She looked back at me.

"Do you have a crew?" she asked again and I shook my head.

"She needs our help, she has no one… just like us." Erin pulled her into an embrace, the sisters' pain clearly fresh. They turned to me simultaneously, but it was Erin that spoke.

“Do you want a crew?” She rose her eyebrows.

I couldn’t help the smile that snaked across my face.

16

RAYA

BURNT LUNGS & RIPPED STITCHES

"How hard would it be to let go?"

- RAYA

"You need to grow up." Khol stood over me, the sun attempting to peek around him. My body ached from hours of sleeping on the cold, damp balcony, my eyes burned, and my throat was dry.

"Are you quite finished being a child?" Khol spoke again, his concern for me clearly turned to irritation. "The quicker you gain control, the quicker you can leave and go back to the people who will most likely murder you." He spat out the words as though they were poison, as though going back to my home with my family was the strangest idea ever to exist.

I rolled my eyes at the lovely wakeup call. Khol strode back into my room, pacing the small space.

"Well?" He stopped moving and starred at me.

"A bath has been prepared." His gaze lingered on me as a maid in loose blue clothes walked gracefully from the bathing chamber, an empty jug in her hands. The heat from the water called to me and I almost stripped right there, aching to feel something other than numbness.

Standing from the balcony, I shuffled to the bathing chamber, glaring at Khol as I moved. Shutting the door with more strength than necessary, I stripped off, leaving my pile of grimy clothing on the tiled floor.

"I'll be out here when you're done," Khol called, the sound of his heavy footsteps telling me that he had continued pacing.

My blue fingers burned as I slipped into the warm bath, my scars stinging as the water lapped over them. I looked down at my body, running my fingers over the scars, old and new. I had never really taken any time at all to look at myself since everything went to hell a few days ago. Although bruised and cut, my skin glowed faintly looking almost smug and satisfied. I traced the scars softly, grimacing at the ones on my ankles, I knew these scars. They had been my enemies for the last twelve years.

I sunk deep into the water, the waves lapping over my head until I was submerged. I relished in the quiet, white noise of being completely still. The water was an old friend, welcoming me home. I starred at the ceiling, mesmerized by the milky scaled texture the water gave everything around me. My lungs ached a little, but I did not mind, I enjoyed the stillness. When my lungs began to burn, I stayed in the stillness, taking a deep breath.

Black spots dotted against my vision and I let my body go limp.

And the world began to fade…

Water rushed over my head as Khol's giant body heaved me up out of the tub. Water spurted from my mouth and my chest shook. Khol turned from me, looking everywhere apart from at my exposed body. He grabbed a towel, passing it to me as he stared as his boots.

"Are you trying to get kill yourself, *Raya*?" he hissed, my name like an insult on the tip of his tongue. I heaved in a deep breath after deep breath, my lungs screaming at me. My hair tangled across my face and blood spread like spilled ink in the water.

"One of your stitches on your abdomen ripped when I pulled you out," Khol said once I'd wrapped myself in the towel, his tone accusatory, as though it was my fault.

Perhaps it was.

He strode out the bathing room toward the gilded wardrobe, tossing out black leather trousers and a long-sleeved shirt. He crossed his arms over his chest and turned toward the wall.

"Get dressed." His tone was final. "Then I'll take you to Elijah and he'll fix your stitches."

"Thank you," I whispered, my throat horse. I stood still at the entry way of the bathing chamber, my towel held in place by my white-knuckle grip.

"What are you waiting for? Trust me, I'm not looking," Khol said smugly.

"Then how do you know I'm not getting dressed," I countered.

"Because I'm not deaf." His voice was unkind. "Your feet haven't moved."

"You're standing in front of my draws." I nodded to the brown chest of draws Khol was leaning on. I moved towards the draws quickly, careful not to get too close to Khol.

"I already got you clothes, Raya." He sighed as if I were the dimmest girl in the entire continent.

"Undergarments, Khol. I need undergarments." My tone was flat and unbothered, and he staggered back.

"They're not going to bite you," I said, rolling my eyes and grabbing the closest set I could find before changing quickly and combing my wet hair.

Once I was ready, I reached for the door.

"Wait," Khol's hand pushed the door shut, his body preventing me from re opening it.

"What?" I said, surprised it took him this long to mention what just happened.

"Are you going to tell me what that was, in the water?" His tone was surprisingly light for such a morbid topic.

"I fell asleep." The lie rolled off my tongue smoother than I expected it.

"With your eyes open?"

I heaved a sigh, remembering myself staring at the ceiling through the water's gaze.

"Can we just leave, unless you want me to bleed to death from my open stitches?" I reached for the door again. Khol slammed it shut.

"Were you trying… what would you have done if I wasn't there?"

"You were there, Khol, so why waste time wondering about things that haven't happened?" Blood began to rush to my cheeks.

"But what if I wasn't?" he persisted.

"But you were!"

"But what if I wasn't?"

"Then I probably would have drowned." My voice came out as a shout, and I wished to cram the words back into my mouth as soon as I had said them. The silence left in the wake of my words was painful, its blunt edges pushing against my skin. Khol starred deeply into my eyes, although it felt like he was a hundred miles away. He opened the door, pausing before continuing down the corridor.

"When will you realize that we are not your enemies?"

And without giving me chance to respond he strode down the corridor, leaving me to scurry after him.

"What happened?" Elijah's tone was concerned as he scowled at Khol.

"I slipped in the bath." Elijah remained uncertain and I reached for his hand. "I am well, Elijah, I promise."

I risked a look at Khol, silently begging that he would not contradict my story. He gave a subtle nod to Elijah who sighed softly, scrubbing his hand over his weathered face before looking up at Khol.

"Fetch your sister will you, Khol?" he said and my face crumpled with confusion. Why would Elijah need Khol's sister? Khol's face seemed to mirror mine.

"I had hoped to avoid using her but since Raya is determined to be my patient forever." He looked at me and smiled. "I think we need some quicker healing, wouldn't you agree?" He looked up at Khol again with his brows raised.

Khol slumped off slowly, and it only occurred to me then that Khol seemed visibly younger when he was around Elijah, Khol had to be a few years older than me, but Elijah made him seem like a boy. I relaxed as Elijah removed the bloody bandage around my open wounds.

"What really happened, Raya?" Elijah did not look up from where he worked.

"I told you, I slipped." My voice remained steady.

"You are a terrible liar," he laughed. "But I am surprised that you managed to get Khol to go along with it." I grimaced at the wave of guilt that washed over me. Khol did not deserve my guilt. He claimed not to be my enemy, but I know people like him.

I knew them too well.

An old, dull pain sunk into my ankles, my scars ached, and my vision danced.

"He probably did not have the energy to argue again. That's all he seems capable of." I rolled my eyes.

"I wouldn't form your opinion on Khol just yet." Elijah didn't look up from dressing my stitches. "He may surprise you."

And as though his name summoned him, Khol strode through the small wooden door, ducking beneath the frame into Elijah's small apothecary. A young girl, no older than eight, trailed behind him, her face bored and soft. She wore a periwinkle dress, loose and flowing from her shoulders to her toes. She glanced at me as though I was just another piece of furniture.

"Elijah!" She squealed before wrapping her arms around his middle.

"Ottie my love, have you grown again?"

"I hope so!' She stood on her tiptoes "I want to be as tall as Khol one day!" Her bored face split into a grin.

"And you shall, my love." Elijah's old face turned young for a moment, his smile earnest and bright. I sat awkwardly in a hard arm chair, my long legs bent attempting to make space in the tiny room.

I felt Khol's gaze hot on my cheek.

Glancing up, my eyes connected with his. His eyes seemed to search mine, as though he was looking for me.

Even though he knew I'd been here all along.

A blush crept up his neck and warmth pooled in my stomach.

I made him nervous.

I couldn't help the small smile appearing in the corner of my mouth.

Oddly, he returned the gesture.

And suddenly the very small room seemed even smaller, the back of my neck became clammy,

And yet Khol did not break our eye contact.

If Elijah was talking, I couldn't hear him.

"Raya!" Elijah snapped and my head shot his way, breaking the connection between Khol and I. Coldness seeped into my bones.

"Where is your head, girl?" Elijah's voice was soft again, he always sounded as though he was on the verge of laughing.

Where was my head? What was I doing?

I shrugged my shoulders.

"…are you sure the message reads *that*?" Faint shouts sounded through the thick door.

"I am sure of it… looking… The girl! … safe…" The voices became more inaudible the harder I tried to listen. Khol's ears were still pricked up and his eyes glassy, as though he could hear the voices loud and clear. Ottie and Elijah had the same placid looks painted on their faces.

"Are they talking abou—" Ottie's voice sounded.

"Enough, Ottie." Khol's voice rang loudly. "We are here to heal her stitches and leave, we've already been here for too long." His voice was bare and rough.

I flinched.

Her.

I leaned back against the uncomfortable chair, resting my head and closing my eyes.

I was truly sick of feeling like burden. I had vowed to myself that I would never be trapped again.

Never feel lonely again.

I ached for the rain on my cheeks. I missed my family and the orphanage.

But mostly I miss Alias. I hated not knowing how he felt

about my mission or my newfound magic. I refused to believe he would have left me voluntarily. How had everything I had come to know disappeared in a matter of days?

I swiped a tear from my cheek before anyone saw it fall. A small hand touched my arm gently as Ottie softly peeled my blood-soaked shirt from my skin, her cold hands making me flinch.

"Remember what we said?" Elijah's voice was small, almost a whisper.

"I am the master," Ottie whispered back, her gazed fixed on my wound. Khol's lips tilted upward as his eyes filled with nostalgia. Nervous energy filtered through my veins. A small hand covered the cut, her pressure stung, and the pain flared to life. I squeezed my eyes shut as my hands balled into fists.

The pain was hot and sharp and then nonexistent. My gaze fluttered to the now almost-fully healed scar on my side. I stared at Ottie in amazement, now jumping on her toes in excitement.

"Be careful, Khol," Elijah mocked. "She's almost better than you," he said with a wink and Ottie giggled.

My body felt unearthly and light. My brain was foggy and cloudy, I felt drunk.

Everything seemed too real now.

The phrase *I am the master* lingered in my head like a bad dream. If they were the masters, what did that make me?

17

JOY

CLOSE YOUR EYES AND THINK OF DAYRA

"We needed supplies, or we wouldn't survive the journey."

- ERIN'S PRIVATE JOURNAL.

By the time the sun began to set and the sky was alight with fire, I knew we had to leave sooner rather than later.

"We should tell Harlow," Jodie stated as we sat on the sand, watching my ship being heaved back into the water, not a scratch in sight.

"Are you insane?" Erin kept her voice low and hushed. "He would never willingly let us go." She rolled her eyes towards her sister.

"Her ship is fixed, he will expect her departure soon enough."

"What is the deal with Captain Harlow? Does, does he… own you?" My voice mirrored Erin's, low and unsure.

"He likes to think he does," Jodie spoke softly. "Everyone in our crew owes Harlow some sort of debt, whether it be money or repayment for a favor." She looked down at the sand.

"If you cannot pay, you must work off your debt." Erin's voice turned soft. "We're working off our father's debt."

"Why isn't he working off his own debt?"

"Dead," Jodie said, a sad smile gracing her lovely face. I knew this pain; it was an old friend. An old nemesis. A wound never to be healed, a bone broken never to be fixed.

A small tear slipped down Erin's cheek, the dark kohl lining her eyes smudging slightly. I nodded.

"How long have you been in the Southern Continent?" My voice was thick with unshed tears.

"How do you know we weren't born here?"

"You don't often see skin as fair as yours." I smiled "Jameson is from the Northern Continent too."

"Jameson?"

"My, uh, 'brother,'" I smiled at the sound of his name being spoken. "My family." The sisters smiled, reminding me of Florence.

Florence.

Where was she?

I hadn't seen her since the previous day, not since we had heaved my broken ship onto the shore and began our wait on the sand.

I stood quickly, if Captain Harlow already had Florence with him, I'd never make it back to Jameson. I looked over at my ship, at the new slightly off-colored wood nailed to the side.

"Joy." A low whisper knocked me from my trance, I saw nothing and no one, but Erin and Jodie stood to join me, looking around for the voice.

"Joy." The whisper sounded again, and a dark brown head

stuck out from the tall weeds separating us and the rest of the island.

Florence waved hastily from within the grass, relaxed now that she had our attention.

"Quick!" she whispered, holding out a hand for me.

Looking around to make sure we were not followed I took Florence's hand, and we walked until each of us were hidden beneath the tall, dry grass. Jodie squirmed.

"There better not be any spiders here!" she squealed and her sister shushed her.

"How did you get away from Harlow?" I asked and Florence shook her head.

"There is no time to explain, Harlow expects your departure by sun-up." I dragged my hands through my hair and she continued. "Our ship is being moved by Charlton, he's going to sail it around the island to the other side as soon as it is dark." I focused on her words, she said 'Our' ship. I shook my head.

"Charlton?" I stared at her.

"He's a good friend."

"Should we trust him?"

"Do we have any other choice?" Florence's voice rose. "I promised to get you to Jameson, and I intend to keep that promise." She turned to Erin and Jodie, as though she had only just noticed them. She smiled brightly.

"You're coming with us?" she asked, her hands resting on each of the girls' shoulders. They nodded and she turned to me.

"You're smart, a FireBringer and a MindWonderer." She turned back to the girls. "Harlow's favorite assets." She turned on her heel and pushed through the grass.

"You are Sorcerers?" I turned to the women as we walked through the grass.

"Yes." She looked back at the trail we had walked, as if checking we were not followed. "It seems we're more alike than you think." She turned, her gaze glued on the horizon as we walked.

"What do you mean?"

"We're almost to the city." Florence's voice cut through the golden evening, and we stopped just before the grass ended.

Music, sweet and longing drifted through the air. Scents of spices and savories filled our nostrils, as I pushed aside the tall grass and a city sprung up around us. Candles lit the night sky and tall buildings stood proud around us. The city was small and cramped but teeming with life. Half broken houses and smashed windows created the skyline, and drunk sailors and dancers kissed in dark alleys.

A FireBringer stood surrounded by children, he created tigers and dragons of fire with his fingertips. Wonder painted my face, and I couldn't stop myself. It was dirty, dark, bright, lively, sexy and, most of all, it was alive. Nothing like I'd ever seen before.

Jodie stepped froward, as though an invisible hand pulled her toward the city. The two sisters shared a longing look and smiled.

Their hands intertwined as they stepped into the bustling city.

I felt Florence's gaze hot on my cheek, her soft black curls lingering in my peripheral vision.

In a swift movement I met her gaze, her brown skin lit by candlelight and her dark eyes full of something I couldn't quite name. I smiled tentatively.

She smiled back.

Her mouth opened, words playing on her lips.

"What are you waiting for?" Erin's voice tore through the

silence. "If we are to find supplies and get to the ship before sunrise then we must hurry."

I nodded, striding toward the women, only looking back at Florence once. We slid into the hustle and mayhem of the night market, not one patron looked up at us. Sellers hollered from their stalls and customers bartered and pushed. There were hundreds of aisles of stalls, each decorated with colorfully striped awnings and littered with candelabras lit with what looked like a thousand candles. We stumbled around like idiots, attempting to grab anything and everything we might need. I closed my eyes, running my hands through my hair.

"Everything alright?" an unfamiliar voice sounded behind me and I huffed a sigh. Turning I came face to face with a neck, his Adam's apple bobbing slightly. I noticed the Sage Guard uniform immediately and a bolt of nerves shot through me.

Why was a member of the Sage Guard on the Southern Continent?

My gaze travelled up to his face, tanned skin, dark eyes slightly slanted, cutting cheekbones and almost black hair. He was striking.

He rose his eyebrows. I had been staring. Staring in silence.

"Everything is fine," I forced a smile. "Just taking a stroll."

Florence jogged to my side, her eyes wide as she took in the stranger's uniform. The guard pulled a sketch from his pocket.

"Have you seen this girl?" His voice was almost sad as I laid my eyes on the beautiful women on the paper, her pale skin, long brown hair, and bright eyes. Without thinking, I shook my head.

"I'm on the island until morning, let me know if you remember seeing her on your… travels." His face did not change from the hard exterior. I nodded and began to turn away.

"If you see her," his voice was stark, "tell her Alias is looking for her."

I nodded as he turned away from me. I didn't know this girl, but I had seen her.

She was the one I had dreamed about for days on end. The one with gravity defying hair.

What did this all mean? And why was he searching for her?

18

RAYA

DON'T TRIP, DON'T FALL

"She is stronger than she knows".

- KHOL'S MESSAGE TO EZRA.

Ezra's terms were simple. There were six tasks I needed to complete before I could return to the 'real world'. Six tasks to gain as much information about The Temple and its people, before Jala dragged me back. Ezra was very clear that I would not be allowed out of the protection of The Temple until I mastered each task. Each was designed to test a different aspect of my being.

First, physical combat, pushing my body and will to its breaking point. Survive that, and then I would been tested on the soundness of my mind. If I were captured and tortured for answers about The Temple, I would need an iron will… and a high pain threshold, that test was designed to test my loyalty, little did they know that information would flow freely from me, no torture required.

Assuming I made it through the first two tasks, the last

four would be surrounding my abilities, my powers. The new force that lurked beneath my skin, begging to be released.

The day after my stitches healed, I marched to the large dining area, hoping to start a fight with Ezra and burn through some of my nervous energy, but she was the picture of calmness and tranquility, focusing on her bowl of porridge, barely noticing I had entered the room.

The other members of The Temple noticed me though, their heads snapping up to meet my gaze. Some of them sliding away from me, some scooching closer. Whispers of distrust and awe mixed together like a god-awful cocktail I wished to smash against the concrete beneath my feet.

I hadn't seen Khol since the day before, I knew he was avoiding me, that much was clear. I was grateful that as soon as Ottie had healed me, she and her brother left the room hastily. Although it was easier to be alone, I had realized that Khol was the only person I had to talk to. Obviously, we argued constantly, and he was a brute through and through, but I was lonely.

Refusing to wither beneath the stares of the Sorcerers' I turned for corridor, striding away. The carpet was warm and soft beneath my bare feet, like a blanket sitting near a roaring fire. I tried to be barefoot as often as I could, it was a tip from Elijah. Being barefoot grounded my power, it could flow freely around my body and into the earth.

Movement in the shadowed edge of the hallway caught my attention.

"Are you spying on me?" I drawled, walking slowly into the dark corner.

"That's very bold of you," Khol whispered as I tucked into the shadows next to him. "I could be spying on a different woman."

I nodded, a sarcastic retort on my tongue. But wrongness twisted within me, was he looking for a different woman?

“But of course, you are the most interesting Sorcerer The Temple has seen in a long while. So perhaps it was you I was looking for.” He shrugged nonchalantly, the movement causing his shoulder to brush mine. I rolled my eyes, ignoring the zing of excitement that rolled through me.

“And why is it that you’re looking for me?” I turned to face him.

“Maybe I just wanted to see you.” His voice was so calm that he took me by surprise.

“I—” Before I could get the words out, he swept my feet from underneath me sending me crashing to the floor, then he pinning my body with the crushing weight of his own.

Ezra strolled past us, glancing at our position.

“Good night, Khol,” she spoke softly, as though seeing me pinned to the ground was completely normal.

“Good night, Mother,” he called out, never taking his eyes from mine.

“What are you doing?” I squirmed beneath him, scolding myself internally. I had been training my entire life and yet I had let Khol take me by surprise? I supposed that my inability to fight him off did play into the role of the ‘scared, weak woman’ that I was masking as in The Temple. Every cloud had a silver lining.

“I’m giving you a little taster.” He leaned in low, our faces only a breath apart. “Get your shit together, our training begins tomorrow. I’ll be at your door at dawn.” And with that he stood up and shot away. Leaving me to question what the hell had just happened.

The moon shone into my chambers as I arrived back to my room, casting a white glow around everything, my head swimming with memories of what had just happened. I shook my head, clearing away the thoughts of him. My gaze landed on my Sage Guard combat boots, left haphazardly against my wardrobe door.

My mind wondered to Alias again.

Was he safe? Did he worry for me? I shook my head again, wading through my thoughts and climbing beneath my bed covers without bothering to change into a night gown. I begged for sleep and this time, she obliged.

A knock at the door woke me hastily, the moon still shone, and the sun was still fast sleep. I laid still until the knock sounded again.

Padding over to the door, fear swept over me, and I lunged for my foreign power buried deep within me.

But it wasn't a threat. It was Khol.

"Can I come in?" he asked timidly.

I nodded, cringing as he walked over to the bed and perched on it awkwardly.

"I- I…" he began. I had never seen him so nervous.

"Wanted to talk about the training?" I spoke for him; he huffed a sigh in relief.

"Right." He wrung his hands, trying to find the words. "I don't know if it's appropriate for me to train you for your trials." His voice was barely audible.

"Why?" I asked harshly, and I couldn't help but feel hurt by his words.

"I don't think I'd be able to concentrate. I haven't been able to think of anyone but you since your arrival."

I opened my mouth to respond but the air whooshed out of my lungs as his lips crashed against mine. He drew me close, his arms wrapping around my waist and our kiss deepening, I opened my mouth, moaning softly as he swept his tongue through my parted lips. I wrapped my arms around his neck, pulling our bodies flush against each other. We moved down, my back now against the soft duvet beneath me, our kiss never breaking, and we fell, Khol's body on top of mine. I whimpered as he pulled away from my mouth, his lips trailing wet kisses down my chin, my neck, and chest. Ripping my nightgown up he began to trail soft kisses up in the inside of my leg, until I was biting my lip and fisting the sheets. He hovered above me.

"Do you feel the same?"

I shot up from my bed, the sun streaming in through the open doors. Sweat coated my body, my hair sticking to my neck and my cheeks flushed, the outfit I wore to dinner still clinging to my skin. My heart slammed against my ribs as I fought against the tingling sensation from last night's dream.

I plunged into the bathtub, enjoying the feeling of the ice-cold water I filled it with. I needed to wash off the dream and the feeling of Khol and the taste of him.

Stop.

I needed to focus on my task ahead.

On exposing The Temple's weaknesses and spilling its secrets.

On letting the Sage Guard hunt the Sorcerers. My stomach turned. Letting them hunt my own people.

Unexpected sadness crept into my mind. I wasn't only spying on The Temple; I was providing a death sentence. In the week I had been here I had become close with Elijah. Would I ever see him again?

Or Khol?

I sat up in the tub, the cold water settling my nerves slightly. I just needed to get through today. I stared at the blue and green tiles on the wall, resting my hands on the rough stone edge of the bathtub. I had not stopped to wonder what my life would look like if I had never entered the gods forsaken safe house. Would I be back at the Foothills with

Alias? Or would I be suffering a worse fate when my power eventually reared its head?

The cold water began feeling hateful, and I leapt from the tub before I could stew in my mind any longer. Dressed and ready, I greeted Nai at the door as she brought fresh linens and outfits for the next week.

"These are beautiful." I picked up an evening dress, it's lilac fabric soft and thin. "Where did you find this one?" I ran my hands over the jewels placed delicately on the bodice. Nai bowed gently.

"I made them." Her cheeks became rosy as she spoke.

"You have a gift, they're truly wonderful."

The door swung open, and Khol smiled smugly as he rested on the door frame.

"You ready, Princess?" His eyebrows rose in question and my skin started to burn softly. I swallowed down the lump in my throat, nodding slowly, my eyes staring at my bare feet. His eyebrows then knitted together in confusion.

"No fight in you today?"

"Something like that." I walked past him, pressing my hand to Nai's shoulder as I did. I couldn't play fight with him; I couldn't argue and pretend. Every time I looked at him, I felt his lips on my mouth, my neck, my legs.

Stop. Focus on the task.

I walked ahead of him, although I wasn't sure where we were going. I sucked in a deep breath and steadied my stance.

A hand clasped on my lower forearm, and I spun toward Khol.

"Are you quite alright?" His eyes studied my own. I nodded.

"Don't lie to me, Princess," he persisted.

"I am not." Heat blushed in my cheeks, betraying me. "Don't call me that," I muttered.

"Tell me."

"There is nothing to tell."

"Raya." And maybe it was the dream, his soft grip on my forearm, or the fact that he called me Raya instead of that stupid nickname, but I relented.

"I had a dream and… it has thrown my concentration."

"A dream?" His gaze narrowed on mine, I nodded.

"Satisfied?" I asked, my voice horse.

"Not at all." His voice was gruff as his grip on my forearm tightened slightly and his face came closer to mine.

"Nor am I," I whispered softly.

"Khol!" Ezra's voice cut through the air, and we parted as though pulled by horses. "You must hurry. Raya cannot waste a moment of time if she is to pass this season's trials. After all, you were the one who insisted on training her." Ezra's floral dress flowed around her as though it was a gushing a waterfall.

"Insisted?" I gaped, my gaze jumping from Khol to his mother.

"Yes. Khol Insisted you be trained by him; therefore, he must follow through on his decisions." She shook her head, leaving us alone in the domed hall where even the paintings held their breathes.

A pregnant silence engulfed us.

"You *insisted*?" I looked up at him. He raked his hands through his hair.

"The only way you'll pass the trials is with a good trainer," he strode forward, continuing down the corridor. "And I am the best. Don't make me some sort of hero."

I caught up with his stride, hiking up my soft, black trousers.

"I am my own hero, *Prince,*" I muttered, using his own nickname against him.

19

JOY

WHEN WORLDS COLLIDE

"Perhaps this is a road we should not have tread."

- JOY WHEN DISCUSSING THE JOURNEY AHEAD.

I stared at the strangers retreating figure. Alias, that's what he said his name was. Florence stood behind me, her hazel eyes watching the figure intensely.

"Do you know who that girl is?" she asked as I stared at the picture taped to the nearest stall.

"Raya." Her name sounded oddly familiar in my mouth, almost like something clicking into place. I didn't know how I knew but there was no doubt in my mind she was Raya. I knew it in the center of my very being. Florence shook her head, looking over at Erin and Jodie, their mouths open, shouting their bids.

"We need to focus," I turned, walking toward the sisters. "If the boat is docking before sunrise, we must be quick."

Jodie turned at our voices, holding out a large sack filled with canned beans, fruit, bread, cheese, and rum.

"Rum?" I rose an eyebrow.

"You might not be a 'real' pirate," she mimicked the word with her fingers, "but we are." Erin couldn't help the smile on her face as she rolled her eyes.

"We have food and… rum, but what of the boat?" I turned to Florence. "Do you know what is aboard?" I asked.

"I'm sorry, I didn't check the contents before I stole the damn thing!" She spoke in a harsh whisper. I flinched as her words but stayed quiet. She had been tense since Alias had spoken to us, looking around every so often to check on the people surrounding us.

"Look, there is a stall across the way." I pointed to a stall at the other side of the market. "Harlow will notice us gone sooner rather than later, I will get some supplies and meet you at the marina, climb aboard, and sail at first light." I began walking toward the stall.

"You're not going alone." Florence grabbed my wrist.

"Only you know what the ship looks like, and I am not separating the sisters," I smiled softly. "I will be back before first light, I promise." I squeezed her hand.

"And if you are not?"

"Then," I looked down at the necklace between my breasts, "save Jameson for me, please." I turned on my heel and fled, not daring to look back. I knew Florence would take them to the ship.

But I didn't know if she would forgive me for leaving her.

I jogged through the market, determined to make it to the stall and back well before sunrise, making the space between us and Captain Harlow as big as possible. The market had thinned out ever so slightly as I finally made it to the large wooden table. An older man sat behind the counter.

"Rope, please, rope, lanterns, binoculars, sage..." I searched the stall. "A map, yes, a map... please." My breath was shallow, and a thin sheen of sweat coated my entire body. The sun would rise within the hour. I bobbed on my feet as the elderly man packed the bag agonizingly slowly.

I jogged back to the place I had left Florence, counting my steps to steady my heart.

But nothing was familiar, everything looked different.

"It's the curse of the city," a women in a purple headdress spoke from behind a stall, a crystal ball in her hands. I heaved the bag in her direction.

"Curse?"

"Everybody gets lost from time to time," she spoke again, her voice wistful and strange. I smiled tightly, attempting to walk away.

"You know her, Joy." I spun at the sound of my name.

"How do you know my name?" I pointed a finger in her direction.

"How does the sun know when she must sleep?" She petted a kitten perched on her matching purple tablecloth.

I knew the sun would rise soon; I knew that I was wasting my time but something inside me pushed me forward.

"Would you like to make a deal, Joy?" Her eyes met mine. "It seems as though you need some guidance." I stared at her wrinkled face, despite the years she was beautiful and vibrant.

"What kind of deal?"

"I'll tell you three truths." She eyed the crystal ball lazily.

"And what do you want in return?" I straightened my back.

"A favor."

"What kind of favor?"

"Oh you needn't worry about that now, I do not need anything yet." She smiled brightly.

I knew this was a mistake, I knew not to get involved with those who knew too much—witches… or those who claimed to be.

I nodded my head.

She reached out and took my palm, slicing a jeweled dagger across it, and deep crimson blood splashed my white trousers. She lifted some blood with her knife, stashing it in a small vile.

"For safe keeping," she said with a wink. I stared at my now scarred hand, smearing the blood with the pad of my thumb.

"What will you do with it?" I asked wearily.

"I thought you were in a rush?" She rose an eyebrow.

"It's true, I haven't much time," I said, looking at the still dark sky. "Will you tell me?" I asked softly. "The three truths."

She smiled and her voice filled the entire space around us as I sucked in a breath.

"One," I cringed as her voice became ethereal. "If you find what you seek, and seek what you find, the lines will blur, and your paths will become entwined."

Her breathy voice rang through my entire body. Seek? Blur? Entwined? It was foolish to expect anything other than nonsense from an old crone. Her voice echoed again. "Two…" For some reason my heart began to beat faster than before, slamming against my rib cage. "Once fair, strong, and wise, with hair of gold and bluest eyes, her once guarded heart will be her demise." My face crumbled in confusion and I played with a strand of my brown hair, this woman was surely insane.

"Three…" She leaned closer toward me. "The most

important one, Joy." She smiled through gaped teeth. "If the seed of doubt is planted and you nourish it so, the truth will remain buried, unable to grow."

I stared at her, unable to fathom the time I had wasted listening to the strangers' riddles. She handed me a piece of parchment, the same words she had spoken written down neatly. I hadn't seen her reach for a quill or begin to write.

"What are you?" I asked, folding the paper and sliding it into my pocket.

"You must not waste time asking of things you already know," she smiled again. "You must make haste, for the ship will leave at dawn, head east and you will find the dock." She stood, beginning to pack away her stall.

"Hurry, Joy!" she shouted and my body began to move.

I ran through the market quicker than I ever though imaginable. It was as though the winds themselves pushed at my back.

I sent a prayer up to the Goddess.

Gold split the night as the sun began to rise behind me, the dawn chased me as I neared the docks. Florence would leave at sunrise, and as soon as light hit the ground Harlow would know we had stolen from him. And so my only option was to run, to race the sunlight and hope that its rays did not catch me.

My feet pounded into the ground and my heart raced. The light lingered behind me.

I wasn't going to make it.

The shadow of dawn danced around my feet.

I would not win this race.

But then a sound entered my mind, a whisper so soft one might think it was the wind.

Just this once, Joy.

The withered witch's voice was there and then gone before I could take another breath.

The daylight at my feet began to draw back, it slithered backward giving me the advantage. The woman, she was pulling back the day, she was slowing down time, slowing down everything but me. The customers and sellers began to slow, their movements tired and soft. I raced through the last of the market, my feet hitting the fragile wood of the docks. I stopped, catching my breath. Hundreds of boats littered the waters around me and just as it had slowed down, time began again. I turned to watch the day race towards me, all of this could not have been for nothing. I heaved the heavy sack back into my arms, sighing at the weight.

It was foolish of me to think I could save Jameson. I couldn't even outrun the sun. Doubt flooded me.

I couldn't save Lolita and I couldn't save Jameson.

Tears threatened to fall as the day light crept closer. I choked on a sob.

"JOY!" I turned at the noise, Erin stood atop a grand ship, her arms waving frantically. Relief flooded me.

"There!" a male voice shouted from behind me, I spun, meeting Captain Harlow's gaze.

"Did you think you could get away from me, Killer?" he shouted, dominance oozing from his every pore.

"JOY!" Erin screamed again. "RUN!"

And I did.

I pushed all my energy into the distance between me and the ship. Harlow and his crew were not long behind me, their grunts and shouts brushing against my skin.

I held tightly onto the straps of the bag, every so often resting my hand over my pocket to ensure the parchment of riddles still resided in there.

Florence, Erin, and Jodie stood at the ship's rear, shouting for me.

I was so close.

"You cannot escape me, Joy!" Harlow taunted from behind me, his fun-loving demeanor gone.

Florence pulled down the sail as I pounded up the gangway and the ship began to move. I had to make the jump.

"Florence! She's not aboard yet," Jodie shouted to Florence as she stirred the ship. My breath became ragged.

"She will make it," Florence shouted back, her confidence pushing me on. I leapt from the gangway to the ship and time stopped. The jump seemed to last forever.

With a jolt I landed on the deck, my legs dangling over the edge. Harlow's men jumped after me, all of them landing in the clear waters below. Erin and Jodie heaved me aboard, my bag of supplies with me.

"This isn't over," Captain Harlow sang in an odd tune, and he began to skip in a circle like a child performing a dance for his parents.

Something cold and wrong slithered into my heart and I knew in my core that he was right. This wasn't over.

20

RAYA

ANOTHER ONE BITES THE DUST

"I cannot. I cannot do this. I am so tired."

- RAYA.

"Contrary to what you might think, your first task is the most important." Khol's voice rang out on the empty training field behind The Temple.

A tall, grey stone wall stared at us from around the field, the wall circled the entire Temple, from the training pitch here, to gardens around other side, and the door at the very front. It had been only moments since our conversation with Ezra, but it felt like hours. Khol had stormed across the grass, leaving me to catch up with him.

"You're not ready to fight with your… abilities yet, so the first test is combat, physical combat." He stood staring at me, his hands resting on his hips. I bit my lip, grateful that most of the previous night's dream had washed away.

Most of it.

I stared at him, willing my eyes to look away but failing.

He picked up a long sword, cutting the steel through the air in quick, elegant movements. His arm muscles tightened, and a thin sheen of sweat gathered on his neck.

I clamped my teeth together. Gods. I wanted to lick it off. I shook my head softly, hoping to clear my mind. I couldn't do this. I couldn't be this person.

"Why are you staring at me?" Khol's blunt voice broke my trance, I stumbled on my feet.

"I'm not staring at you," I said defensively, backing up slowly. He rolled his eyes.

"Pick up the sword," he pointed to the sword on the grass beside me. "If you can handle that." I threw him a cold smile.

Clearly, he was not daydreaming about me.

I mirrored his positions, feigning an inability to fight with a sword the best I could, I had picked up a long sword before I had picked up a pencil. The weapon felt like an extension of myself. I fumbled with the metal like a child, dropping it.

"Pick up your feet!" He jabbed my shin with the handle of his sword as we begun sparring.

"I thought you said you were trained in the Sage Guard?" I ignored his words… if he only knew. I could cut him down without a thought, I could hold his life between my fingers. Swinging and swooping, quickly wiping off the sweat that soon pooled on my forehead. I made my feet stumble.

"No wonder they are all dropping like rocks in a pond. They're unprepared and sloppy," he muttered under his breath as he easily blocked my blow. My blood raced and my heart pounded.

Something in me clamped tight and I knocked the sword from his hand without thinking of the consequence. I threw my own sword down, stabbing the earth with its metal tip.

"Those people are my friends!" I heaved my body toward

him, shoving him backward, hard, and forgetting to hide my training.

The ground began to shake.

"How dare you speak of the dead and dying in that way?" My body shook, and tears began to well in my eyes. For some reason his words had cut deep, so deep that the well of power that sat in the middle of my stomach began to overflow. I was once a part of that team, of the Sage Guard, those people were my friends.

But would they welcome me back? Even if I brought them information, would they still treat me like one of their own? Or would I be cast out? A member of the Sage Guard, but no longer a member of their team.

"Why would you say that? I knew you were a brute, but I never thought you cruel!"

I smashed my foot against the grass and the earth split next to us.

The world opened. A gasp got stuck in my throat, and Khol wobbled on the earth's edge, almost falling into the cavern I had created.

"They may hunt our kind, but it is only because they don't know any better. They are only human." My verbal assault continued. Thunder cracked and rain, heavier than a wet blanket, fell atop us. We were soaked in seconds.

"While you sit here and pray to your Gods, hiding your power, innocent people are dying." A sob shot through my body as I thought of my slaughtered team.

"My people are dying." My voice was a whisper.

A gust of wind blew my hair around my face wildly.

Khol stared at me and I heard his heart beating so loudly the sound hurt my ears. I backed up a step, squirming at the sound.

"Why can I hear your heart beating?" I asked, and the

earth stopped shaking but the rain fell as heavy as it had before.

I felt a tremor of fear shoot through me, but it did not belong to me.

"Are you afraid of me?" I asked, my voice almost getting lost in the wind.

"I don't know," he whispered, and I stepped forward.

He flinched.

I stared at him. Then my hands, at the scorch marks that never let me forget.

"I'm sorry." The words left my mouth before I even had chance to understand them.

"I'm sorry." This time to spoke to myself.

In my mind, I wanted to ask where the rain had come from, why the thunder cracked and why the earth split, but I did not need to.

I knew that it had come from me.

I fought to calm my erratic heart as Khol knitted the earth back together with a wave of his hand. With everything that had been going on, I had barely noticed the ease of which Khol used his power.

"I thought you were a MindWonderer?"

"I can get inside the mind of any living thing," his voice was quiet and closed. "Even the earth." I nodded, trapped in the silence between us. My pulse skittered.

MindWonderer, EarthShaker, SkyChanger, FireBringer.

But how was it that I could wield all four? How could I, an untrained Sage Guard soldier, a woman full of mistrust and betrayal, wield all the gifts from the Goddess?

"Are you familiar with The Prophesy?" Khol asked a moment later. I scoffed; everyone was familiar with The Prophesy.

"The bedtime story?" I raised a brow, feigning indifference.

"It is more than a story, I think we both know that," he whispered softly, as if he were any louder it might be true. "No Sorcerer can manipulate all of the elements, no one until you." His voice was small.

"Perhaps…" He looked away, staring at the storm clouds slowly softening. "Perhaps you are one of them? One of the Celestial…" I stared at him as his words trailed away, eyes wide and brows crumpled, how had he spoken of such things so casually? Nervousness sat low and heavy in my stomach. This was madness. I was not the one they waited for.

"But The Prophesy states there are to be two," I countered. "And I do not have anyone else." The hard truth slammed into me like a rock. "Even Alias is gone."

Khol nodded softly. He lifted his sword again and we sparred. This time he was distant and his movements soft. I tampered down my training further to prevent causing him harm. The image of him flinching away from me played over and over again in my mind as our swords clashed together halfheartedly.

"I wanted to join the fight," he spoke again, his voice soft as a whisper, and my sword paused midair. "The war, but my mother won't risk it, if anyone found out about us, about any of us…" he paused as if catching his breath. "We will be hunted until they find our home, until they find The Temple." Sorrow and loss filled his eyes. "We cannot lose anymore, we have already lost so much."

In that moment I thought I understood Khol. Everything he did was for his family, every choice, every move, everything. I hated the envy that flooded me, why had no one protected me this fiercely? Not even Alias had stopped Jala when she tortured me.

My hatred for Ezra burned a little brighter. Placing such high expectations on a man only a couple years older than I, it wasn't fair. Nothing is fair for those of us who were different.

"I do not think even our power would stop the war in Zetka." The war that had raged for over one hundred years. "I suppose I was talking more to The Goddesses than to you…" I stepped closer and rested my hand on his arm. "How could they be so cruel?" A soft wind floated over the grass, brushing my hair over my face. Reaching over, Khol swept the hair behind my ear.

"I'm scared, Khol," I whispered. "Why has this… power, only manifested now? Why didn't it show itself before when I was angry or sad?" I would not let myself cry, not now. I had been punished for less.

"Most of us, our power, it awakens when we are young," he stumbled over his words. "We do not have it when we are born, a single tantrum could split the earth in two." I smiled at his words. "My power awoke on my eighth birthday, three years after everyone in my training." His face turned placid in the way one does when they are bringing forth a memory. "And yours awoke now, sometimes it is buried so deeply that it never wakes." I soaked up his words, determined to learn everything there was to know about the new life I was living.

We strolled back to The Temple's main building. Khol laughed at my ever-present questions and hatred for short answers. We drank tea from the grand food hall, we talked and walked and talked some more until the sun began to set.

"And what about me?" I asked, bowl of curried lentils in hand. Khol paused, stuffing a large spoon of lentils into his open mouth.

"I don't know." Despite his words he looked calm, almost serene "You are something different, I haven't quite figured you out yet." I laughed, rolling my eyes.

"Let me know when you do." I reached for the book beside me and flipped through the pages.

PART 2

The Spark

We were learning.
We were striving for something better.
We were trying.
Just not hard enough.

21

JOY

HOW FAR IS TOO FAR?

"What happened that day? When the sun died, and the waves stilled?"

- FLORENCE

The sky was black, darker than the sea floor. Erin and Jodie sailed better than anyone I had ever met, they swooped around the ship, swinging on ropes, and tying unbreakable knots. The ship rocked, salty ocean water spilling onto our decks. Despite our trip through the markets, we had nothing to protect us from the rain. Our first day sailing had suddenly become a very wet one. As each drop of frosty water burned my skin, I stared at the achingly melancholy sky, and I couldn't help but think of Jameson. He loved the rain and he constantly complained about the lack of it in Dayra.

"When are we sailing back to the Northern Continent?" he'd asked me the day before Kai'd, the day before he was taken, and everything changed. I smiled softly at him; he was the only person I could truly be soft with. To the rest of the world, I had to be brave, calm, and strong, but Jameson never cared about those things; only that I was happy.

"A week after Kai'd," I told him. "I thought we would wait until rainy season has begun." His smile split his face in half, the sun bounced off his golden hair as he leaned back in the broken armchair, his face tilted to the heavens. We had not yet been to the Northern Continent without Lolita; she was the one who knew the path we had to take.

"I wonder if Romy has even glanced at his map yet?" I asked, thinking out loud. Jameson lowered his head so that our gazes met.

"He says he has, I don't know why he won't just let us look at it." Jameson walked over to the edge of the boat where I stood. "That is if you believe a word that comes out of his mouth." He laughed, nudging me with his elbow.

"Are you not excited to get out of this heat?" he asked me.

"You're the one of us who is actually from the Northern Continent, you can't handle sun, and I..." I tied my curls into a messy knot on the top of my head, "can't handle the cold."

"The rain isn't always cold, you know, sometimes it's warm, refreshing." It was my turn to nudge him and his silly response.

"Are you alright?" Florence caught me standing in the middle of the ship's deck, my head tilted toward the clouds as I let myself be soaked by freezing rainwater. I nodded.

Since our crew was extremely small, we anchored during the night, letting us all get our well needed rest. It would add a few days, maybe even a week onto our trip, much to my dismay, but I would have been no use to Jameson if I could not even hold a sword. The sisters passed out as soon as their heads hit the pillows. Their bodies shoved together on one of the only two beds. Florence and I shuffled into the other bedroom, tripping lightly as the ship rocked dramatically.

Our shoulders brushed slightly, and I leapt away from the touch, ignoring the warmth that spread across my body. The ship rocked again, and we bumped against each other.

But this time I didn't jump away. Instead, I actually leaned into her touch ever so slightly. Relishing in the feel of her skin against mine. She sighed deeply, a sound that reminded me of relief, of comfort.

We stood next to each other, swaying back and forth slowly with the movement of the ship.

A stick snapped in the fire that sat in the corner of the room. Pulling us from each other immediately.

"I'll sleep on the floor." Florence's voice was rushed and thick. Why was there only one bed? I cursed Kai'd inwardly, feeling as though I was in a romance novel or something.

"Don't be ridiculous, we both need a decent night's rest," my heartbeat quickened.

Icy water dripped down my back, it was as though my entire body was frozen from the inside out. Florence shook beside me, her teeth chattering ever so slightly. We were grown women, surely, we could share a bed without it causing a problem.

"Florence," I stated loudly. "Take off those wet clothes, your chattering teeth are starting to make me feel colder."

She laughed, and we shared a small smile. The hatred I felt for Florence had started melted away slowly, a little more every day. She was scared and alone, I understood what it meant to feel that way. I turned from her and began peeling off my wet tunic. My wet hair slapped against my back and I gasped loudly.

"Are you alright?" I felt Florence's hand against my bare shoulder.

My skin warmed around her touch.

I nodded, sucking in a deep breath.

"Just not used to the cold."

She pulled away her hand and my skin began to freeze again. When my breathing returned to normal, I opened the wonky draws next to the bed and pulled out two large shirts, clearly belonging to sailors that lived here last.

"I hope this is okay," I said, throwing Florence one of the shirts. I couldn't help looking at her bare skin, the deep brown seemed to be everywhere and nowhere at all once. I longed to reach out and touch it. Faint scars littered her skin, her now braided hair falling to the middle of her back. She pulled the shirt over her head and her naked skin was gone.

I swallowed against my dry throat, picking up a spare blanket to dry my braids. We stood in silence, both of us dressed in large shirts falling only to the tops of our thighs. I cleared my throat.

"Do you have, uh… an…" Florence pointed to the bed awkwardly.

"A preferred side?" I laughed slightly at her mumbling. She nodded, laughing along with me. I patted the sheets on the left side, instantly regretting the weird decision to pat the bed sheets.

What was I, an eighty-year-old woman?

"Good, I sleep on the right," she spoke, touching the sheets as awkwardly as I had.

"Oh, how lucky!" My voice sounded too loud and too enthusiastic.

We stared at each other again. I knew she was waiting for me to get beneath the covers first, but I couldn't. Not straight away. I hadn't shared a bed with anyone, never mind someone… like Florence, since Lolita died. Sliding beneath the blanket felt like I was losing a small part of her. I flipped my braid over my neck and squared my shoulders.

Lifting the blanket, I slipped between the soft fabrics. Resting my damp head on the pillow. I had forgotten how long it had been since I had a good night sleep. I closed my eyes, faintly hearing the sound of Florence sliding between the sheets.

Our knees touched beneath the sheets but neither one of us pulled away. I knew we were touching and she knew we were touching, but both of us were going to pretend otherwise. She hummed a goodnight, but I did not have the chance to answer, for sleep pulled me away and I let it.

I felt the drool against my chin before the I saw the sun peaking though the thin curtains, the ship rocked gently, and the gulls called to one and another. It was, coincidentally, the kind of sleep you dreamed about, and I knew that once I sat up, I'd feel the imprint of my pillow on my cheek. I wriggled softly, feeling something heavy upon my waist and I turned swiftly.

It was an arm, Florence's arm to be exact.

She must have rolled in her sleep and latched on to me for warmth, or maybe she was dreaming of someone else and had mistaken my body for theirs.

Something sharp twisted in my gut.

I hated myself for enjoying her touch. I had vowed that I would not touch another until I met Lolita in the next life… if I met her. I stared at Florence, unable to look away. Her braids, finally dry, fell around her neck and face.

She sighed deeply, her leg sliding over mine. My

breathing hitched. I reminded myself that she was asleep and completely unaware of what she was doing.

Right.

Breathe.

Inhale. Exhale.

The large shirt had ridden up in her sleep, showing her deliciously black thighs and soft stomach. A ring pierced through her belly button. I fought the urge to reach out and touch it.

"Do you like it?" Florence's croaky voice startled me, my eyes shot to hers, but she didn't move away from me.

"Sor-ry," I stuttered. She laughed lightly, like the soft sea foam that sat atop the water.

"Don't be." She rolled the ring around her fingers.

"Did it hurt?" I looked at the piercing again.

"Not really." She turned, lying flat on her back. "Every one of my friends has one, it was like a rite of passage." She smiled softly as if remember her life before Captain Harlow and the crew.

"It's something that bound us together." She looked at me, our gaze never breaking. "We believed that sharing not only love, but also pain, brought us closer together."

I watched her toy with the belly button ring, her bare fingernails stark again her dark skin.

"Where are they now?" I asked, turning to lie on my back, staring at the swaying ceiling above us. She swallowed the dryness in her throat. Her gaze darted from mine.

"They're… here and there," she almost whispered and I nodded. "They burnt our village to the ground a few years ago, some children were being taken away or some just killed, my mother got us out but we couldn't all stay together. It was too risky."

"Were they searching… were they searching for Sorcerers in your village?" I asked softly, Florence nodded.

"My mother, father, and I fled to the Northern Continent to escape the pillaging, but it only followed us there."

"You lived in the Northern Continent?" I sat up, and Florence mirrored my position.

"Yes, we moved right after the attack."

"I am so sorry, Florence, I do not understand why they would target your village and make you suffer." My head dropped into my hands.

"Because it was true." She shrugged softly, her eyes never meeting mine. "They were searching for Sorcerers and my family were the perfect targets. We are Sorcerers, Joy." Her chest heaved at her honestly.

"I am a Sorcerer, Joy."

22

RAYA
RUN AWAY

"We cannot trust her if we do not learn to understand her."

- KHOL

A hummingbird perched on a tree outside the training barracks as I began our daily training. I stared at it through the window, its heart pattering so quickly. I wondered what it would be like just to live from moment to moment. To not have this new life spread in front of me.

Every day we woke at first light and ran around The Temple twice. We ate massive bowls of porridge and began working on my 'poor combat skills'. This would be my first task, my first task that would take place in one week. Already dreading our run, I stared at the rack of weapons in front of me. Picking up the bow and arrow, feeling its weight in my hand, I let out a sigh. I'd always had a soft spot for this weapon.

"Know how to use it?" I started at the sound of Khol's

voice as he entered the barracks, and I dropped the weapon. It clattered loudly.

"I'm not completely useless," I stated bluntly, retrieving the bow from the floor, its weight familiar and comforting.

Could I show him a slice of my abilities, blame my skill on luck? As I pulled the string taut, Khol came up behind me, wrapping a hand around my waist, his warm palm landing on my stomach.

"What are you doing?" I breathed, looking at him over my shoulder. Our gazes collided, every thought falling from my head.

"Tense your muscles." His grip tightened on my abs, his eyes never leaving mine.

The warmth from his palm spread from his body to my own. My grip on the bow weakened ever so slightly as Khol rested his other hand on my lower spine, his pinky finger sliding beneath the waistband of my trousers, sending a shiver of pleasure through my body. My toes curled against the soft mat beneath our feet. I sighed softly, as I watched Khol's pupils grow larger and larger until they almost eclipsed his entire eyes.

My arms began to shake, my muscles begging me to release the bow string as it strained against the arrow.

But I couldn't move, I didn't want to break the spell that had somehow been cast over us. Even though I should've walked away, I found myself leaning toward his touch. My back brushing against his chest. Our faces moved closer together, only a breath separating us.

"Raya," Khol breathed. And the snap of a bow string woke me from my trance. My gaze flying to the target.

"Impressive," Khol's voice was thick and deep as he stared at the arrow embedded in smallest red circle. I stifled a laugh. *Bullseye.*

"You hit the bullseye without looking," he mused.

We stood for a moment, both of us unsure on what might have happened if I hadn't let the arrow fly. Although the bow was now by my side, rather than held in my arms. Khol's hands remained on my skin, burning me softly. His pinky finger brushed the top of my underwear and my pulse spiked. The steady pounding of Khol's heartbeat against my back sped up, both of our chests rising and falling raggedly.

"You're going to be the death of me." Khol whispered, his voice brushing against my ear. And my blood turned to ice in my veins. He was right, wasn't he? He didn't truly believe I would be the death of him, but if I carried on with this mission from Captain Jala and they found The Temple, Khol would be hunted. I was going to be the death of him. I stepped away from him, out of the warmth of his arms and turned to face him. A flicker of hurt washed over his face.

Swallowing the thickness in my throat, I did the only thing I could think of. I swallowed my feelings and pretended they didn't exist.

"We should probably get started." I cringed at the high-pitched sound of my voice. Khol nodded, clearing his throat for what felt like the hundredth time. Awkwardness surrounded us, wrapping us in its cold embrace.

"It's dawn," he pointed outside. "Time to run." I couldn't help the groan that fell from my lips. Running? Again?

"Are you trying to kill me?" I winced at my words. Why did my brain stop working when I was around him? "Perhaps you could show me more of The Temple?" I asked, trying to ease the tension around us.

"What happens if you're being chased in the test?" he asked smugly and I returned the facial expression, thankful that the unease between was vanishing

"By one person?" I laced hurt through my voice and the

earth cracked slightly next to us, Khol rolled his eyes before knitting the earth back together with a wave of his hand.

I smiled sweetly and curtsied. It was in moments like this that I truly forgot why I was in The Temple. I wasn't just Jala the little spy, I was a Sorcerer, the most powerful one alive today.

"What if you were being chased by 40 people?" He stepped closer, I rolled my eyes.

A pause.

"Okay, what about 400?" he lessened the gap between us yet again, and the all the tension that had been between us only a moment ago reignited.

"You underestimate me, Khol," I sighed. "I know how to run."

I somehow became a different person when I was around him.

"Look who suddenly became so confident," he mocked, slowly circling me like a lion about to descend on its prey. "You're getting complacent." He looked me up and down with something like disgust and lust.

"I am getting *stronger,*" I countered.

"But not strong enough," he shook his head at me.

"If I were chasing you," Khol motioned to the training field around us, "I'd catch you and you know it. I'd kill you before you had the chance to blink." His words cut deep as he stepped into my personal space. I was stronger, faster, and more deadly. But he could never know it. He could never know the truth about my time at The Temple, and my life before it.

I lifted my arms to push him away, but he caught my wrists, pulling me to him forcefully.

Our bodies pressed together; my heart slamming against my ribs aggressively.

"Never allow your opponent to catch you like this," he motioned to his hands with his chin, I nodded, swallowing a scoff. Matron Clara had taught us this when we were children, maybe I would show him that I wasn't completely useless.

Reaching up on my tip toes so that we stood at eye level, I looked his face up and down. I didn't pull away, I didn't fight. His brow creased in confusion and for a split second his grip on my wrists slackened slightly. Hooking my leg around his, I sent him crashing to the floor before he could think to stop me. Smiling smugly, I rested a knee on his chest and pinned his wrists to the cool mat beneath us.

"Never allow your opponent to distract you," I whispered as he looked at his pinned hands in almost disbelief, I bit my bottom lip to stop the laughter than erupted inside of me.

"I thought you said you were not taught to fight in the Sage Guard," he asked looking up.

"We were trained with some weapons," I tucked a rogue strand of hair behind my ear. "And in some combat." The lie rolled off my tongue. His eyebrows rose, awaiting a real answer. I sighed loudly. "As I said, I am not completely useless, I know a few self-defense moves." I released the pressure from his chest and allowed him to sit across from me.

"That was a move?"

"Well not a much a move, just putting my womanly wiles to use," I said batting my eyelashes. He chuckled softly.

We sat in soft silence for a moment, our knees brushing against each other.

"I notice you've got a handle on the Earthshaking," Khol's voice sounded, filled with promise and hope. I nodded.

"This is good, Raya." The sound of my name in his

mouth sent shivers up my spine. "It means our training is working."

"We've been training for weeks," I said softly, staring at my boots. "And the only thing I have a handle on is cracking the earth." I stood heavily, pacing the room. "My lightning is out of control, I set two fires last week and don't get my started on the three-day storm I created." I ran my fingers through my hair, sighing.

"What am I doing?" I whispered to myself. Khol sat in front of me, watching me, his face tight.

What if she fails?

"What?" I turned, facing Khol sternly.

"What?" he repeated back.

"Did you just say something?" I rested my hands on my chin as he shook his head.

I don't think I could go through with it.

I don't think I could watch it.

Should I tell her?

Would she want to know?

I felt cold air brush against me. Was I listening to Khol's thoughts?

"What happens if I fail the tests, Khol?" I crossed my arms over my chest, my eyebrows raised. Khol opened and closed his mouth, and then opened and closed it again. Dragging his hands through his hair, he blew out a deep breath.

"You have to understand, you will pose a threat against all of us." His voice came out hushed and quickly, as though his mouth could not keep up with his mind.

"What happens if I fail the tests, Khol?" I repeated, my words stern and cold.

"You will pass them, I know it." He blocked the question yet again.

"Khol." My chest heaved in and out.

"Tell me," I touched my hand to his forearm. "Please."

His eyes focused on my hand on his skin, his gaze flicking from it to my face.

"If you don't not pass the test, you will not be able to become a threat to our kind."

My breathing shallowed, fear skating along my spine.

"What do you mean?"

"They will," he swallowed. "They will put you down."

I nodded, attempting to keep my fear in check.

"And everyone has to take the test?" My voice wobbled slightly. He nodded.

"Does everyone pass?"

He shook his head.

"The Temple allows this? Allows the murder of their own kind?" I stood, pushing past him, resting my hands on the wall, sucking in a deep breath. Jala would get me out if I failed the tests, wouldn't she? If I died, so did her information.

"They must, to ensure our survival," Khol spoke again.

"Survival? That's rich." I spun to face him, my anger boiling my blood.

"You wouldn't understand, we have lost so much already." His voice remained level and hallow, as though someone had sucked all of the life from inside of him.

"And you will lose more." I pushed his chest with my hands, catching him off guard, he stumbled. "I understand loss, *Prince*, I have known loss, I have known what it is like to belong to a family, belong to a home and have that all go up in flames." I pushed him again but this time he was prepared, his body remained still.

"And you think I have not?" He stepped toward me,

closer and closer until I stepped back, hitting the cool wall behind me.

"Do you think I wish for this to be my life?" He leaned forward, his hands against the wall, encircling me.

"You think I wish to see you hurt? Especially… when I…" he mumbled off. Although I thought it impossible, he leaned closer to me. Both of us heaving heavy breaths, our eyes burning into one another. Khol pushed off the wall, turning to stare at the large wall that encased The Temple, his hands resting on the back of his neck.

"My brother did not pass the tests." He spoke quietly, his voice shaking. My face crumbled in confusion.

"What do you mean?" I whispered.

"We took our tests together, he was one year older, so he waited for me." Khol sat on the mat where we had fought only moments ago. "They did not tell us what would happen if we failed the test." He turned to look at me as I sat down next to him. "But I think Rafael knew." silver lined his delicate eyes.

"Your parents, they are the leaders of The Temple, surely they could've saved him?" I asked, as if it was possible to go back and stop it from happening.

"They could not treat us any differently, here at The Temple we are one, none of us different or special." Khol smiled to himself.

"Rafael was special," he looked up at me again. "I couldn't watch them… I couldn't watch him die," he heaved a shuddering breath. "I should've been there for him, I should've made sure he did not die alone." Regret swam between us, we both had things we regretted, he was human just as I was.

"He did not even get a chance to live." I saw the torment swirl behind his eyes, I knew he blamed himself. "I think you would've like him," He almost whispered and I couldn't help the tear that slipped from my eye.

"I think I would've too." I smiled.

Our eyes met and, in that moment, I saw him differently.

In that moment, I finally understood him.

With my mind swirling, I didn't notice Khol getting closer until he kissed me. His touch was soft and fleeting.

As soon as our lips met, he dragged them away again. My eyes widened.

"I apologize." He stumbled to his feet and headed for the door, not turning to look back.

The breath left my lungs.

Khol felt something for me, and I was going to betray him.

23

JOY

WHAT LIES BENEATH

"Maybe she is a Sorcerer, maybe she is not. It is not my business, and it is not yours."

- JOY WHEN ASKED ABOUT FLORENCE

"Why didn't you tell me this sooner?" My voice came out harsher that I intended it to. I walked to the bedroom door, shaking the handle, checking we would not be disturbed.

"This is why I didn't tell you, Joy," Florence whispered through her teeth, pulling me down to sit on the bed beside her. "I wanted to tell you but…" Florence fought the words in her mouth, opening and closing it until finally finding the words. "I did not know who I could trust, after what happened to Jameson…" She scrubbed her hands over her face. "After what I did to Jameson, I didn't know if you would use this against me." The words hit me like a fist to the gut. She was scared, I had caused her fear.

"But when I saw how open and accepting you had been towards Jodie and Erin…" She trailed off, her words lost.

She believed I would have sold her out, she believed I would have given her up to be slaughtered.

Disgust balled in my stomach.

"I'm sorry," I whispered lightly, "I'm sorry." More words threatened to flow from my lips, but my mouth refused to form them. I knew her pain, I knew her fear and loathing and self-hatred.

But through all of it I had Jameson by my side, telling me every day, even when I refused to listen, that I was loved.

That I was safe with him.

That I was enough.

I reached toward her, tugging on her shoulder until she let me wrap my arms around her.

Silence radiated around us as we embraced. I forced all the safety into the hug, hoping my clinging arms radiated how sorry I was. My shoulder started to feel damp as Florence began sobbing.

"I miss my brothers," she said softly. "I miss them so much." She crumpled as she finally let a few tears fall. Guilt burrowed into my chest; Florence had lost everything. Her family separated just because of their ancestors.

"Do you… have your… do you know?" My words failed me, yet again.

"Do I know what I am?" She lifted her head so our eyes could meet. I nodded, my nose grazing slightly over her cheek. She sighed, her breath causing goosebumps along my skin.

"I am a 'SkyChanger'." Her eyes darted around the room as she spoke.

A SkyChanger. I moved back from her and crossed my legs beneath me.

"What's it like?" I whispered, unsure on how to ask such a question. She pondered the question for a moment, then smiled deeply.

The smell of the ocean breeze, fresh washed bedsheets and brewed coffee filled my nostrils. Light rain knocked against the windows around us, making the world both loud and quiet at once. She released a breath.

"It's like being away for so long, and then coming home." Her eyes fluttered shut as the rain continued its steady beat against the windows. Her power bringing rain to our part of the world.

"You make it sound so good," I whispered.

"It is," she opened her eyes to look at me, a grin splitting her face. "It is unlike anything else in the entire world. I would let myself be hunted a thousand times over, just to feel this power once." Mesmerized by her words, I reached out to grab her hand.

"I am not sure, I think I might've made it rain when Harlow crashed into our ship." She clasped her hand around mine, soft calluses and scars sliding over my own.

She smiled softly. "So I can make it rain and use my power in combat but that's the extent. How can I help us get to Jameson? Start a sandstorm?" She rolled her eyes.

"You're more help than I am, I can't do anything." I smiled as she squeezed my hand.

"You've brought us here, you saved Erin and Jodie, you're travelling across continents to save your family, you're saving everyone." Her voice was soft like velvet. "You've already saved me countless times," her whisper blew hot air against my cheek and, in that moment, I realized how close we had become. Thighs pressed flush together, arms brushing, hands still firmly encased in the other's.

"You saved…" my voice broke, I heaved in a deep breath

and blew it out. "You saved yourself." My whisper barely made it past my lips. She reached out, twining one of my braids between her fingers. Staring at her now, really staring, the breath was knocked from my lungs at her sheer beauty.

"You are beautiful, Joy," she spoke, as though taking the words from my mouth.

A blush crept from my neck all the way to my cheeks. In that moment I knew that I could not stay angry at her, I could not blame her for Jameson's kidnapping any more than I could deny the feelings blossoming in my chest. Despite all of this I had to be smart. Jameson was still at large, and my crew were waiting for me back on Dayra. I rested my hand on her cheek, my calluses slipping over her smooth skin.

"I should go," I said, even though the words begged to stay in my mouth.

"I know," Florence nodded. But we didn't move, we stayed still, staring at one another. I knew I couldn't stay in this moment, but I also knew I didn't want to leave, so I was stuck. Stiller than the waves on a calm day.

"Mooooorrrningggg!" Jodie yelled, wooden planks creaking beneath her feet as she made her way to the deck. I moved slowly, letting Florence rest her forehead against mine for a fraction of a moment, before heading for the door in only the old t-shirt.

Erin joined me in the hallway, opening her door as I did mine.

"How did you sleep?" I asked, pulling her in for a hug, she resisted at first, only to wrap her arms around me a moment later.

"Not bad," she smiled to herself. "This ship is a hell of a lot quieter than Harlow's." She glanced up and down the corridor as if looking for the rest of her crew.

"I miss the noise too." I nudged her softly with my elbow.

"On the loudest nights, when the crew sung drunkenly or Jameson brought home… company for the night, Lolita and I would bring our blankets and sleep on the deck, just staring at the stars." I laughed softly.

We walked onto the deck, stomachs grumbling as Jodie tore at hunks of bread and cracked open cans of peaches.

"Lolita, she was your partner?" Erin asked as we sat on the warm wood next to Jodie.

"Oh yes, I'm sorry I thought I mentioned her before." A blush crept up from neck. "She was my partner, she was my everything." For once I felt like smiling at her memory rather than crying.

"She passed last winter." I nodded to myself, plucking a peach from the can.

"Oh, Joy, I'm sorry," Jodie said softly, resting her arm on my knee momentarily. I smiled back at her, resting my hand on top of hers.

"I hope to someday love someone the way you love her." Erin clasped my other hand, and maybe it was the way she said 'love' instead of 'loved' or maybe it was the unbelievably sweet gesture the sisters were showing me, but love burst within me and the words fell from my mouth.

"I don't think I could ever love anyone as much as I love Lolita, that kind of connection… it is not severed through death." A creak on the boards behind us sounded as Florence approached us warily.

Guilt rushed through me, but I didn't know why, I was not ashamed of loving Lolita, but a part of me didn't want Florence to know that. I cringed.

"Hungry?" I asked by way of greeting, shielding my eyes from the sun as I looked up at her.

"Starving," she replied, plopping down on the other side of Jodie.

24

RAYA

KISS AND... RUN?

"I need to focus; my life is hanging in the balance. I cannot allow myself to be distracted."

- RAYA'S JOURNAL ENTRY

I stood, staring at Khol's retreating figure, wondering what the hell I was supposed to do. I could still feel Khol's lips against mine, could still feel the burning heat of his intensity, his desire. I closed my eyes and breathed deeply, clamping my bottom lip between my teeth.

How had this insufferable brute turned into a man who decided to kiss me? How had I turned into a woman who wanted to be kissed? Did I want to be kissed?

I shook my heading attempting to shake off the feeling of his hands on my shoulders. I picked up the bow and arrow, inhaling and exhaling softly before lining up the shot. Closing my eyes, I knew the target, I saw the target. Goosebumps covered my arm as I imagined Khol's hands sweeping across them gently, and I swallowed against my dry throat.

I let the arrow fly. My eyes snapped open as the arrow hit the center of the target. Again.

Calmness settled over me, I was still a solider and I was still loyal to my people.

"Maybe we should wheel you out at the ball and show you off." Ezra leaned against the training room's entry way. I took a deep breath, praying that I could keep myself in check.

"Khol says you're doing much better." She strolled across the room, standing in front of the target.

Oh, don't threaten me with a good time.

I paused at the sound of Khol's name.

"You spoke to him?" I asked as nonchalantly as I could.

"Yes, just now, he says he believes you are more than ready to take the first test next week." Something warm and sweet pooled in the center of my stomach.

"But," Ezra spoke starkly, "I am not so easily convinced. You see, I am worried, Raya, worried that my son is getting too… personally involved in your testing." She stalked around the room like a dragon eyeing up its next kill. I rested my hands on my hips.

"I do not think your son is any more involved than you are, I assume you want to see me succeed as much as he does?" I quipped.

Take the bait, Ezra, I know you want to.

She paused for a moment, assessing me slowly.

"Of course," her voice was emotionless and cold, then she turned to leave.

"You mentioned a ball?" I called after her.

"A day after your first test," she continued walking. "Assuming you survive." Ezra strutted out as though the world fell at her feet.

I supposed it did.

Slamming the bow down, I left the room, Ezra's threats

sticking to my skin. My blood sang and my head swam. Did she speak to everyone this way? My pace quickened as I headed to find Alias.

I stopped dead in the middle of the corridor.

Alias wasn't here, he was never here. I had been gone for almost two weeks and I hadn't heard a peep from Alias, or anyone from the Sage Guard. Captain Jala hadn't even written to check on my progress. A maid scurry past me, her footsteps pulling me back to reality, and all of Ezra's threats swarmed me again as I stormed to Elijah's apothecary.

I pushed the door open hastily, making Elijah jump.

"I think Ezra's trying to kill me!" I wailed dramatically, walking into the room. Only to see Elijah was not alone, Khol sat uncomfortably on the too small chair, in the too small room.

"Khol," I said quickly. "I didn't—" I babbled embarrassingly.

"What did she say to you?" Khol stood quickly, scanning his eyes over me as if checking for injuries.

"Nothing, really."

"Raya," he said sternly.

"Khol," I repeated back.

We stared each other down, it was like gravity slowed, like I could reach out and touch the dust that was falling between us.

"She said something about wheeling me out at the ball, as a party trick or something," I spoke softly. Khol rose a brow.

"But she said I would only be at the ball if I, if…" I tripped over my words again.

"If what?" Khol demanded, his stare ablaze.

"If I survive the first test." I slumped into the chair Khol stood from, scrunching up my long legs to fit. Khol muttered a string of curses to himself.

"She's just trying to get in my head, and I'm only telling Elijah about it because… because he is my only friend." I laughed softly, shooting Elijah a grin.

He winked back.

"Well, as you're one and only friend, we must take a trip into town and find you a dress." Elijah began emptying his seemingly always full satchel.

"Elijah," I said, a deadpan look on my face. "There is a chance that I won't be attending the ball," I said, attempting to add humor into my voice. He reached a hand toward me.

"I have known many warriors in my life, Raya, and I have no doubt in my mind that you will be in attendance at the ball." I smiled at his words, fear slowly seeping back down into my stomach.

"Will you be my date?" I asked Elijah hopefully.

"Oh, my love, I'm afraid I cannot," he brushed his thumb over my cheek. "I promised my husband I'd go with him." The wrinkles by his eyes crinkled as he smiled.

"You're married? Why do you never tell me anything?" I nudged him. "Congratulations," I whispered.

"My dear girl, your congratulations, although touching, are not necessary, we've been married almost twenty years." Light shone in his eyes as he spoke, and warmth filled my chest.

"Well, I'd love to meet him, although I am sad I will be attending alone." I touched my hand to his arm momentarily and turned toward the door, walking straight into Khol's muscled torso. I had completely forgotten his was in the room.

"Sorry," I mumbled, looking up to meet his eyes. It felt as though a hundred little fires were set alight beneath my skin as our gazes lingered on one and other.

"Khol!" Elijah stated loudly. "You are not escorting

anyone, are you?" Khol's eyes finally jumped from mine to Elijah's, and he rubbed the back of his neck with his hand.

"Ah, well… I… no. I'm not escorting anyone," he stuttered out finally.

Elijah clapped his hands together gleefully and sighed.

"Perfect, then you can escort Raya." Both of our gazes shot to Elijah as the words left his mouth.

Khol? Be my escort?

I knew that Elijah was just attempting to help, but he did not know that Khol had just kissed me and that the last thing we should be doing together was attending a ball.

Unease crept into my bones.

"I'm sure Khol has a mass of people wanting to go with him to the ball." I smiled awkwardly.

"Not unless you count Ottie," Khol laughed gruffly before looking over at me again. "It really isn't a problem, unless you would rather go with someone else?"

There was no one else, and I think Khol knew that too.

"Okay, let's go to the ball," I said quietly.

"Well, first you need to survive the test," Khol teased, nudging me with his crossed elbow.

Khol's mood swings struck me like flying rocks, first he kissed me, then ignored me, and then he's teasing me again? My neck ached with the whiplash of it all. Shutting the door of Elijah's room behind me, I leaned against the wood, slowly attempting to get my bearings.

"Do you suppose Khol will tell her? He seems smitten," voices trickled in from further down the corridor.

"Don't kill my hope completely, I'm still hoping he'll fall for me," another voice joined the chorus.

"Dream on," the first voice spoke again. "I can't believe they're actually making her do the tests." My breath hitched in my throat. "We all know Ezra will not let her survive the trials, she's a threat and we all know it." She laughed quietly. Laughing as if my life truly meant nothing.

The words cut me. Was I being betrayed, again? By the people that were supposed to be my own?

The Sage Guard didn't want me. The Sorcerers didn't want me.

She's a threat. The words cascaded over my skin.

If they only knew how much of a threat I was.

The two voices trailed away, taking my hopes with them.

The breath left my lungs slowly, my energy depleting as the adrenaline fell away. I was so sick and tired of being the outsider. I had always been lethal, someone to fear, but now I was nothing but an untrained liability.

"You can't be serious, Khol," Elijah's muffled voice sounded from through the door I still leaned against.

"Your mother has the entire Temple behind her, she has all of the Sorcerers behind her."

"But I cannot let her carry on with this, this… crusade!" Khol's voice rose ever so slightly.

"When does this end, Elijah?" His voice returned to a whisper. "I stood by when she murdered Rafael." His voice turned grave and deadly. "I won't do it again, not with Raya." Fear ran cold through my veins. He knew. Khol knew that I was not to survive the trials. The uncaring armor I wore vigilantly for the last twenty years began to crumble.

But despite the desperation in his words, he had lied to me, they had all lied to me.

When would I realize that the only person I could trust, was myself? I had been foolish and blind and about a hundred other things I didn't have the energy to name. I never wanted to become a woman that depended in the decisions of others, especially the decisions of men. My mother flashed in my mind.

I hadn't seen her since my blood loss induced hallucination when I first arrived at The Temple. Missing her was like a wound that never healed.

I had let myself get distracted. I had, for a moment, let myself forget my mission. Jala's words sounded in my head.

Infiltrate, gain their trust, learn their secrets and report back.

Alias's life was at stake and one moon cycle had already passed. Pushing off from the apothecary door, I flew down the corridor, twisting around the bends and dips until I found the door to my room. Throwing it open I began pulling out draws aggressively, searching for parchment and a quill. Lighting a candle with a wave of my hand, I sat down next to the bookshelves.

Anger coursed through my veins like never before. I was not some pawn in a game or something to sacrifice.

I was a badass fucking woman.

And I would save my best friend's life. Dragging the quill across the page aggressively, I scribbled everything I had learned about The Temple, secrets one could only learn from living within it. I had yet to find a way in and out of the building, but I assured Jala that my success would be imminent. Addressing the letter, I hid it away. A weapon to be used when the time was right.

"That was intense." My eyes snapped to Khol leaning against the door frame, his pupils dilated as the anger radiated off me. Had he seen what I had been writing?

"Get out of my way, Khol." My words were curt and passive, I didn't have time to waste on pleasantries.

"What's gotten into you?" he asked, noting the change in my demeanor. I ignored him, grabbing my belongings from around the room aggressively.

"Where are you going?" He lounged against the doorway; his arms crossed leisurely.

"I'm leaving." I attempted to push past him, but he knocked me back softly, "Get. Out. Of. My. Way." I spoke again, quiet threats laced between my words.

"No." Khol smiled smugly. I ground my teeth as lightning sparked softly in my hands. Khol looked down at them and raised an eyebrow.

"Impressive," he said sarcastically. I stepped closer to him.

"You wouldn't know impressive if it hit you in the face," I whispered. He stepped toward me, our chests brushing slightly.

"Is that right?" he whispered. I nodded; rage still hot in my chest.

"Khol," I whispered. He hummed a response. "Move," I pushed against him, but he didn't budge. "Or are you going to kiss me again and then run away?" As soon as the words left my mouth, I knew I touched a nerve. But instead of backing down like I thought he would, he didn't balk.

"Is that what you think I did? You think I ran away?" He lifted his hand and twined a strand of my hair around his finger.

"Do you have a different explanation?"

"I didn't want to distract you." He tugged on the strand softly and my breathing hitched. "This is a very important time for you."

"You think highly of yourself," I said softly. "You don't have the power to distract me." I swallowed against my dry throat, knowing that my words were lies. He spun me quickly so that my back was flat against his chest, his arm caged around my chest. I began to argue but then I noticed the glowing light, every single candle in my room was alight.

"How did you do that? I thought…" I whispered softly.

"I didn't do anything," his lips murmured against my ear. "It was all you." He tightened his grip around my chest. "They lit as soon as you saw me." Shivers ran down my spine as his words ran over me.

"I suppose I do have some effect on you." Annoyance spiked in my veins at the smug sound of his voice.

"Or maybe I don't have control yet."

"Oh, you definitely don't have control yet." He laughed softly behind me, and warmth pooled in my stomach.

"You're doing a terrible job of distracting me, Khol." I turned in his arms, his hand now splayed on the top of my back. "I'm still leaving." I raised my eyebrows.

"Elijah will be crushed; he was so excited about finding you a dress for the ball."

"I suppose he'll have to get over it." I attempted to pull out of Khol's grasp, but he only held me tighter.

"You know I can't let you leave," his voice was solemn.

"You can't stop me."

"Don't make me do this, Raya, I don't want to do this," he spoke softly.

"And I don't want to die." The words almost hurt to say, the truth always had a funny way of making its way out at some point or another.

"I'm not going to let that happen."

"You can't stop it, Khol, you couldn't even save your—" I stopped the word before causing more pain that necessary.

"I couldn't save my brother," he repeated back to me. "You needn't shy away from the words, Raya. I couldn't save my brother, but I can help you save yourself." He spoke solemnly, his hand loosening from my back. I did not move an inch.

I heaved a deep breath and finally stepped away from

Khol's touch. No matter how much I denied it, his touch and his presence distracted me, and I could not afford to break my concentration.

"I can't stay," I whispered, wrapping my arms around my middle.

"I know," Khol spoke softly.

"And I can't leave," my voice was full of cracks and unfulfilled promises.

"I know."

We remained still, staring at each other. Knowing that we couldn't move from these positions without a decision being made. So, we stood, hundreds of unspoken words floating between us.

25

JOY

TIME TO REACH THE SHORE

"I held my breath for Jameson, for my new friends. For my new family."

- JOY'S JOURNAL ENTRY

"Wake up!" Florence shook my body so vigorously I fell to the floor, hitting the wooden slats with a thump. She pulled the thin sheet from me, allowing the cold air to rush at my warm skin. Goosebumps trailed from my toes to my fingers.

Cold air.

I shot up to a seated position and swung my legs over the bed.

"You're going to need more than that," Florence stared at the long t-shirt I slept in.

Moments later, suited and buttoned into huge, musty fur coats and fleece trousers we had found in the cupboards full of cobwebs, I braved the outside. To my surprise, ice coated the floor of the deck.

"How did this happen in one night?" My startled voice was almost lost to the howling winds of the Northern Continent.

"We passed into the Northern Continent early this morning when I was on watch," Florence spoke, snapping an icicle from the railing.

"Why didn't you wake me?" I asked sharply.

"What would that have achieved? A grumpier version of you with less sleep? No thank you," she shrugged.

"I don't know if you are aware but my friend, my brother, is somewhere, trapped, alone and afraid." I stomped closer to her, careful not to slip on the ice. We stood eye to eye, so close I could feel her warm breath against my frigid skin.

"Next time, wake me up." I spoke through gritted teeth. I turned to walk away, but she grabbed my arm, spinning me back toward her.

"What is your problem?" she asked, suddenly defensive and loud.

"My problem?" Anger bubbled inside of me, what was my problem? Who did she think she was? "My problem is that as soon as I think we're on the same page or you're even a remotely decent person and not just the careless fool who allowed Jameson to be taken in her place, you go and do something stupid without even thinking about the consequences. This is not some sort of trip or adventure or vacation, we're on a stolen boat, with a crew of four people, hunting my brother who could already be dead for all we know." I huffed a giant breath, allowing some of my anger to leave with the air.

"It was a mistake, Joy, I was afraid!" Her voice was strained and low. "Must I live with this guilt forever? Will you ever trust me? I have spent my entire life running from those who wish to kill me just because of something I inherited. I have been running, just like Erin and Jodie have, for so long that I have forgotten what it is to stop and be still. I have forgotten how not to be selfish, and I will not apologize for being a survivor, I will not apologies for becoming the person that they made me become." A fat tear slipped down her cheek, and she wiped is fiercely.

"I am sorry about Jameson, I really am, and I will do everything in my power to get him back to you." She rested both of her hands on my shoulders softly. "But you cannot blame me forever, I won't let you." Her molten eyes were stark and clear. She was standing her ground, and I had no choice but to let her. I nodded softly.

"Okay," I whispered; I was wasting precious energy blaming Florence when I should have been focused on Jameson.

"Okay," I repeated more to myself than Florence.

"Burning hell, it's freezing out here!" Jodie skidded across the decks in her attempt to run toward us.

"Careful!" I chided, reaching for her. She righted herself and swung an arm over my shoulder.

"Don't worry, baby, I'm always careful" she winked softly.

"Is this your attempt at flirting?" Florence said, tapping her finger against Jodie's nose.

"Yes," she turned her gaze to Florence and rose an eyebrow. "Why, do you like what you see?" She pulled out her best smolder and the three of us burst into fits of laughter as Erin walked out onto the icy deck. She took one step forward before falling, gracelessly, onto her butt.

"Smoooooth," Jodie drawled, her arm still resting on my shoulder.

"Oh, piss off," Erin muttered.

We laughed and lit felt so good, even as our toes became numb, and our eyes became misty.

But then suddenly Florence stopped laughing. Her gaze fixed on the darkening horizon. A small voice wriggled between my bones softly.

Turn back, Joy. Turn back now.

I sucked in a deep breath, attempting to calm my racing heart.

"We're here," I looked over to Florence. "Aren't we?"

She nodded solemnly.

"This is the place, if Jameson is anywhere, he'll be here," she stuttered. "With the Sorcerers." Something other than wariness crossed her face, something almost like relief or familiarity.

I turned to Jodie and Erin; the sisters huddled close.

"This is where we leave you," I stated, I would not risk another person I had come to love.

"No," Erin stepped forward. "We all go or none of us go." She reached up her hand and rested it gently on my cheek.

"You don't get to play the hero all by yourself," she looked over to her sister and then back at me. "And you don't have to, we're in this. We're with you, until the end."

"You can't, it's too dangerous," I argued, petrified of losing one more person, let alone two.

"We've been in danger every day of our lives, what's a couple more hours?" She smiled and I rolled my eyes.

"Yes, but going headfirst into danger…" I gestured to the massive island coming to view beside us, "Might be pushing it a bit, don't you think?"

The sisters looked at each other and then back at me, before shaking their head.

"So, we're doing this? All of us?" I looked between the

women that stood before me, their heads held high and their hearts completely wild and free.

"Okay, write your love letters and send 'em home." I smiled and looked over to Florence, her face a mixed of worry and fear and something else I couldn't quite place.

"It's time to save my brother."

Strapped with knifes, powers and prayers, we docked our ship behind a cluster of Spruce trees and began to trudge up the sand. Florence pulled a small gust along with us, wiping away our tracks while Jodie kept us warm with individual fires in each of our hands, hot enough to beat the chill but not enough to burn. The sea sloshed gently behind us as Florence finally released her hold on the wind and we darted into the nearby trees.

"I've been here before, many years ago." Florence's eyes grazed for a moment before returning to us. "Follow my lead. The entrance is up ahead. Maybe two or three miles. Once we reach the doors, Erin, I need you inside the minds of the two guards at the gates while simultaneously making a hole within the front door," Erin stared at Florence, her eyes wide.

"Can you, do it?" Florence had become cold and serious once we reached the shore, no more fun or games once we set foot on the damp sand of the beach.

"Yes," Erin stated.

"Jodie," Florence turned to her, and she beamed back, "I need you in my back pocket, no unnecessary fires and you wait for my signal." Jodie's face sank slightly. "The best chance we have in saving Jameson, is if we do it quickly and quietly. I don't want a repeat of the Marley's tavern incident of three summers ago," she stated, and Jodie smiled, folding in a laugh.

In all the chaos I had almost forgotten that these women had known each other for years, they had lived together and fought together. A new kind of hope spread within my heart.

"Joy," finally Florence turned to me, "I know where the dungeons are, but I also know that they are huge, I need you to seek out Jameson, use your bond and pull on the tether that is tied between you. You can find him; you need to find him."

Worry crept over my face. Find Jameson? Pull on our bond? Did Florence know that I was powerless? Did she know I was only Human?

"How?" I asked. Florence took my hand and squeezed.

"Close your eyes and think only of him," her voice was so smooth as my eyes fluttered shut.

"Think of the time you've spent together, of how much you love him," she whispered. "You may not have powers, but magic lives within us all." The enticing smell of magic filled me once more.

"Find your brother, Joy, it's time to bring him home."

Determination ran through my veins as I reached for him. Where are you, Jameson? Help me find you.

26

JAMESON

COME HOME

Joy…?

Is that you…?

I can… I can feel you.

Hurry, please.

They'll be back soon.

27

RAYA

SHOULD I STAY OR SHOULD I GO?

"What happened that evening? When the decision was made?"

- QUESTIONS UNANSWERED BY RAYA

Khol stood outside of my room for three nights and three days. He thought it was for my protection, but I knew it was my imprisonment. The day of my first trial had loomed like a bad headache for what felt like years. And then the day arrived, like days always do.

My energy had died out, I had not used my power in days. Realization dawned on me, I did not really care whether I passed or failed. Whether I lived or died.

Nothing really mattered anymore. The three days I had spent without any contact with the outside world had cut me deep. It all seemed so pointless. Ezra was going to kill me; it was only a question of when. Maybe today or tomorrow or next week, so why bother trying?

Alias would find a way to survive without me, I was sure of it. Jala surely couldn't punish him for my death.

I slugged out of bed, dressed in my fighting leathers, and tapped on the door.

"Right," I huffed a deep breath. "Let's get this over with." I rolled my eyes as I walked past Khol, and his face crumpled with confusion.

"Have you eaten?" he asked, jogging to catch up with me.

"Have you seen any food delivered to my door?" I pointed to myself with outstretched thumbs. "I'm a prisoner, remember?" I laughed soullessly. I enjoyed not caring. I really enjoyed it.

Suddenly everything seemed like one big, colossal joke.

One big, massive fuck up.

What's the point in caring when you've probably already seen your last sunset?

What's the point in even trying when you know you are dead whether you pass or fail.

I laughed again at the thought.

"What's wrong with you, Raya?" Khol asked softly. I hated that the way he said my name still sent tingles throughout my body.

"What do you mean?"

"You're not acting like yourself," he stated, his eyes trained on the long hallway ahead of us. I stopped in my tracks.

"Stop acting like you know me, Khol." I folded my arms over my chest. "All you are is an overqualified prison guard, don't pretend to know me, don't pretend to care."

"You think I don't care?"

I shrugged, moving to lean on the wall opposite him.

"I think you want to care; I think you want to be better

than your mother." I rolled my ankles and cracked my neck. "But I suppose the apple doesn't fall far from the rotten tree."

Blood rushed to Khol's face, and a small pang of guilt buried its way into my heart. I wasn't angry at him, not really. But it seemed that he had become my personal punching bag. I opened my mouth to apologize.

"No," Khol cut in before me. "It's my turn to speak." I closed my mouth and leaned further into the wall.

"You don't get to decide to just give up, every day will be hard and every day you'll question why you are even trying." He took a deep breath. "But that's life and we're the ones that are lucky enough to be living it." He stepped toward me a little and lowered his voice.

"I'm not going to let anything happen to you." He echoed his words from three days ago. This statement, although bold and filled with conviction, was false and we both knew it.

"You can't stop this, Khol," I stifled a shudder. "I heard the maids or guards, whoever they were. I know why I am here, but I don't know why your mother is wasting her time on this charade of a trial." I attempted to sink deeper in the brick behind me.

Khol stepped forward again.

"What are you talking about?" he whispered.

"That—" I began to speak but he shushed me quickly. My voice became a whisper. "I heard some maid talking in the hall. They said that I didn't even need to do the trials, that your mother wouldn't let me live either way," I whispered.

"That can't be true," Khol stated, still whispering. "Perhaps the voices you overheard were just rumors? Think about it, why would she do that, to one of her own kind?"

"She had her own son executed, Khol," I whispered, letting the words settle between us.

"Can't you see that she is dangerous?" I stepped closer to him, our breath mixing softly.

"She is my mother, Raya." Khol's eyebrows knitted together, and his jaw ticked once. Twice.

"Am I supposed to believe the word of a girl I barely know over my own family?" As he spoke, it felt as though each of his words hit my chest like tiny, vicious knifes.

I swallowed against my throat. Standing up to my full height.

"No, I guess not." I swept past him, stalking down the hall toward my first trial. A new fire now blazing in my veins.

Not caring felt good, it felt freeing. But using the unbridled power that lived within me? Well, that was Gods damn delicious.

Crowds piled into stands all around a makeshift arena. I had heard the hammering and stamping of feet before I saw it. It was a stadium just outside of The Temple's wall, and the crowd were hungry for a performance. A decision on whether I lived or died.

Just as I began to wonder how such an extravagant event would be shielded from the humans, Ezra pointed to sixteen MindWonderers posted around the arena. If a human stumbled upon or found their way to us, all they would see is an old, abandoned farmhouse, unable to be opened. My own interest irritated me, I wish I didn't marvel at the new world I stumbled into.

Despite the over-enthusiastic assembly, the task was simple.

I was placed in a ring, on my own, and told to fight and win.

Rather anticlimactic if you asked me.

I categorized the area around me. The floor was dust,

which meant harder to run and easier to slip. There was one half fallen-down brick wall standing in the center of the ring. Debris from, assumably, previous fights scattered around it. My years of training lessons with Matron and the Sage Guard jumped around my mind. I could use the wall to hide or to collect momentum or… or…

It suddenly dawned on me that the feeling making its way up from my toes to my shoulders was fear.

I was scared, scared for my life and what it would mean to die.

I turned the words over in my head.

Jala wouldn't let me die. She needed my information. Ezra needed me alive to bargain with, right?

But she also needed a good show.

Gates creaked and the crowds' cheers went from loud to near deafening. A man, around my age and height, swaggered from the dimly light gateway at the edge of the arena, his arms raised waving to the crowds. Women and men alike began screaming with pure glee. A man fainted. A woman threw her underwear into the arena. It was madness.

He had ridiculously toned arms and a smile that suggested he knew exactly how handsome he was.

I was a damn solider of the Sage Guard, I couldn't let myself lose to this… show pony.

Raya

The whisper in my head startled me but I immediately looked around for Khol. He stood stoic and tall next to his mother.

You fight until one of you can't carry on. Remember what we practiced, you're ready for this.

I nodded, before Khol spoke again.

Look at him he's a… a show pony.

I laughed quietly as Khol repeated my own words back to me.

I've seen him fight before, he goes for the impressive moves to show the crowd, he's not here to kill you, he's here to embarrass you. Fight dirty and fight hard. You can do this.

With Khol's words running through my mind, I squared my shoulders and stole one more look at him. And winked.

What I should've said was thank you. I should've told him that he was the one I wanted to celebrate with.

But instead, I settled for a wink, attempting to convey my feelings through the gesture.

"Jasper Garner," my opponent shouted across to me, bowing low but never taking his eyes off me.

"I'd introduce myself," I shouted back, my voice laced with sweetness. "But you already know who I am."

"This'll be quick, don't worry, sweetheart." He smiled cruelly.

"Oh, I bet you say that to all the girls." I smiled back, then turned my head toward Ezra at the sounds of the deafening trumpets.

Ezra stood gracefully, a waterfall of technicolor robes swirling around her.

"Begin," she shouted, her lack of words catching me off guard, as well as the hard punch against my jaw.

I stumbled back as Jasper swung for me again, planting my feet in the dust and shaking off the punch.

Goddess, my jaw stung.

Jasper turned and waved to the crowd, not even worried about turning his back on me.

I couldn't tell what the bigger insult was.

I leapt forward, sweeping my leg underneath him, pinning his body to the ground. Dust quickly covered us as he struggled against my hands on his throat. If I could just get him to pass out, then this would all be over.

But he did not give up that easily, soon he spun us, his hands now closing on my throat.

Thunder clapped overhead and the once blue skies turned grey. I knew that using our magic was forbidden in the combat trial, but I didn't have complete control yet.

And Ezra wasn't really playing by the rules now, was she?

Heavy rain fell in sheets, soon turning the dust beneath us into thick mud.

In a moment of weakness, the rainwater made Jasper's hand slippy and he loosened his grip. Air whooshed into my lungs as I rolled away, jumping to my feet.

"Nice trick, Raya," Jasper sneered. "Or should I call you 'O mighty queen'," he mock bowed, his gaze narrowing in on mine. We circled each other slowly.

"You can call me whatever you want, although 'O mighty queen' might be harder when I've knocked all your teeth out." I smiled again, jumping out to throw a punch.

He blocked it easily, catching me on my cheek. Blood leaked slowly, falling over my lips. What was I doing? I had spent my entire life training and fighting and becoming a weapon? And now I was letting Jasper punch me?

Wake up, Raya.

Darting behind the half-broken wall, I swiped the blood from my lip. *Focus*, I chided myself. Nineteen years of training had prepared me for this. And I wasn't going down without a fight.

Grabbing the bricks for momentum, I swung around as Jasper approached, my feet slamming into the center of his chest. A strained cough sounded from his chest as he attempted to rise. I smashed my fist against his nose, the bones crunching beneath my hand. Blood, hot and thick dripped down his face. He rose again, his pride forcing him to go on. Swinging at me, I let him hit my face. The Temple needn't know how deadly I was just yet.

My skin parted on my cheek, blood seeping down into my mouth.

"It really is a shame to ruin such a pretty face," Jasper choked, reaching for me again, this time I blocked him easily, throwing a punch to his groin.

"Aw, you think I'm pretty?" I sung sarcastically, watching him attempt to steady his balance. My hair stuck to my shoulders as my rain continued to fall. The steady beat of the drops calming me, the knowing that I created them filled me with confidence and ease.

I could break this world apart if I really wanted to.

So, I did.

As Jasper lunged for me again and smashed my foot against the mud and cracked the earth with a battle cry, Jasper realized too late that he was heading right for the hole in the earth. I reached for him, grabbing his hand just before he plummeted down into the earth.

"I'm bored," I sighed, holding his entire life in my hands. "Yield and I won't let you fall to your death."

"You bitch," Japer spat, I loosened my grip ever so slightly.

"Wait, wait! Fine," he looked around at his once adoring fans. "I yield!" he shouted, and I plopped him back on solid ground.

Turning to Ezra, I fell slowly and steadily into a bow.

Khol raised his hand to knit the earth back together, but I beat him to it, waving my hand.

I wasn't sure it would work, but I was so high on power that I tried it anyway.

And the earth fell back into place.

The crowd sat still and silent, unsure what to do with themselves. And then suddenly, all at once they jumped to their feet, screaming, shouting, clapping, and stomping. The arena began to shake. I turned back to Jasper curled up and panting on the floor.

"Don't take it personally."

28

JOY

IT TURNS OUT YOU CAN GO HOME AGAIN, BUT IT'LL COST YOU

"He appeared in my life, his hair messy and short, and his heart big and wild."

- RAFAEL'S JOURNAL ENTRY

Seconds turned into minutes as I waited for any response from Jameson, anything other than the embarrassment that began to seep into the bottom of my trousers and crawl up my leg.

"This is useless," I sighed, opening my eyes.

But everything had vanished. The sisters and Florence, gone. The tilted trees and the soft splashes from the ocean.

All gone.

In their stead was four concrete walls that seemed to suck the life out of an already lifeless place. Movement in the corner caught my eye, a lump shivering.

"Jameson?" I whispered, too afraid to hope. The lump shivered more aggressively but did not roll over. I crept toward it slowly, hand extended to pull back the blanket.

"Joy?" A small voice sounded from behind me and I spun to face it. "I wouldn't move that blanket if I were you, Rafael is a miserable sod on the best days and downright insufferable on the worst." Jameson's signature grin hung lopsided on his face. The breath caught in my throat and the blood drained from my face at the sight of him. My dear friend, finally found. I raced toward him, opening my arms to embrace him.

But my arms swung right through him, as though I was made of air and nothing more.

I stared at his battered face, dried blood cracking on his now hollowed cheeks. How long had it been since he ate? Drank clean water? The concrete walls around us leaked black water, and the feeling of damp crawled inside my throat. Hay bales sat in sad piles as makeshift beds; bruises bloomed on Jameson's shoulders from nights of sleeping on the hard floor.

The shape, Rafael I supposed, shifted beneath the blanket only to still again.

"Joy," Jameson sighed. "Is it really you?" I nodded franticly.

"It's me," I laughed at the absurd joke my life had become. "I am here, almost." I marveled at the confidence behind my own words. "I projected myself to you." A small smile tucked itself in the corner of my mouth.

Jameson stared at me, his eyes wide and unblinking.

"How do I get to you?" I reached a hand out, only for it to fall through his shoulder again. Jameson continued staring, unmoving.

"Am I dreaming?" His whispering voice bounced around the room. My eyes softened as I fixed my gaze upon him.

"It's me, sweet boy." Tears blurred my vision and

realization dawned on me. I had done it. I had found my brother and I was going to bring him home.

Relief, sweeter than honey-glazed apples, settled into my skin. A life without my beautiful friend was a life not worth living. And now he would return, no doubt with extreme dramatics. A smile, deep and bright, spread across his face and if I had any skills with a paint brush, I would have painted the sight. It was, quite possibly, the most beautiful thing I had ever seen.

"How?" he whispered, glancing behind my head for listening ears.

"I couldn't possible explain it all at once." I could not seem to form any other words. And somehow Jameson seemed to understand.

"I'm coming to get you, brother," I vowed. "And we will return home to our family." His eyes were lined with silver as he nodded and begun reciting the maze that was the prison. It would not be easy to get in and it would be even harder to get out. There was a very real chance that we would not make it out at all.

Once he stopped speaking, I felt a tug on my arm, but turning, I found nothing there.

Another tugged pulled at me and I almost toppled over.

"I think I need to get back to my body."

"One more thing," Jameson started just as I began to close my eyes again. "Rafael comes with us, I won't leave him here."

His loyalty made my heart squeeze.

"Do you trust him?" I eyed the sleeping heap.

"With my life."

I nodded.

And then I was back in the tall, twisty trees, Florence and the sisters on my right and the ocean behind me.

"Wow," I whispered, reaching out a hand to get my balance. "That was the most incredible thing I've ever experienced." The words toppled from my mouth before I could stop them.

"Yeah, you can say that again." Erin held out a hand for me to grab.

Once the world stopped spinning and the ground stopped whirling, I stood up straight, taking a slug from Jodie's water canteen.

"How does he look?" Florence almost whispered from behind the sisters, guilt fresh in her eyes.

"He's alive. Half-starved and bruised, but alive." I smiled and tears sprung from my eyes.

He was alive. He was alive. He was alive.

I chanted the words in my mind over and over until my tears dried.

The ocean slapped against the shore as though it was agreeing. The ocean loved Jameson and I; it sounded strange, and I had never said it out loud, but I knew it was true.

As water returned to water, I knew we would soon return home.

A secret promise shared between two old friends.

"Jameson is adamant that the prison is easy to navigate. He was blindfolded when he was brought in, but he overheard the guards stating that there is only one way in and one way out, baring a jump from a sixth story window. He took one left, then a right, went down forty steps and turned right again. He was pushed into a cell, and he's been there ever since. Surviving on questionable water and even more questionable bread." I looked over at the women, each of them forming a plan in their minds.

I looked up at the mammoth fortress before me, its walls black and thick, with the occasional glass platform sticking out harshly. Vines snaked up the walls, its thorns glinting in the sun.

"They remind of a story mother told us once," Jodie said softly, staring softly at the vines. "About a girl who pricked her finger on a thorn and fell asleep for many years." She looked over at us, waiting for the rest of the story.

"A princess travelled across the continents, climbed the walls, kissed her and the girl woke up. They married and lived happily ever after." She smiled, looking once again at the vines.

"I've never heard that one before," I said, reaching into my pocket to run my fingers over the shell hidden there. A little piece of home.

29

RAYA

YOU'VE AIN'T SEEN NOTHING YET

"What are we going to do about it? We can't let her get away with this!"

- EZRA'S ADVISORS AFTER RAYA'S TRIAL

Staring in the mirror, I knew the cut on my cheek would scar. I had enjoyed my glory for all of twenty-four seconds before two guards ushered me from the arena and back inside The Temple. Everyone was talking in hushed voices, and no one dared make eye contact with me. I knew why, I knew that once the crowds had dispersed and the excitement died down, I'd probably be executed anyway for violating the rules of the trial.

I began the tedious task of scrubbing layers of mud, dust, and blood from my skin, hair and fingernails. Elijah had stopped by earlier and stitched my face, his words few and far between.

"You're not angry with me to, are you?" I looked up at his almost gray eyes and smiled.

"I'm not angry, Raya, I'm scared for you. If you keep pushing," he sighed softly, "Ezra will push back." He returned to cleaning the cut on my face and a chill ran through my entire body. Had I really been careless? Or foolish? Elijah had taken me in and kept me safe after the incident at the safehouse. But The Temple had also kept me imprisoned, lonely, and scared. Not to mention the ones who intended to use me as though I was cattle at the market.

I had stared at myself in the blue tiled bathing room until Khol knocked on the door.

"She wants to see you," he said before even looking up from the book in his hands. His eyes quickly found mine before darting to the stitches across my left cheek. Suddenly one hand was on my cheek and the other was lifting my hair to get a better look.

"Are you alright?" He looked closer, our faces only centimeters apart. "Jasper is such a bastard! God, I would love to pummel his entitled, little face," he muttered, still staring at the scar but also checking the rest of my face and body for injuries.

"Be my guest, part of me wishes I'd thrown him into that cavern," I sighed.

"You should have," his hands slipped from my cheeks, but his face stayed right next to mine.

"Your fighting today, it was…" he whispered.

"I know, I broke the rules."

"Raya, shut up," Khol put both his hands on my shoulders. "It was amazing, you looked amazing out there, like you were born to fight, born to survive." I smiled inwardly at his words, if he only he knew how right he was, how much I had survived in my twenty years.

"I'm quite proud of you," he smiled, and his words were so genuine I almost started to well up.

Almost.

"Thank you," I said after swallowing against my dry throat.

"I wish I could be brave like you." His words came out has a whisper, his warm breath against my cheek. He hands slowly ran down from my shoulders to my forearms and then, finally, to my hands.

"You're plenty brave," I whispered, my voice breathless. He shook his head.

"I have never done anything like that." I stared into his eyes, his words wrapping me in a warm blanket of security. My head was screaming at me to pull away, that I knew better.

"You are—" I cut Khol's words off by pressing my lips against his.

As soon as our lips touched, I understood what it felt like to come home. Wrapping my arms around his neck, I opened my mouth for him, his tongue swept against mine as he pulled me close. Strong arms snaked around my waist as he lifted me up to his full height and my legs instinctively locked around him. Our bodies were touching in every possible way but I wanted more, I want to be closer to him. To be enveloped by him.

A dormant emotion stirred beneath my skin, I ignored it. Focusing on the feeling of Khol's hands digging into my hips, hard enough to bruise.

Lips, tongue, and teeth, a breathless groan sounded at the back of Khol's throat as I nipped his flesh with my teeth. Everything inside me felt gooey and bright and new. His lips felt like dying and living all at the same time.

We broke apart, our foreheads resting against one another, our breaths the only sound filling the room.

"I should have done that on the first day I met you," Khol

whispered against my lips and a warm shudder filled my body.

"That was…" I couldn't find the words.

"Agreed."

We stood for a moment, my legs still firmly wrapped around his waist.

"Your mother…"

"Ouch, you're thinking about my mother right now?" Khol reared back with a smile.

"Well, what were you thinking about?" I asked defensively.

"Oh, we're definitely not there yet," he said smugly, setting me down on the floor. I stared up at his swollen lips and messy hair.

"We should probably get going," I said, smoothing my own hair down and then reaching up to smooth his.

He nodded. I was digging a hole inside my brain as I walked from my chamber into the hallway. I did not have the capacity to think about what this meant for Khol and I. What it meant that a letter addressed to Captain Jala sat in a draw only a few feet away, heavy with secrets and betrayal.

Something had been building between the two of us for weeks, but I would still be leaving The Temple when Jala came for me. So why did leaving The Temple now feel like ash inside of me?

The Temple was filled with people full of hatred and revenge like Ezra, but it was also full of people like Elijah and Khol and Ottie. Sorcerers whose only goals were survival and happiness.

A war raged on within my head.

Khol had made it very clear that he trusted his mother's words over mine, so where did that leave us? I shook my head, clearing my thoughts as I walked down the hallway and entered a new room I hadn't noticed before.

Purple and gold tapestries lined the walls and golden lanterns swung in the faint breeze from an open window. Incense burned close by.

Ezra sat behind a large wooden desk, books, crystals, and papers scattered around her.

"Raya, how pleasant to see you," Ezra spoke without looking up from her journal. "That'll be all, Khol," she dismissed her son without a glance upward. "I wish to speak to Raya alone." She finally looked up and made eye contact with me, a slow smile on her face.

"Mother," Khol started.

"Shut the door behind you, please," she spoke, and her word was final. Khol turned to leave, sending me an apologetic look as he did so.

"That was quite a show today." Her eyes locked on mine. "Jasper isn't usually beaten." She stood from her desk and walked around it slowly, her eyes never leaving mine.

"Well, I know that you like to keep the trials… festive." I smiled sweetly. "The crowd loved it."

"Yes, they did. I, however, did not." She leaned against her cherry wooden desk, her golden bangles sliding up and down her wrist.

"This trial was combat only, your little stunt was a blatant act of disobedience, not to mention the rumors that have already started swirling. You are foolish, Raya. A foolish and reckless little girl. If it weren't for your abilities, I would…" She stopped herself short as if catching the words before they could leave her mouth.

"You'd what?" I pushed. "I know that you don't want me here, so why keep me?" I asked, wanting to rile her, wanting to bait her.

She pushed off from the desk and walked up to me, our gazes locked. She grabbed my chin between her thumb and finger, digging in her nails hard enough to draw blood.

"This is my Temple, my home, if you EVER pull this kind of stunt again, whether it be in front of the crowd or not," she seethed and spoke through a clenched jaw, "I'll kill you myself." Her words were cool and calm. She pushed my head back and licked a bead of my blood from her thumb, before turning to her desk.

"You wouldn't dare," I spoke nonchalantly, and she whipped around and smacked the back of her hand across my cheek.

"Know your place, girl. I am the leader of The Temple. You. Are. Nothing," she spat before walking to her desk and returning to her piles of pages. Blood rushed to my cheek and my skin began to sting.

"You're dismissed," she said without looking up.

I walked away, not knowing that the slap across my face was the least of my worries.

Exactly one week later I stood in the dressing room of one of the finest boutiques in the Northern Continent. The handprint on my cheek had faded into almost nothing, and the scar across my other cheek had settled nicely.

I shivered as I stood in only undergarments waiting for the next monstrosity to be handed through the curtain. Elijah, although a talented healer, was no stylist. Even the seamstresses looked worried when he picked out a black funeral dress for me to wear to the ball.

"I thought it looked classic," he had protested.

If I had to stuff my body into another frilly, pastel dress I was going to scream. I had already dealt with the stick thin seamstresses that eyed my full hips, stomach, and bum like I was muck on their shoe.

"I don't think this one will… fit," she had spoken loud enough for the shop to hear, when Elijah had held up a satin pink dress.

I crossed my arms over my chest at the thought.

"Raya?" a familiar deep voice called through the curtain.

"I'm naked," I yelped, attempting to further cover my exposed body with my arms.

"O-kay," Khol said oddly and then paused for a moment.

"Did you need something?"

"Elijah had me sent here, he wanted me to see the dress."

I sighed deeply. Covering my face with my hands.

"There is no dress, Khol, only ugly, frilly pieces of fabric I can barely squeeze into!" My voice came out like a little girl, I was throwing a tantrum. About a dress.

Talk about loss of priorities.

Elijah pushed another awful dress through the curtain and greeted Khol sweetly.

"I don't think this one's going to work," I pushed it back through without giving it a second look.

"What about this one?" This time it was Khol that handed me a dress. My fingers grazed his forearm as I grabbed the soft fabric from him.

It was midnight blue, with a pinched waist and flowing skirt. The thin straps were crested with tiny diamonds and the billowing skirt was dotted with the shining gemstones too. I slipped into the gown as though it was tailored just for me. The material hung onto my every dip and curve and my breasts were held firmly inside the fabric.

"It's… it's…" I stammered.

"Let us see it!" Elijah protested and I slung back the curtain.

The men stared, silent.

Elijah reached out to touch the fabric, his hand trembling ever so slightly.

"It's beautiful, Raya, you're beautiful," he rasped, wiping the corner of his eye. I smiled deeply, reaching out a hand for him to grasp.

Turning to Khol, I noticed his eyes tracking up and down my body, stopping on my face.

"You're breathtaking," he said, because for him there was nothing else to say.

For a woman who did not care much for 'things' because she never had the luxury of having them, I felt as though this dress had become an extension of myself. Deep in my belly something unraveled and a plant pot by the window began to bloom brightly, its leaves growing wide and healthy. Khol turned to watch my gaze but instead of awe, his face filled with dread.

"Raya," he hissed, pushing me into the dressing room forcefully, shutting the curtain behind him.

"Are you insane?" His wild eyes searched my face. "We are not in The Temple now!" He spoke through gritted teeth.

Just like his mother had.

"She warned me this would happen," he spoke softly.

"Who?"

"My mother, she said you weren't ready to be out with the humans, I should've listened!"

"Khol, it was one flower, and we are the only people in the boutique!" I whispered angrily.

"That's not the point, Raya, and you know it. You cannot be so careless! Just because The Temple doesn't matter to you, it doesn't mean it doesn't matter to me!" A deep breath whooshed from his chest. I stumbled back as though his words had hit me.

"Is that what you think?" I whispered, "that I do not care?"

"Raya… no… that's… you have to understand…" he stuttered.

"You should go," I whispered, pulling away from him and folding my hands over my chest.

"Raya—"

"Now." My word was final, and he knew it. Turning abruptly, he fled from the store. My moment of happiness gone and forgotten.

But he was right, wasn't he? I didn't care about The Temple, right? In a matter of weeks, I would be sharing everything I had learned with Captain Jala, I would be sighing their deaths.

Wouldn't I?

30

JOY

LOVE AND MONSTERS

"I saw it straight away for what it was. A reunion"

- JOY'S PERSONAL JOURNAL

The plan was set and underway. I stared at Jodie and Erin's retreating figures as they started their trek around the building. They were waiting for our signal, waiting to scale the walls incase our plan failed.

Florence and I were taking the front doors.

"I've been here before, remember? They know my face," she said to me as we bent low and hid within the trees. Her steps faltered from time to time, her mind somehow elsewhere. Her face a mixture of feelings I couldn't decipher. But one was clear, guilt.

"The guards that took Jameson, they must have been newly trained because they didn't recognize me," she winced, and my chest tightened for a moment. The first lie she ever told me. The biggest lie she ever told me. I nod, eager to move on.

"I…" she struggled to find the right words, "escaped from them once and they'll probably be pretty eager for the chance to have me back in The Te…" she cleared her throat, "in the dungeons." She flipped a braid over her shoulder, attempting to be nonchalant.

"Perhaps they will remember me and escort me straight to the cells." She continued to fumble with her words, as if unable to work out what she was saying. "You can sneak in behind me." Her eyes lit up excitedly.

I stared at her in bewilderment.

"You want to get yourself thrown in jail, so then I must save you, as well as Jameson? I am I getting that correct?" I rested my hands on my hips.

"It might work." She shrugged, and I gaped at her. "Have I ever let you down?" She nudged me with her elbow. I scoffed at her words.

"Yes, repeatedly," I answered, raising my eyebrows.

"But have I ever purposely let you down?" She nudged me with her elbow again. I rolled my eyes.

"No."

"Exactly." She smiled deeply.

"Exactly what?"

"The plan will work!"

"No, it won't."

"Well, I don't think you have a choice, I don't see you coming up with some grand plan!"

I turned away from her, hoping to see Erin or Jodie walking in the distance. But they were too far gone, too out of sight. The setting sun painted the black fortress a myriad of orange, yellow, and pink, I wanted nothing more than to be back at our ship, laid on the sun-warmed deck, watching the sunset. My arms draped around Lolita's body, Jameson's head resting on my thigh. All of us together but none of us speaking.

We had never been religious and neither had our families. But now I wished for one or both prophesied Celestial Queens to come and save us from this life. From the heartache and loss I knew would follow our family everywhere we went.

"Okay," my voice was barely a whisper. "If you believe this plan will work, and save my family, then I'm on board." I looked over at Florence, her face solemn and red. Something odd lingering behind her eyes.

I wrapped my braids and knotted them on the top of my head, attempting to get ready for anything this plan might throw at us. Worry nibbled its way into my stomach, would Jodie and Erin be safe? I had told them everything I knew about scaling a wall… which wasn't much but something felt wrong. Something felt off and I couldn't put my finger on what… or who.

"Are you ready?" Florence said, resting her hand on my shoulder, it was shaking ever so slightly.

The doors to the dark fortress were as intimidating as I expected them to be. Perhaps the hunters were overcompensating for something? I smirked.

"What?" Florence snapped; she had been on edge ever since we arrived at the door. I supposed it was because she was about to give herself to the enemy. I had never felt more grateful to be powerless than I did in that moment. Blissfully ordinary.

"Nothing," I shook my head, we continued to stare at the door.

"What now?" I prompted. "Do we open the doors? Knock a secret coded message?" She glared at me, but I smiled anyway. I couldn't help feeling lighter now than I had during our entire journey. I was getting Jameson back and I knew he was alive. I was bringing him home to our crew.

"This isn't a joke, Joy," Florence scoffed, rolling her eyes at me.

"I wasn't the one who got us into this situation, Florence, was I?" I bit back, irritation scolding through my blood.

"I did you a favor," she whispered under her breath.

"Excuse me?" I whirled on her.

"You heard me, this journey saved you from yourself. From your own grief about Lolita," she spoke.

And I snapped.

I grabbed her shoulders, digging my fingernails into her dark skin as I pushed her against the castle doors ferociously.

"Do not," I scolded, "say her name ever again." It took me a moment to figure out that the wetness on my cheeks was tears. "You didn't know her, you don't know me or my family. You did not do me a favor." I pushed her one last time before letting go. "You took someone else from me." I wiped my face with the back of my hand aggressively.

Just when I thought we were working toward the same goal, Florence changed. She shifted into someone I didn't recognize.

"I'm…" she began, her words quiet.

"Stop, I don't want to hear it, let's get Jameson and go. Then we can go our separate ways."

A creak sounded, as loud as a fallen tree hitting the ground, and the two of us fell silent. The doors began to move at an agonizingly slow pace, as though being pushed by two gigantic tortoises.

"Move," Florence leapt towards me, pushing me out of sight. I hit the floor with a thud, my skin scraped against the rough ground.

“This wasn’t the plan!” I whisper-shouted over the still creaking doors.

“Plans change, Joy!” She mimicked my own voice back to me. What was she doing? Was she buying me time to sneak inside? I stumbled into a crouch position, hidden behind a thorn bush.

Even the vegetation was unfriendly.

It was the most ridiculous situation I had ever been in, and I had spent my life drunk in taverns with Jameson. We made a plan, only ten minutes ago, and it had already gone out the window. How was this possible? Energy spiked inside of me as I stood up. I would reason with Florence, help her understand that we were a team and we needed to stay together.

But then the doors stopped moving and a woman stepped toward Florence. She must’ve been a good twenty years older than us, her hair peppered with gray, and a snake tattoo twisted around her bicep.

“Florence,” she spoke, her voice crisp, clear and incredibly lethal. “Welcome home.” She forced a smile to her lips.

All the air whooshed from my lungs in one fell swoop. This had to be a mistake. Welcome home? Was it a taunt? Welcoming her back to the prison? Black spots clouded my vision.

The two embraced and I knew it was all wishful thinking.

She had betrayed me. Again.

“We’ve missed you,” the older woman spoke.

“I’ve missed you too, Mother.”

31

RAYA

DANCE UNTIL YOU DROP

"This cannot continue. They must give each other up!"

- EZRA TO HER HUSBAND, JONAS

I thought of the flower, now probably dead and drooping, while sitting on my bed. Nai had rolled my hair in hot rings and left me to change into the new dress. It laid flatly on the desk, daring me to put it on. I hated the thought of letting Khol down, but I hated the thought of letting myself down even more.

He had no right to speak to me as though I was a child, but I understood his concern. I was being thoughtless. So lost in my own power that I let myself forget. I had let myself forget about my real reasons for being at The Temple. The letter sat unsent in the top draw. I could have brought to town when we shopped for the dress. I could have slipped into in a messenger's satchel on ten separate occasions, but I did not.

I could not.

A soft knock sounded on the door and Nai slipped through.

"You're not dressed!" she stated. I smiled and laughed softly.

She scurried to the desk and held the gown in her hands as though it was The Goddess herself.

"Elijah says you look beautiful in it," she spoke softly, not taking her eyes from the dress. I looked from the dress to the open double doors that lead to the balcony. I could leave if I really wanted to. I could run and never turn back. I had all four elements on my side, I was the most powerful Sorcerer in this Temple.

"Come on now, Raya, you must get dressed quickly before you're late!" Nai stated and lifted the dress into my arms.

The silky fabric sway around my hips as I made my way to the banquet hall. A faint trickle of music wrapped around the air and soon I stood outside of two heavy wooden doors. The same doors I stood outside on my first night here. When my body was battered and bruised, and my questions large and unanswered.

"It reminds me of the first night you stayed here," Khol spoke softly, standing a few feet away from me. Clad in black dress pants, a white tunic and a black over coat, I had never seen him look more incredible.

"What was it you said?" He laughed to himself, light glinting off the golden hoops in his ears and nose, matching the gold rings collecting on his fingers. "Ah yes, you thought we were going to sacrifice you." His voice was interrupted by a fit of his own laughter. The sound touched my toes and ran all the way up my body. His eyes crinkled and his whole body shook. If it were possible to drink a sound, I would get drunk on his laughter every night.

"You should laugh more," I said without truly thinking first. As his laughter died, he looked up and our gazes met. His look was deep, as though he was staring directly into my soul.

"You should too."

I wanted to say more to him. We had been tip toeing around our kiss since it had happened the day before. With everything going on, it was hard to even fathom what was starting to build between us. I opened my mouth to tell him everything I was thinking and feeling, but we were interrupted.

"Well don't you both look dashing!" Elijah spoke from behind us, his husband proudly on his arm.

"I could say the same for the both of you!" The two men were utterly perfect in their black pants and gray overcoats, white tunics hidden underneath them. Each of them had a purple lily in their front pockets.

"It's beautiful," I whispered.

"Conan preserved the flowers from our wedding with his gifts, we wear them at every special occasion." Elijah turned to his husband, years of love still present in his eyes. I turned to Conan and smiled deeply.

"We haven't met, I'm Raya," I held out a hand and he shook it.

"I have heard so much about you, I feel as though I already know you! I'm Conan." His tanned skin and angled eyes reminded me of Alias, and a pang of guilt resided in my chest.

"You're from the Eastern Continent?" I asked.

"Yes." He looked over at Elijah. "But when I saw this young jumper on the battlefield, I knew I would follow him anywhere." They shared a quick kiss and a lump formed in my throat.

I wanted what they had; something easy and simple. I looked over at Khol who watched them with a small smile on his face.

"We should go in," he held out an arm to me as I smoothed my skirts.

"Do I look alright?" I asked, finally pulling the white gloves up over my elbows. Khol swallowed and barely met my eyes.

"You look beautiful."

The memory of my carelessness in the boutique surfaced.

"I'm sorry," I whispered as the tall doors were pushed open. "About the flower earlier, you were right, I wasn't thinking clearly." He met my eyes and nodded.

"I'm sorry too, my reaction was perhaps a little… over the top."

A world of glitter and luxury poured into my senses as we stepped into the grand hall. Glasses of champagne were stacked, overflowing with amber liquid. A cake, taller than me, sat in the corner. Lilac flowers were swirled in icing. Floor to ceiling windows covered the wall to my right, thick lilac curtains draping around their edges. Two of the windows were flung open, many people strolling The Temple's walled gardens. To our left stood several round tables, with chairs filled with guests sipping or eating or chatting.

If I were better with words, I would have probably found a wonderful way to describe the sight before me. Instead, all I could say was, "It's beautiful."

And it was.

Khol nodded beside me.

"What are we celebrating tonight?" The changing music brought me back down to earth. I looked at Khol, only now noticing how his midnight blue tie matched my dress perfectly.

"Ah, well," he scratched the back of his neck nervously.

"It's my birthday," he said quickly and quietly.

I stopped in my tracks.

"It's your birthday? Why didn't you tell me?" I whispered through my teeth.

"It seemed as though you had more important things to think about." He pulled us through the crowd, toward the stack of champagne glasses, one of which he handed to me.

"Khol," Ezra stated as the crowds parted for her and her husband.

Looking at Khol's father, Jonas, I realized how much the two men looked alike. Their dark brown skin, stark against the green of their eyes. They were very handsome men. Some may say that beauty on men is abnormal or strange, but no one could deny these men. Khol stood a few inches taller than his father, his hair solid black without the streaks of gray his father wore.

"You look lovely, Raya," Jonas stated, smiling sweetly. "As do you, son." He held out a hand and forearm for Khol to clasp. It was clear enough in that moment the men had grown together while Ezra had been leading The Temple.

Watching Khol interact with his father made me ache. I felt a deep sense of loneliness thump against my bones. It settled beneath my skin. Sitting oddly like oil and water. Khol's eyes met mine and the world turned to mist around me.

She is breathtaking.

The words echoed in my head like a tune refusing to be forgotten.

"Shall we get this celebration started?" Elijah's voice softly cut through our gazes.

Khol guided me throughout the room, glasses of sparkling wine in our hands.

Sorcerers from all over the continents had visited The Temple this evening. Khol had shared that most of them had arrived via the underground river beneath The Temple or used powerful magical disguises to arrive without notice. As gnarled, thorned trees surrounded The Temple and the island it was on, only invited guests could find it. It was the Continent's best kept secret.

"I like your tie," I spoke under my breath without looking up at him. We had been stuck in a Goddess awful conversation with a man whose name I hadn't bothered to learn.

"I thought you'd appreciate it," he said, his tie glinting in the candlelight.

"I asked for my grandmother's empanadas," Khol whispered to me softly as we stopped at a table for another glass of wine.

"Where are they?" I looked at the glorious table.

"They won't be there," he shrugged. "I ask every year but they no longer 'trust' my grandmother so…" his words trailed off and I made a mental note to probe him for answers later.

"Khol," a woman with golden hair, around my age sauntered over to us, her skintight dress a deep red. "Happy birthday," her voice was sultry and low.

"Nora, it's good to see you. Thank you for coming." Khol's voice was low and hushed.

"You're welcome," she said before winking. "It's always nice to celebrate with an old… *friend*." The word sounding unnecessarily sexual in her mouth. She eyed me curiously.

"Perhaps we'll talk later?" she asked, turning on her heel before Khol had chance to answer.

I moved further down the table and popped a macaroon in my mouth.

"Are you sleeping with her?" I spoke around the food in my mouth as casually as I could.

Khol choked on his mouthful of fizz.

"What?" His voice was high and quick. "Why would you think that?"

"Who is she?" I tried my best at being nonchalant.

"We were schooled together; I've known her for years."

I swallowed a gulp of wine, the bubbles filling my head softly. I stuffed another sweet in my mouth. Another gulp of wine. Then wiped my hands against my dress before I could stop myself. I was a trained fighter after all, not a princess that went to balls.

"Do you want to dance?" I turned abruptly to find Khol already staring.

"With you?" He cocked his head to the side.

"Who else?" I asked, a mocking tone on my voice. Khol's lips formed a tiny smile as he chuckled softly, reaching out his hand to take mine.

Jealously was not very flattering on me.

Our bodies touched and a fire smoldered within me. I tripped over my feet, stamping on Khol's toes a few too many times.

"I am a solider, never learned to dance," my voice was clipped. Red dancing on my cheeks in embarrassment.

"Just relax, I've got you."

Songs flew by, one after another and we danced and danced. Ezra watched from the sidelines, Jonas whispering in her ear.

"Jealousy looks good on you, Raya," Khol's deep voice rumbled across my skull as we danced with our cheeks touching.

"I don't know what you mean," I teased.

"I thought you were going to rip Nora's head off or choke on a macaroon." A laugh burst out from my chest, and I tamped it down quickly.

"Maybe I just really love sweets," I argued.

"Maybe," his hand slipped from the top of my back to the base. "But I don't think so."

A sucked in a breath hastily. I had to stop this.

I couldn't let Khol develop feelings for me, and I definitely couldn't let myself feel anything toward him.

"I'm still leaving, Khol," I said. "When I complete the trials, of course," I corrected myself, forgetting the lie that lived within me. Pulling my cheek away from his to look at him, a cold breeze hit me. Couples danced around us and glasses clinked, men and women laughed, and people snuck off into dark corners, but we may as well have been alone.

"I don't want you to," Khol whispered, pushing a strand of my hair behind my ear. My traitorous heart stumbled over itself.

"Please don't do this, Khol, don't ask this of me," I begged quietly, our bodies still dancing with muscle memory.

"Stay with me."

The air was knocked from my chest and my knees began to wobble.

Because I wanted to.

I wanted to stay with him.

I wanted to burn that Goddess forsaken letter in my draw.

I stepped back from Khol, walking backward one step after another until I knocked into a man and spilt his drink.

"I'm sorry." I brushed past him and bolted toward the glass doors, desperate for the night's cool air.

How had I let myself become so distracted? The Goddess only knew if Alias was still alive, and what of Captain Jala?

How had I forgotten that the Sorcerers were 'vicious?

How had I even believed that in the first place?

I had become complacent.

I had somehow become tethered to the power that begged to be released. That begged to destroy.

This was no Temple. It was a double edge sword, a poisoned betrayal bound to end in bloodshed.

32

KHOL

RUN AWAY LITTLE BOY

"Would I follow her?"

- KHOL'S PERSONAL JOURNAL

I watched her tall figure retreat until she was lost within the crowd. What had I done? Asking her to stay with me? I had never been more selfish in my life. I knew what staying here was doing to Raya, I could see the unease that sat just beneath her skin. Like a decision that needed to be made. I could try to reason with my mother, demand she release Raya. Surely, she was not the monster Raya thought she was.

I walked across the room quickly, carefully avoiding Nora's sultry stare and Elijah's warning gaze, attempting to remain the always elegant heir to The Temple while letting my long legs eat up the ground beneath me.

"Have you seen Mother?" I caught Ottie by her arm as she swirled past me. She paused, noting the urgency in my voice.

"Just a moment ago, I believe, talking to a guard about something or other." She pulled her arm from my grip, swishing onto the dance floor yet again.

Looking for my mother, I came up empty handed. She wasn't even in the room. Neither was my father or their closest advisors.

"Where is my mother?" I caught the collar of the guard Ottie pointed to as he attempted to hurry past me.

"I do not know, my lord," he spoke, and I scoffed at the title.

"Where?" I demanded, my gaze burning hot and unforgiving, I dipped into his head and forced the answer from his lips.

"In her office but she is not to be disturbed," he stiffened his upper lip. "My lord."

I dropped his collar and headed for the thick wooden doors ahead. Pushing them open with enough force to splinter them, I strode down the hall.

Pacing outside of her office doors, a speech formed in my mind.

She was still my mother, surely, she cared about my feelings.

Rafael popped into my mind. *Perhaps not.*

But soon voices joined me in the lonely hall. A maid scuttled out of my mother's office leaving the office door open, just a crack.

"…if the people find out about this," my mother scoffed. "The girl will be made into some sort of hero. You and I both know that she is dangerous and that she could be this Continent's undoing." Her words were sharp and cutting.

"But Ezra, she could also be the one to end this war, to bring light to the darkness that had plagued us for years," a strong voice interrupted. It took me a moment to realize that it was my father's.

"You saw her with Khol tonight," my father spoke again. "If she is the one to fulfil The Prophesy like you say she will, wouldn't it be in our best interests to have Khol by her side?"

My heart stopped in my chest.

The Prophesy.

When I had mentioned it to Raya all those weeks ago, it was a passing thought, something absurd and fantastical that belonged in my sister's story books.

My mother truly believed Raya could fulfil the Prophesy.

The champagne in my stomach turned and curdled.

"She will not fulfil the prophesy, that I know for sure," my mother's voice was laced with hate and iron and something akin to jealously.

"It is to be done tonight," my mother's voice got louder and quieter as I pictured her pacing around the room. "The world will have to find another person to be their savior." She heaved a sigh.

"It is decided. Raya will be dead before sunrise."

My heart sped up, beating so fast I thought it would jump out of my chest.

Raya had been telling the truth.

My mother had never wanted her to be part of our world, of our family. Her own jealously fueled a hatred that burned hotter than the fire Raya summoned in her hands.

I had known she was different; known she was more than just a late blooming Sorcerer. Raya was special and everyone who met her knew it.

I had known it. The moment I had met her.

Reality slammed into my chest as the last few moments settled into my mind. All her life Raya hadn't understood why her village had been burned, why her mother was murdered, and she was spared. But now it all makes sense.

Now I knew why her life had been saved, why she has been searching for something untouchable for so long.

She was our rightful ruler. She was made to end the war.

Raya was a Celestial Queen.

33

JOY

LIE, BETRAY AND DECEIT! OH MY!

"I'm glad to be home. Aren't I?"

- FLORENCE'S PERSONAL JOURNAL

My entire body was numb. I stayed still, crouched behind the thorn bush until my legs cramped and sweat began to bead on my forehead.

I had let myself become a fool, again. I had let myself believe her, again. I watched as the two women embraced awkwardly, Florence smiling bitterly at the woman she had called mother.

I've missed you too, Mother.

Her words rang in my mind, like an off-key bell that never let me forget. How many times does she have to betray me before I stop forgiving her?

Hurt buried into my chest. Was everything she told me a lie? All of it false, all of it a deceit? My heart thumped wildly as pain bled into my entire body, I hadn't seen it coming. Despite every betrayal, every lie that she had told me in the short time we had known each other, I had still believed that she was a good person beneath it all.

Red bloomed in my cheeks, embarrassment coating me. We shared a bed; we had awoken tangled around each other. Surely, she had felt something unravel between us, something urging to live, like a candle in the winter wind.

My body swayed in the bitter cold, foolishly I had thought the lack of snow would mean a slighter warmer temperature.

But the Northern Continent was still the Northern Continent, and it was still freezing. The sound of the heavy doors closing and locking, knocked me back into reality.

This was really happening. Florence had really left us.

But why? If she wished to return to her 'Mother', then why bring me with her? How did Jameson play a part in any of this?

My mind whirled uncomfortably.

The tall dry grass brushed against my legs. I turned back to the ocean that always seemed to follow me, staring at the 'borrowed' ship, wondering if I should give up.

Why did I think I could do this? That I was strong enough to do this? Did the crew back in Dayra think us dead? At the beginning of the journey, I had counted the days and nights but with all the chaos that seemed to follow our group, I had lost count, I guessed three months. Maybe four.

I sighed softly, what happened to us? To all of us.

I gasped out loud.

Erin and Jodie. They were scaling the prison's walls. I shot up on shaking legs and began sprinting around the fortress. My arms pumped as my body shot across the barren plane. I needed to tell Erin and Jodie what had happened, that Florence was no longer to be trusted. Sweat pooled at the bottom of my back and my muscles barked in protest but I did not stop. I would not stop until my friends were safe.

My arms ached by my side and my heavy footfalls echoed behind me, as though encouraging me to keep going. The wispy grass tickled my thighs as I leaped and hopped through the thick forest, avoiding puddles of black water and grass that was burned on the tips.

What had happened out here? Blood roared in my ears and my heart slammed against my rib cage.

I halted abruptly at the sight of a heap of rope on the floor. Had they fallen? Or fled?

My head spun.

Had they been captured? I swung my head around, eager to catch a glance of them somewhere. Jodie's long blonde hair or Erin's bright blue eyes. But nothing.

I didn't think I could survive another loss. I collapsed into a heap on the floor, catching my breath as fat tears began streaming down my face. Why is nothing ever easy? I found myself constantly asking why. Why me, why my family? Why do the people I love always seem to leave me? The tears dampened my tunic.

"I knew she loved us!" a familiar voice chirped from behind me. Jodie's head popped out from behind one of the trees surrounding the huge fortress. Air whooshed into my lungs, the feeling of relief almost overwhelming.

I pushed to me feet.

"Are you hurt?" I called, rushing towards the sisters, pulling them both into a huge embrace.

"I thought something terrible had happened!" I whispered into the sisters' hair.

"So did we," Erin spoke softly, her eyes lined with silver. "We saw Florence push you to the ground…" she began.

"How did you see from so far away?"

"Who was that old woman?" Jodie interrupted; my question forgotten.

"Yes," Erin eyed her sister with annoyance. "Who was she? We saw her embrace Florence and then something felt wrong."

I shared the tiny shreds of information I had gleaned from the interaction between Florence and her supposed mother. Erin shook her head, disappointment clear and stark on her lovely face.

"We decided it was probably best to wait for you before carrying on with the plan," Jodie said softly, blinking back the tears in her eyes, I smiled.

The air stilled for a moment, as though letting of us catch our breath.

"What now?" Jodie asked, gazing up at the castle towering above us. The eternal question stuck to our skin like honey.

"I can't leave without Jameson," I spoke softly, almost apologetically.

"You don't have to stay with me, I understand if this is all… getting too much." I winced at the pathetic sound of my own voice.

The sisters shook their heads in unison, resilience tattooed into their minds, just like the 444 tattooed on their bodies.

"Don't you dare," Erin looked at me, straight in my eyes.

"We're in this together." Jodie rested her hand on my shoulder.

"And when we probably die during this mission to save your brother," Erin raises her brows, "at least we'll be ghosts together!"

I laughed at her words.

"And I'll mock you mercilessly for the rest of eternity for dying over…" She fake vomited, "a man," she mockingly spat the words out, making a small burst of laughter fall from my lips.

I thanked any God or Goddess that would listen for throwing me onto Harlow's ship with Erin and Jodie.

They had truly brought me back to life.

I took a deep breath and set my shoulders.

We dried our tears, retied our boots and scraped back our hair.

And then we picked up the rope and tried again.

I watched in awe as Erin used her MindWonderer power to lift the rope up into the air and wrap it around an iron bar sticking out of the wall, about three feet below an open window. I latched onto the rope, ready to plant my feet on the stone wall in front of me.

"If I fall, can you use your magical magic to stop me from smashing against the ground?" I smiled, looking over at Erin.

"Magical Magic?" Erin mocked, raising her eyebrow.

"Yes…?"

"I can try, but no promises," she laughed. "It doesn't really work that way." I tried to ignore the sinking in my heart.

I heaved my body up onto the wall, my feet shoulder width apart and I began to haul my body up. Taking small steps, edging closer to the window. The rope burned against my hands.

"I don't understand why you can't float me up to the ledge, like you did with the rope?" I whined as sweat dripped down my forehead.

"I already told you," Erin shouted from down below, "it doesn't work like that!"

"But I am a living thing!" I protested.

"If I try to manipulate you, it might break up your insides and possibly destroy you," she cringed.

"What is the probability of that happening?" I asked, sweat making my hands slippy. I was distracting myself and we all knew it. I moved as fast as I could, focusing on ending the pain in my hands and muscles.

I could see the iron bar now, not too far.

And then my leg slipped, scraping my knees and my body slammed against the wall. My heart kicked up, galloping like a fearless horse. The rope began slipping through my fingers, my expose skin grazed against the rough brick and my palms burned from the friction. I gritted my teeth until I felt as though they would crack.

Squeezing my hands against the rope, I grappled with my feet until they found the wall.

I finally stopped moving. Blood dripping down my wrists.

I heaved in a breath.

And then another.

I looked up, the iron bar now even further from my grasp. My biceps screamed for me to let.

Give up.

"Joy?" Jameson's voice seemed to whisper in my ear. I almost dropped the rope in shock.

"You must keep going. Don't go soft on me. Don't quit."

If I fell now, I would not survive, there was no escaping it.

A strange calm settled over me. If I gave up now, I wouldn't just be giving up on myself but on my entire crew, my entire family.

I didn't know if I was hallucinating from the pain or if the strange magic that helped to find Jameson before was in play again.

But I planted my feet on the wall. Squared my shoulders and thought of Dayra, of home.

Biting my lip hard enough to draw blood I pulled with all my might.

My hand wrapped around the cool metal of the iron bar only moments later and I pulled myself up, into a balanced sitting position.

“What now?” I shouted down to Erin, hoping my voice wouldn’t carry into the prison.

“You have to jump up, reach for the ledge.”

“Jump!? Are you crazy?” I looked up at the window, it felt so close yet so far. “Why didn’t you tie the rope up there?” I wobbled on the metal bar, my breathing hitching.

“There was nothing to tie it to, this was the best shot!” Fear for my life coated her words. I nodded.

Clutching the wall with shaking arms, I stood up, balancing on the bar.

Don’t look down. Don’t look down. Don’t look down.

I tied the rope around my waist and prayed to every Goddess that I wouldn’t fall.

And then I jumped.

34

RAYA

BIRTHDAYS GONE WILD

"The smell was overpowering. Damp and Dirty."

- KHOL AND RAYA

I stormed out of the palace, my ridiculous dress swirling like smoke beneath me. I had never visited the gardens at night, but I was too angry to appreciate the blooming white roses and glowing pink lilies. I scoffed at the sky-high walls that surrounded the entirety of The Temple, *for safety* Ezra had said.

Now I know she means imprisonment.

I stared at the windows placed along the walls, they looked lonely. I had walked within the walls before; it was like a long corridor that stretched the entirety of The Temple's perimeter. I had stood up there, staring at the miles and miles of tangled trees. I could've jumped, fled, never looked back.

But I didn't, I had instead turned on my heel and hastily ran to my training session with Khol.

Khol.

I paced through the lush garden, flowers brushing against my hands and I shivered as the night air made its way along my exposed spine. Stepping out of my heeled shoes, I wriggled my toes against the soft earth, and I was suddenly grounded. A flower bloomed at my touch and a tree groaned as it grew taller at my request.

"Raya?" Khol called from somewhere behind me. His voice sending a million different shivers through my veins.

I turned toward him, noticing his face was pale and grave. My body tensed immediately. Khol stepped towards me, attempting to grab my wrist. I pulled from his touch and marched further into the gardens. Something happened after I left the ballroom. I could see it on his face.

Stopping next to a pond, I waited for him to catch up.

"I won't do this anymore," I whispered into the silence of the garden, furiously wiping tears from my eyes.

"Won't do what?" His voice was frantic as I stared at the tiny ripples in the pond water below me.

"Raya, please just talk to me," he pleaded. I spun at his request, all my anger and frustration exploding into words.

"It is killing me," I almost shouted, and his face remained blank. "Being near you and feeling the way I feel is killing me." I fisted my hands through my hair, messing the sleek waves given to me only hours before.

"I care for you, I care for you so deeply that I wish I had never met you." Blood rushed to my skin, heating my cooling cheeks. Khol started to reach a hand toward my face but lowered it hastily.

"I've been forced from everything and everyone I know, and your mother is trying to kill me and all I can think about is you. I truly am pathetic." I heaved a deep breath and turned toward the white lilies scattered around the garden, attempting to hide my shame.

Silence engulfed both of us for a few moments, and I wasn't even sure that Khol was breathing. Faint music from The Temple's open doors reminded me that a celebration still raged on inside, but I wasn't part of it. I never was.

"Do you think I do not feel the same? Do you think that I look forward to hours of frivolous attention from everyone in this Goddess forsaken place apart from you?" His words flew from his mouth faster than I thought possible before he spoke again, this time his voice was so quiet I wasn't sure I had heard anything at all.

"I feel like my heart will burn a hole in my chest every time I look at you."

I turned back to face him, and he strode forward, closing the space between us, our faces so close I could smell the wine on his breath.

"Sometimes when I look at you, I cannot breathe." He edged his head closer. I stared at him, wondering how such soft words could come from such a brutal mouth. The corner of his lips turned upwards as though he could hear my thoughts, the movement causing his lips to brush over the corner of mine. I took in a deep breath, my entire body shivering at the small contact.

"Does this scare you? My feelings for you," Khol whispered, his hand trailing up one of my exposed arms. I nodded, aching to feel his lips against mine. He chuckled slowly as I stopped nodding.

I trailed my hand up his torso and rested my palm above his heart. The sound of my name on his lips was ethereal, his breath hot on my cheeks, and his hand began trailing from my shoulder, down my torso, all the way to my thigh. My eyes fluttered shut.

"Khol," a guard shouted from The Temple's doors. My eyes snapped open.

"Not now," he shouted back, not breaking eye contact with me for even a second. "Tell my mother I will be back in a moment." He smiled at me and I gasped, his smile was so rare that it completely changed his face.

But then his smile fell, and he cleared his throat softly.

"Raya," he threaded his fingers through my hair slowly, as though he was categorizing everything about me. I rested my hand on his forearm. "Raya, I'm so sorry." He closed his eyes. "You were right about everything." He looked up at me again.

"About what?" I whispered.

"About my mother, about the trials. Everything you said is true. She… she means to…" he stumbled over his words, not daring to say them out loud. "She means to sacrifice you at first light." He dragged his free hand through his hair. "I'm so sorry," he repeated.

Even though I had suspected Ezra's conspiring against me, it still wasn't easy to have it confirmed. My lungs became tight and my breath shallow. The realization that my life would be cut short caused pain to grow within me. I was trained to deal with this, I had been training to risk my life for years. But actually facing it was completely different.

I didn't want to die, I wasn't ready.

"Raya, it's going to be alright." He placed a hand on either side of my face and stared into my eyes. "I'm going to get you out. Tonight." His quiet confidence was almost calming.

"I choose you, Raya." And for the first time in my whole life, I suddenly and irrevocably knew what it felt like to have a home. I thought I knew the feeling, with Alias and Matron, but this was different. A deep sense of anchoring, a tether that

I knew would never break, never wither. Home wasn't a place; it was a person.

It was Khol.

And then all his words caught up to me.

"Khol." I couldn't let him give up his family for me, not without knowing the truth. No matter his feelings for his mother, he loved many who resided at The Temple.

"There is something you must know before we go any further." Guilt and nervousness coated the inside of my mouth. I hadn't touched the letter in my desk draw for weeks, I couldn't. Every time I opened the draw, I had been met with so much guilt I had almost collapsed from the pain.

"I was sent here, by the Sage Guard." My words trickled out slowly, not wanting to leave the warmth of my mouth. Khol nodded, he knew this part of the story.

"But not because I belonged with the Sorcerers here." My eyes cast away from Khol's, not daring to hold his gaze.

"Raya, what do you—" he interrupted.

"Please, let me finish. I can barely get the words out." The pain in my voice was clear, and Khol nodded solemnly.

"I was sent here to learn about The Temple, to find its weak spots." I dared a glimpse at Khol's slack face. "Once my power had bloomed, the Sage Guard no longer trusted me." My voice trembled. "And I had to do anything I could to get that trust back."

"You betrayed us?" he whispered in disbelief, before quelling his emotions quickly. "You betrayed me for people that didn't want you?" Khol's voice was deadly and quiet.

"They threatened my friend, the boy I had grown up with. They tortured me, cursed everyone I cared about," I pleaded with the man in front of me, reaching out to touch his shoulder.

"I had come here to get infor—"

"*To spy,*" Khol corrected.

"It doesn't matter what you call it, I didn't do anything. There is a letter in the top draw of my desk. I wrote it weeks and weeks ago, it contains all the information I had learned from my time in the Temple, from my time with you." I fisted the lapel of his jacket. "But I didn't send it, I could've, when we went to the human village for this dress." I looked down at the midnight blue wrapping around me.

Trying to portray everything I felt for Khol, I looked him deep in the eyes.

"Please believe me, Khol," I pleaded. "I would never betray you now, never betray Elijah." Small tears slipped down my cheeks and neck.

"But don't you see? You already have," he spoke in a voice I didn't recognize and then realization dawned on his face.

"I spent my time training you, did you even need it?" I winced at his words.

"I have been training to fight for the last nineteen years." Guilt buried a hole in my chest.

"You are a liar," Khol whispered. Disappointment sat so nakedly on his face.

"I'm sorry," I said, because there was nothing else to say. "But Khol," I rested a hand on his cheek and surprisingly he let me. "I choose you too," I whispered, hating the fact that I spent so long fighting my feelings for him, so long lying to him. We gazed at each other, knowing that time still surged on, but pretending it did'nt.

He closed his eyes, heaved a breath, and pulled away from my touch.

"Meet me in the dungeons in one hour, pack light."

"You're coming with me?" I asked, hating how hopeful I sounded. He glared at me.

"I can't stay here," he looked back at his home. "Not now I know what my mother is capable of." My heart broke softly for him.

"Thank you for under—"

"I do not understand. You feel like a stranger to me now," he whispered, and his words hit like rocks. I swallowed back the tears, knowing now wasn't the time to try and change his mind.

"How are we going to escape in the middle of the ball?" I whispered, afraid to talk too loudly. Khol no longer trusted me, he no longer wanted me.

"It's the perfect distraction, no one will notice we're gone until morning, we have all night to get as far away as possible." His voice was gruff and distant, like the brute I had met on my first night here.

"Khol, I don't think you understand…" I stepped out of this reach. "If you leave with me."

"I can't come back," Khol finished for me. He turned from me slowly, kicking the grass under our feet hard. I flinched.

"Something is not right with my mother, with this place, and I think I've known it for a while now. I can't stay here and wait for things to get worse, I need to do something." He turned back to me, nodding softly.

"Khol—"

"I need time, Raya, I know you didn't send the letter, but you still wrote it. You betrayed me. I need time." He heaved a sigh.

"Okay," I spoke, nervousness wet against the back of my throat.

"I still haven't figured you out," he whispered, more to himself than to me.

"Take your time," I whispered back, trying to convey all

my feelings of remorse, guilt, sadness, happiness, and something new that I couldn't quite put my finger on with only a few words. "I'm not going anywhere."

35

JOY

YOU JUMP, I JUMP, JACK

"This is the worst plan I've ever heard."

- ERIN TO JOY

My body slammed against a stone floor as I pushed myself through the opening at the top of the wall, gulping down mouthfuls of air, one after another. The relief that covered my body was hot and sweaty, I had made it. Looking down at my bloodied hands, nausea swept through me. The climb was possibly the easy part of our rescue mission, and it had almost killed me.

Looking ahead it became clear that I was in some sort of watch tower that wrapped around the prison, light music filtered in from the cracks between the stone. A party in a prison? Festive.

Finally catching my breath, I stood, leaning over the edge of the 'window', beckoning Erin and Jodie to follow me up the tower.

The scuff of stone against shoe echoed throughout the

tunnel as I ventured deeper into it. Where was everyone? Surely the prison needed at least one person as a lookout. Chairs dotted around the tunnel suggested that soldiers usual sat, playing cards or drinking ale, but today, it was barren, empty, deserted.

Jodie yelped as she slipped, almost losing her footing on the wall. I sprinted back to the window, leaning out with my hand stretched toward her. She reached the bar, her chest heaving and her hands shaking.

"The hard part is done," I reassured her. "Just grab my hand."

I anchored myself by gripping the wall tightly, leaning further toward her.

"Jump," I said sternly, she shook her head. "Jodie. Jump. Now." She looked up at me, fear seeping into her pores. "I've got you, I promise." My voice was unwavering and strong. She nodded. Keeping one hand clasped on the wall and another reaching up toward me.

Our fingers brushed. So close.

"Jump, grab my hand, I'll pull you up and you need to grab the wall." I wasted no time being polite. This was life or death, and no one was dying today. She took a deep breath, stealing a look down at her sister and jumped.

Our fingers brushed. I reached, locking our fingers together, her weight pulled at me, and my hand threaten to let go of the anchoring wall.

I gritted my teeth. Feeling the blood pour from my already broken skin.

"Joy," Jodie gasped, her hands slipping on the blood.

I pulled with all my might, her hand flying up to grip the wall next to me.

And finally, she was over, safe. I didn't realize I was

crying until my cheeks became wet. Jodie wrapped her arms around me, her body trembling and her breath shallow.

"One more time, just one more," I whispered into her hair, and we turned toward her sister, our arms outstretched.

We all laid in a heap on the floor as we pulled Erin into the hollowed wall. Blood, sweat, and tears coating all of us.

"We look *delightful*," Jodie looked at all of us. "We're going to need new clothes when we finally leave this place, Joy smeared her blood over us both." She laughed. Smiling at her, I noticed the music again soft and rather beautiful.

"Do you guys hear that?" I asked them, the sisters nodded.

"A party?" Erin asked.

I shrugged, walking to the window on the other side of the watch tower. A luscious garden sprawled out down below, large windows saw couples dancing, drinking, and laughing, all of them in fine clothing.

"Do you think Florence tricked us? Took us to the wrong place?" Jodie asked softly. I shrugged again.

"I still don't understand why she needed our help in getting here if she was just going to betray us? Surely, she could sail here alone, back to her… family?" Erin began pacing the stone floor.

"Jameson's here, I know it." I attempted to calm them both.

"I saw him, remember?"

"But what if it was just another trick?" Jodie's voice became high and rushed. "We know she is a Sorcerer, maybe she isn't a SkyChanger, but a MindWonderer? What if she got inside your head?" Tears began trickling down Jodie's pale skin.

"How could she have done this to us? After everything

we've been through?" The tears began dropping faster and faster.

"He's here." I wrapped an arm around her shoulders. "I know it and once we have him, you and Erin are coming home with us, to our family." Erin's eyes became glassy, and she nodded softly.

I headed down the hallway, careful that our footfalls did not echo through the empty tunnel. It seemed to go on for miles, until it we arrived at a fork in our path. We took the right, following the music. The music got louder and louder as we neared a wooden door, cobwebs and dust flew about as we heaved the heavy wood aside. Ornate, gilded decorations sat on every table and hung from every ceiling as we entered the empty sitting room, irritatingly there was no signpost that directed us to the prisoners. Why can't anything be easy?

Brushing the dust from our linen trousers, we walked further into the room.

"Do we split up?" Erin asked.

"Are you crazy?" Jodie whispered through gritted teeth.

"Jodie's right, we stay together," I said. We rounded corner after corner, following the music until a huge tapestry came into view.

A young women stood, light in her hands, her hair floating around her as though she was underwater.

I knew this girl. I had dreamt about her.

"It's half of the prophesy," Jodie whispered, "she's the one with the power, most people say she's the most important, but the one without the power was always my favorite, because she is ordinary." I smiled at her.

"She's beautiful, isn't she?" a male voice sounded from behind us, breaking our focus on the tapestry.

We all knew this voice; we all dreaded this voice.

Spinning on my heel, I faced him, squaring my shoulders.

“No Florence?” Captain Harlow drawled, he dragged his finger along a desk, smearing the dust between his fingers. “I told you she was slippery.” He smiled; his eyes transfixed on me.

“What are you doing here, Harlow?” I ask, stepping in front of Jodie and Erin.

“Isn’t it obvious? I followed you here, you took some things that belonged to me,” he eyed Erin and Jodie. “And I want them back.” His tone sounded bored.

“I can’t let you tak—” the air squeezed from my throat, I gasped for oxygen, but it was like everything had disappeared. I sunk to my knees, my hands turning white as they clawed at the carpet.

“Harlow, please!” Jodie cried, kneeling beside me.

Black spots began clouding my vision and I was suddenly so tired.

I coughed, pain lancing through my entire body. My head felt as though it was going to explode and I closed my eyes.

And suddenly the air dragged itself into my lungs. Coughing and spluttering, I began breathing, tears streaming down my cheeks.

The pain, now softer but just as biting, needled across my skin. Erin lifted Harlow off the ground with her mind and fire found its home in Jodie’s hands, her long hair swishing and her once blue eyes now a deep, burning orange.

A fireball struck Harlow’s arm, and the smell of burning flesh filled the room.

“We,” Jodie spat, throwing another ball of fire, “do not belong to anyone!” Erin threw Harlow’s struggling body against the wall, blood spirting from his forehead.

His hand flew up, throwing Erin against the wall and keeping her there. She coughed violently as water began to spill from her mouth.

He was drowning her from the inside out.

"Erin!" Jodie's shouted, her scream feral and raw.

I finally stood, swiping a solid gold letter opener from the desk next to me.

"Harlow!" I bellowed, running at him as he turned toward me. Erin's form dropped, the water disappearing from her lungs.

I plunged the letter opener into his thigh, I had no plans to become the killer he called me.

I twisted the blade, pushing it further into his leg as he clawed at me.

"Leave my family alone," I spat, pushing the blade one last time before knocking him out with a smack to the temple.

"We need to go," I whispered out of breath. "He won't have travelled alone, someone will come looking soon."

The girls nodded and we raced out of the room, travelling deeper into the fortress.

36

RAYA

KEYS & ALLIES

"Can we trust them? Should we trust them?"

- RAYA TO KHOL

The air in the dungeon was stale and cold, a metallic taste coated my mouth and shivers danced up my spine. The smell of ash clung to my hair, I had blazed the incriminating letter about The Temple in my hand with my FireBringer magic.

"Khol?" I whispered. The words bounced off the walls. I walked deeper into the room, and prisoners stared at me from behind bars.

"Khol?" Had he changed his mind? Decided my traitorous self was not worth helping.

Voices travelled down from the opposite entrance, and I slipped into the nearest open cell.

"How are we going to get him out of the cell? Do you have a key?" a young female voice floated through the room.

"No, I'm just hoping the lock is old," another voice sounded.

"That's the plan? Hope the lock is old?" a third voice chimed in. The door creaked open, and three girls crept in, weapons up.

"Jameson?" The tallest girl whispered, her curved body and black braided hair swishing as she moved.

"Are you sure this is where you saw him?" The shortest girl spoke, her pale skin peppered with goosebumps as she hugged her chest.

"Raya?" Khol's voice sounded from further down the tunnel. I closed my eyes and sighed softly. I couldn't call back to him, but I couldn't let him believe that I hadn't showed up. After everything we had been through, I couldn't allow myself to be caught now, not when I was so close to being free.

My heartbeat became rapid as he called my name again.

"Should we hide?" The middle girl with short blonde hair whispered.

Khol's voice was closer this time.

The women fled into the only empty cell as Khol's voice began filling the room.

The empty cell that I was currently occupying.

I cringed as the leader tripped over my barely covered form.

"What the hell?" A dirty tarp was pulled off me as Khol walked into the dungeon. I stared up at the three girls, women, all of them looking tired, scared, and worn. They reminded me of myself.

"Who are you?" the tallest girl asked me, her eyebrows raised.

I opened my mouth to speak but the words refused to surface.

"Who are you?" Khol asked back, finally walking into the cell.

"Where is Jameson?" The girl ignored Khol's question and looked back at me. "Get up." She held out her hand for me to grab.

I stood at my full height. A small smile tugged at the corner of the strange woman's mouth as I rose to her eye level.

"Are you members of The Temple?" I asked, risking a glance toward Khol.

"The Temple? What is The Temple?" the woman asked.

I looked at Khol again, both of us scrunching our eyebrows. Questions turned over and over in my mind as we left the cell, all of us standing in the middle of the dungeon, staring at each other.

Now I saw them in better light, it seemed as though the two blonde girls were related or from the same village. Their hair and eyes almost identical.

"Where is Jameson?" The leader spoke again, her dark brown skin wrinkling as she frowned.

"We don't know," I spoke.

"How did you get in here? What do you want from us?" Khol asked, placing a hand on my lower back. I felt the fear that coated his entire body, and realization racked through me. I hadn't felt anyone's emotions but Khol's and I hadn't felt his since our argument on the field. When the lightening had struck, and the rain had soaked the earth.

Even when he hated me, he protected me. He feared for my life.

"We're here for Jameson and once we have him, we'll leave," the shortest girl spoke again. Her hand firmly locked with the other fair-haired girl.

"Raya, we need to go," Khol looked down at me. "Elijah,

he's waiting for us." Sadness crept into my mind, I hadn't even thought of Elijah, my dear friend.

"Elijah," I whispered, just as the tallest girl said, "Raya?"

I turned to her. Now it was my turn to drown in fear.

"I've heard your name before, I've…" Her voice trailed off.

"Someone is looking for you," she spoke again. "I saw him a moon cycle ago. Alias." She turned the name over in her mouth. "I think he said his name was Alias." Sweat began pooling in my palms. "Do you know him?" she asked.

My heart smashed around my rib cage, turning ragged and wild.

"Alias," I whispered, relief sliding into my heart. Alias was not a prisoner. He was free.

"Alias?" My voice shook. "He's alive?" I almost laughed.

"Well, he was alive when I saw him last. That or he was a ghost," she shrugged.

"Who are you?" I asked, and finally, they told us their story.

Her name was Joy, she and her companions, Erin, and Jodie, had travelled for weeks in search of Joy's brother Jameson.

"And how do you know this 'Jameson' is here?" Khol asked after we heard their story.

"I saw him," Joy spoke, looking at her feet. "In a cell with a man named Rafael?" Khol's head shot up.

"Rafael?" he whispered before raking his hands through his hair, his breath came out in slow, shallow breaths. "Did you see what he looked like? Did he have dark skin like ours?" he asked Joy, he stepped closer to her, pleading clear in his eyes.

She hadn't seen his face, and Jameson hadn't told her

about him either. We didn't bother asking how Joy had 'seen' into the cell without entering the building.

Enough crazy shit had already happened.

We began searching each cell. I knew what plagued Khol's mind. Rafael. Was it Khol's brother? Or just another man with the same name? Dripping water echoed throughout the dungeon, each room we ventured into bigger and wider than the last. Rust and mold made its home on all of the bars and stone walls.

"Jameson?" I whispered into each cell. "Rafael?" Murmurs and grunts were thrown in my direction. Many of the prisoners were laid, sleeping. Some of them still enough to be dead.

Some assumably newer prisoners stood at the front of their cells, arms stretched over the decaying bars.

"Hey beautiful," a toothless man lisped in my direction. I hurried past, almost slipping on something that smelt suspiciously like human waste.

"I found them!" Jodie whisper-shouted from an adjoining room and I ran toward her voice, thanking every Goddess in existence for the chance to leave this Godforsaken place.

37

JOY

TRUST?

"Nothing mattered more than getting home to our family."

- JOY'S JOURNAL ENTRY

I ran from my line of cells, sprinting to the source of Jodie's voice. And then I saw him, skinner than before and dirtier than ever, but wholly Jameson.

"Joy," Jameson whispered from where he stood at the door of his cell. Disbelief and astonishment painted on his soot ridden face. Tears sprung in my eyes without warning, streaming down my face as I ran toward him, attempting to wrap my arms around him and the bars. A half-hearted chuckle racked him as he attempted to hug me back.

"Are you alright?" I whispered, tears clogging my voice. I catalogued his face, noticing how his protruding collarbone peaked out of the top of his tunic. The same tunic he wore the day he was taken, all those weeks ago.

"Much better now," he smiled, smudging the dirt around his forehead with the back of his hand.

"Stop being so loud, Jameson!" a male voice whispered, his figure staggering up from where he was once laid, sleeping.

"It's the middle of the night!" His voice was scratchy but clear, almost regal. Jameson's eyes hooded slightly at the sight of him.

"You must be Rafael." I smiled as the man joined Jameson at the bars, confusion painted on his face. Scenes played out behind his eyes, hope and fear mixed like a cocktail of confinement.

"Jameson, what's happening?" Rafael turned to Jameson, ignoring my words, and placing his hand on the bars.

"We're getting out," Jameson's tears continued to fall. "We're going home."

I stared at Rafael, smiling brightly at him, then he let out a huge breath.

And scoffed.

Turning back to his makeshift bed, he sat with a huff and took out a bent paperback novel from his pocket, once that must have been read a hundred times.

My eyebrows crumpled as Raya and Khol finally made their way into the room. The latter severely out of breath.

"Is he alive?" Khol panted.

"I hope so," I said, throwing a thumb in Jameson's direction. Khol rolled his eyes, getting closer to the bars in effort to see into the darkness. He dragged a hand through his hair.

"Not him, I need to… if he's alive…" Khol's breathing became more and more shallow.

"Calm down," I stated. "Give me a moment to pick… or break the lock."

Khol wrapped his hand around the decaying bar, not taking his eyes from mine.

The bars turned to dust in front of our very eyes. Jameson fell into my arms, his quiet sobs echoing in the huge dungeon.

"You're a MindWonderer," Erin spoke as Khol stepped over the threshold into the cell.

"Rafael?" Khol whispered, as though he was afraid of his own voice. I understood his fear, the fear of the unknown.

'Hope is dangerous' my mother used to say. I had said it once, to Florence, on a day when the ocean was still and the sky clear.

She asked me about my parents.

"I was nine when the sea swallowed my parents and I," I told her, my back straight, "I can still feel the scrape of salt against the inside of my throat," I whispered.

And the sounds of my parents dying screams.

"They were so young." I smiled at nothing in particular.

"We were swimming," I scoffed at the story, how pathetic it sounded in my feeble voice.

"The ocean turned on us, the waves rose, and the rain poured." I looked up at her. "I couldn't do anything to stop it, we drifted apart, they screamed for me and I for them." Wetness blurred my vision. "I must've passed out because when I woke up, I was laid on driftwood, washed up on the beach," I said in a matter-of-fact voice, aggressively wiping a tear drop from my cheek.

Florence stared at me, lifting her hand, only to drop it again. A familiar ache bloomed in my chest. Waves of physical pain slammed against me as I recalled my parents' death. I lived every day with the guilt of my parent's demise staining my hands. They drowned trying to save my life.

"Happiness does not thrive in the cruel water, it suffocates and withers," I said, meeting Florence's eyes.

"And yet you spend more time in the ocean than anyone

I've ever met," she argued, not the first to question my time in the ocean.

I still heard their whispers.

"Because I am not afraid," I stated and we both remained quiet.

"I command myself not to be afraid," I whispered to myself.

And there was nothing more to say. My parents were gone, and they had been, for a long, long while.

I blinked back the tears as Rafael stood from his makeshift bed.

"Khol?" His voice was hesitant.

Khol stood dead still at the threshold, where the bars used to reside. He took a deep breath, tears already wetting his deep, brown skin. Rafael took a step forward and then another and another, arms outstretched.

It happened in slow motion, the two striding toward each other, arms reaching. Their embrace was fierce and strong and everything in-between. A pang of sorrow resided within me; I missed my crew more than words could say. I missed my family.

"Brother," Rafael whispered. And the words hit me like a battalion ship heading into war. I hugged Jameson closer.

What was Khol's brother doing in the dungeon? Who were these people? Staring at the fine clothes on Khol and Raya's back, I had assumed they were part of the party that raged on above us.

"What are you doing down here? I thought you dead!" Khol's voice cracked as he embraced his brother again.

"I think it is time for some answers," I murmured in Khol's direction, the brothers still embracing.

"I think it's time we leave," Raya interjected. "Answers

later." She looked up, the faint sound of footsteps carried down through the room.

We moved as a group, weaving through room after room until we found ourselves in the place in which we started.

"This way," I called over to them. "This is the way we came in, over the wall." Khol shook his head.

"It's too risky." Khol's gaze met mine before landing on Raya's, he lingered for a moment before shaking his head and looking away, something akin to hurt in his eyes.

"Elijah is waiting, he has a way out for us." A smile of relief spread across Raya's face.

I paused; distrust now so common within me it was like an extra limb.

"We don't need to leave together," Raya spoke, reading my body language. "If you do not wish the travel with us, we will not stop you from leaving on your own."

Silence engulfed the dungeon, dripping water, and scrambling rodents the only sounds. I rested my hand on Jameson's shoulder. His gaze trained on Rafael.

"Then we must go," I spoke. The sisters and I turning toward the door.

"Thank you," Khol spoke, breaking the silence. "For bringing my brother home."

I nodded.

"Thank you for helping me find mine," my words were barely a whisper.

Khol turned to a set of stairs in the corner of the damp dungeon, Raya following close behind. An unfamiliar ache pounded into my chest as Raya turned away from us, almost like a string pulling taut between us. I took a small step forward and at the same time she stopped walking. Turned on her heel and looked right at me.

And then her hand caught ablaze.

"Raya," Khol said through gritted teeth. She remained still, staring only at me. Without thinking, I walked towards her and grasped her inflamed hand. But the flame did not burn me.

Smoke whirled around us, our hair floating above us although we were one with the water. My heart slowed, beating softly like footsteps in sand. Thoughts poured into my head, but they did not belong to me.

I can feel your emotions, Raya whispered into my mind. *What are you?*

A bright sky bloomed overhead, the blue giving birth to electric oranges and reds. I knew this sky; I had seen this sky before.

Images blurred past me. Memories that had once been locked away, the key swallowed.

Manacles on thin wrists, skin rubbed raw. Two girls, tears dripping like melted candle wax. Death coating the very walls around us. Then pain, not physical, something stronger. A pain that felt as though my heart would explode. As though I was being ripped away and a new person was forming in my absence.

And then darkness, a lantern lighting the way. A decision made.

"Raya…"

Light blinded me as we found ourselves in the dungeon again. Khol placing his hand on Raya's shoulder, extinguishing the fire.

With our hands still clasped, we stared at one and another. Our breaths sounding at the same time.

"We must go, Raya," Khol's voice was filled with hurt. "Elijah will think something has happened to us."

"I'd say something has happened…" Jodie whispered

under her breath. "Or are we going to pretend that Joy didn't just offer her hand up to be barbecued."

Raya stared at me; our hands still joined.

"What was that?" she whispered.

"I have no idea," I whispered back.

In that very moment the words from the old crone in the marketplace came running back to me.

If you find what you seek, and seek what you find, the lines will blur, and your paths will become entwined.

Did she speak of Raya and I? Did she know that when I found Jameson, I would find Raya too?

"We can't stay here," Raya spoke, breaking my trance and turning to Khol and Rafael.

But Rafael stood still, as though his feet were stuck to the floor.

"Raf, we need to go," Khol spoke in a gruff voice.

"I won't leave without Jameson." His voice was stern and unmoving, his gaze not breaking from Jameson's. Khol glanced from Jameson to Rafael, dragging a hand through his hair, again.

"Come with us, please," Khol begged. "There is a river that runs under The Temple, it will bring us out at the next town. We have boats," Khol pleaded in my direction.

"The river?" Rafael asked, at the same time Erin asked,

"What the hell is The Temple?" from behind me.

All the unanswered questions bubbled up inside me as the footsteps above us became louder and hurried. We were running out of time, and I couldn't leave without Jameson or without answers. We had been in the dungeon for all of ten minutes but all of our lives had changed in that short time.

I looked at Khol, my lips a flat line.

"Okay," I glanced from him to Raya and then to Jameson. "Let's go."

38

RAYA

BLAZE OR GLORY?

"Promise me you'll take care of each other. I love you both."

- ELIJAH

Fallen leaves, blown in from Goddess knows where, crunched under our feet. All of us ducked low to fit beneath the low walls of the tunnel. Khol, Joy and I practically bent in half. Barely able to see our hands in front of our faces, we stumbled and tripped, our eyes never really getting used to the immense darkness.

I reached for Khol's hand instinctively, wrapping our fingers together.

He pulled his hand away quickly, as though my skin had charred his. Wretchedness crawled under my skin like insects, how had I been so foolish? Why hadn't I confessed to the truth months ago, when my heart stirred and twisted for the first time?

Forgiveness seemed too far away for me to grasp.

"How much further?" Jodie whispered from behind us.

"We're almost there," Khol whispered back, tripping over a rock.

A laugh poorly hidden by a cough sounded from Joy's throat, I marveled at how similar we were.

"You're not afraid of the dark, are you, Jodes?" Joy whispered. Everyone's voices sounded far away and extremely close at the same time.

"No…" she whispered timidly, causing a few laughs from people around me. But I couldn't even bring myself to smile. Each step Khol took reminded me that I had betrayed him.

"You guys are awful," Jodie pouted, which only made the others chuckle more.

"I like the dark," I claimed, desperate to rid myself of my own thoughts. "It was good for stealing food from Matron's kitchen."

"Good for picking pockets," Jameson agreed.

"Good for hiding from murderous mothers," Khol dropped in casually.

"Good for plotting to murder *your* mother," I mumbled.

"You guys are *really* awful," Jodie spoke again, her voice littered with humor.

Light spilled into the abandoned tunnel, the sound of moving water now slipping into our ears. Elijah stood in what looked like a hollowed-out cave. He was hidden beneath a brown cloak, a hood draped over his head, next to a row of canal boats, most of them crumbling through rot and decay.

"Elijah!" I whisper-shouted.

As all seven of us spilled from the opening, Elijah's hood dropped, and surprise plastered against his wrinkled skin.

"Khol, what is—" he began, before his eyes found Rafael, standing sheepishly in the corner.

"Rafael?" The word caught in his throat, tears already

threatening to spill from his silver eyes. “Is that really you?” He stepped forward uneasily, although he was afraid to move.

“It’s me, Elijah,” Rafael said. “Not a ghost, I promise.”

A laughed bubbled wetly in Elijah’s throat.

“Rafael my boy, I thought… I thought you…”

“You thought I died,” Rafael smiled sadly. “It’s okay, Elijah. That’s what my mother wanted.” He wrapped his arms around the old man. “She did not have the guts to kill me, so she locked me away,” he glanced up at Khol, “and threw away the key.”

A somber chill settled over the room, all of us unsure how to proceed. Elijah rested a hand against Raf’s cheek.

“You must go, get away from here before your mother finds out you’re gone.” Elijah spoke in a hurried whisper, handing a cloak to Khol and I.

“Your clothes are too recognizable, you’ll either be robbed or discovered, these are better.” He smiled as we pulled the fabric over our bodies. The blue dress now covered, a mark that our night was truly over.

“I’m sorry I did not bring any clothes for… for your… friends?” Elijah spoke, motioning to Joy, Jameson, Erin, and Jodie.

“You have done more than enough, Elijah,” I spoke, kissing him on the cheek. He smiled, silver lining his eyes.

“Quick, quick,” he ushered us with his hands, I knew it was because he did not wish to cry again.

“I have packed you enough food to last a month…” He looked over at our expanded group. “Perhaps a week.”

He heaved at a rope, pulling the biggest canal boat I have ever seen toward the concrete edge we stood at. A large tunnel sat at the front and the back of the room, I didn’t know where we were going, but anywhere had to be better than here.

One by one we stumbled into the boat. Jameson with his hand outstretched for Rafael, Erin patting the bench next to her for Jodie and Joy, Khol's hand shaking gingerly on my waist as I stepped onto the vessel.

Forgive me, I wanted to shout. *Forgive me, please.*

He removed his hands as soon as my feet touched the wood, sitting as far away from me as possible.

Elijah stood watching us as we began to drift.

"Thank you, Elijah, for everything," Khol said gruffly.

"Promise me you'll take care of one another. I love you." Elijah's voice cracked softly.

"Thank you, Elijah, you saved my life." I smiled. "In more ways than you know. I love you." Tears filled with love wetted my cheeks.

The tunnel drifted closer as Khol steered the boat toward the entrance of it. The journey ahead hung high in the air. Elijah smiled once more before pushing the rusty boats on the canal back into place.

"What of Florence?" Jodie said as Elijah turned toward the tunnel to the dungeons.

"I have no idea," Joy replied flatly.

"Florence?" Khol and Rafael said at the same time. Joy nodded.

"What is she? Your long-lost wife?" Jodie joked, her head falling into her hands.

"Not quite," Raf laughed.

"But she could possibly be our sister," Khol spoke nonchalantly. "Mother's favorite, she's been gone for years in—"

"In the Southern Continent?" Joy asked, rolling her eyes. "I can't believe she created this elaborate plan just to hitch a ride home," she scoffed.

"I suppose Captain Harlow was in on it too," Erin mumbled.

"It doesn't make sense, we knew Florence, we lived with her. She was part of Harlow's crew for months before she escaped. Why would Harlow search for her if he was in on her plan?" Jodie's head swayed in her hands.

"My head feels like it's about to explode," Jameson groaned.

The tunnel enveloped us, all our figures blurred slightly in the darkness.

"One day she was in training with us," Khol spoke softly, "and the next she wasn't, mother said she had completed her training and taken the trials in secret."

"She just left?' I asked him. He nodded softly, shrugging.

"We need to regroup," Joy said. "We can't keep going off half stories and blurred truths." She looked around each of us.

"We need to know how each of us got to this very moment," she spoke again. "I'll begin… It was Kai'd, the day we celebrate the Goddess of the sea…"

One by one we shared our stories, I told them about my burst of power, Alias, and The Temple.

Khol spoke of his mother, of what he had overheard from her study.

Erin and Jodie shared their time with Captain Harlow and their journey with Joy.

Jameson and Rafael explained their time in the prison.

"She put me in the dungeon because she feared me. She feared my power, what I could do." He looked over at Khol.

"She wanted to be the most powerful person in The Temple, in the entire world," he heaved a sigh. "No one *fails* the test, Khol," he whispered.

"She takes the most powerful of us all and drains us of our abilities, she takes it for herself," he choked on his words.

"She took mine." A small sob found its home in his throat. "I have almost nothing left." We watched as a tiny fire spluttered in Raf's hands, barely big enough to light his face.

Jameson wrapped his arm around Raf's shoulder as he began to cry.

Although we knew each other better now, we still had so many unanswered questions.

Was the war in Zetka related to Ezra's hunger for power? Did the other Sorcerers know about this?

Surely the humans knew about this.

Why did Florence lie about her intentions and why had she been gone for so long?

How had Ezra been stealing power from others?

My eyes began to spin behind their lids.

Another question pressed into my mind. One that asked,

What had happened between Joy and me? When our hands touched and our minds became one?

The moment had seemed to last a small eternity.

Time was afraid to tick by when we were joined.

PART 3

The Flame

We were one.
We had strength behind us.
We fought for answers out of our reach.
We set the fire.

39

FLORENCE

TRUTH TIME

"We have trained you for too long, you should be stronger than this."

- EZRA TO FLORENCE

The Temple had not changed in the years I had been gone. The same dusty floors, the same heavily robed elders, the same ominous tapestry reminding me that I would never, ever fulfil the Prophesy. I shook out my hands.

A SkyChanger.

The weakest of all my siblings.

At least Khol had the power to manipulate minds and Raf, Goddess bless his soul, had the greatest fire power I had seen when he was alive. Even Ottie could heal faster than everyone I had ever seen. I stood at the threshold of what used to be my brother's bedroom, I missed Rafael dearly.

The curtains surrounding his bed were still placed in mourning, gathered with dust and un-had dreams. The silk of my deep purple dress hissed against the floor; I had forgotten that tonight was my mother's ball. We had thrown this ball so many times I had almost forgotten what we were celebrating. Almost.

It was Khol's birthday.

Standing in my late brother's bedroom, I remembered that Rafael had always loved birthdays, being the eldest of the four of us, he always begged mother to throw a ball.

He was the parent we never had.

When the trial had deemed his life no longer his own, I had begged my mother to spare him, to save him, to do anything she could to keep him alive.

"It is out of my hands, Florence!" She scolded me years ago, pushing me away from her.

"Do not make this any harder than it already is," my father whispered in my ears, his words always softer than my mother's.

Tears dripped from my chin on to my upraised palms as I prayed to The Goddess.

"Stop that, Florence." My mother batted my hands down. "The Goddess does not have the time to answer a petulant girl's wishes, your brother failed the trial. His is a threat to The Temple." She pushed papers from her deep cherry desk onto the floor, stood and began pacing.

"Send him away then," I cried. "Lock him in the dungeon! Just do not kill him!" She stopped pacing as sobs shook my body, and my father began dragging me from the room. I watched my mother's head tilt and her brows furrow, and then the doors slammed in my face. I didn't see my brother again.

Never saw his smile again.

Shoes smacking against the floor behind me brought me back to the present, I'd know my mother's gait anywhere.

"Standing in his room will not bring him back, Florence," my mother said, not look up from where she to knelt to fix her shoe. I nodded anyway.

"Find your brother for me, will you?" She looked up and met my eyes, I winced.

"Which one?" I countered childishly; I couldn't help it.

She ignored me.

"He's probably cavorting somewhere with the half human," she examined her perfect reflection in the mirror. "She truly is a tiresome girl," she scoffed.

"Half human?" I asked, slipping from Raf's room and into the hallway where slow music sounded from the party below.

"I am afraid so," she shrugged, turning to look at herself in a cracked mirror. "The humans left her on our land, half dead, almost five moon cycles ago. She had performed a Graceling without even knowing."

"A Graceling?" I whispered. I had never been able to complete one, not even when my mother starved me for days as punishment.

My mother hummed her agreement.

"But once she arrived here, I… I realized she wasn't what we thought she was, she was something else entirely." Her primping paused momentarily. She recentered herself. "But your brother is taken with her, infatuated with her I suppose." She shrugged again, as though her words didn't mean a thing.

"Speaking of, there is a man downstairs I want you to meet, fetch Khol and come meet him, it is time you married, Florence." She checked her appearance once more before turning to leave, as though she was simply asking me to pass her the morning paper. I had been expecting an engagement once I returned, but the words were so blunt, so emotionless. Pain unfurled in my gut.

"Aren't you curious to why I returned?" I asked sheepishly. She turned, her steel eyes meeting mine.

"You completed your mission did you not? I've read your report on Captain Harlow's crew, it's very impressive. I'm glad you brought them to me. We knew only you could *charm* the captain" she said the word 'charm' as though it was an insult, and disgust bloomed in my stomach as my mother spoke.

"And now we have the information on Harlow and his crew, we can start negotiations with him. Would be a shame for him to side with the humans." She rearranged her skirts, moving to leave.

"I do not wish to marry, Mother," I said, changing the subject abruptly. She paused before stalking toward me, smoothing my hair with the palm of her hand.

"I know it is scary, but Bennett is a nice man, a FireBringer. I believe you could grow to like him." She smiled, spinning, and beginning her walk down back toward the party.

"No, I could not. I do not wish to marry any man," I whispered. She stopped walking, standing still. She did not turn. She did not move.

And as though I hadn't said a thing, she began walking again. My words lost in the wind.

Heat flowed through my blood. I did not go looking for Khol and his half human, I stalked down the corridor after my mother, my steps hurried.

"I met someone," I stated, my words louder than I imagined. Ezra turned to face me finally.

"Someone I thought would lead me to Harlow again. I had no boat you see, no way of sailing across the ocean." I walked a circle around my mother. "So I sent for the humans, the hunters that trusted our family, thinking us humans too. I told them of a Sorcerer in Dayra, and they were more than happy to come a collect. I have to say mother, it is very impressive the way you made the hunters believe The Temple was a prison for Sorcerers, instead of a home." My voice was sickly sweet and mocking.

"But," I returned to my story. "I had seen a woman on her ship the day before Kai'd, I followed her to a tavern and pointed out a member of her crew to the hunters. My name was Dahlia then." My mother tapped her foot against the floor, she never was a patient woman.

"I'll skip to the end; she needed help finding her friend and I conveniently knew where he was being held. I knew it was only a matter of time until we found Harlow. He was more than happy to see me again." I heaved a deep breath.

"But something happened on our journey, we had two of Harlow's girls join our crew and I… I grew to love them." I looked up at my mother, her snake tattoo stark again the white of her dress.

"But with Joy it was different," I refused to break eye contact with her, "I feel although I fused with her, like a part of my soul now lives within her and hers in mine. And now she believes I have betrayed her, again, and I suppose she is right." I shrugged.

"But I cannot marry another, you see." My mother's eyes narrowed. "For I think I am in love with Joy."

I felt the sting before her hand made contact with my cheek.

"I raised you better than this, do you think I care whether you marry a man or a woman? I do not." Anger radiated from her body. Heat making her hands glow a burnt orange, she never really had full control over her FireBringer power.

"But for you to have feelings for a *human* is disgraceful. We have trained you for too long, you should be stronger than this." Her face was inches from mine. "I have never been more disappointed in my life."

40

RAYA

SINK OR SWIM

"Are we going to talk about that?"

- JODIE TO HER SISTER, ERIN

"If I'd known how annoying he was, I don't think I would've rushed to help save him," Khol huffed as Jameson began the song again from the start.

"There once was a girl who always looked her best. The village thought her beautiful, especially her br—"

"Enough!" Erin stated. "I can't listen to this again," she cried.

My eyes had adjusted to the dark well enough to see the wide grin on Jodie's face. We had been floating in the unyielding darkness for a lifetime, tension keeping almost everyone quiet. Almost.

"I'm trying to lift the mood, Erin," Jameson stated, elongating the sounds in Erin's name. "I'm the one who's been locked up for the last one hundred years," he mumbled under his breath.

"I think a hundred years is possibly a bit of a stretch," Rafael spoke from beside Khol, who had not looked at me once during our journey. I could feel the anger radiating from him.

The seven of us sat in silence for a moment, still unsure whether to trust the people we had embarked on this journey with.

"How much longer?" Joy asked, wrapping her arm around Jameson. Khol lifted a hand and plunged it in the water.

"The river is warming; we should find the light soon," he stated quietly.

"Are you going to talk to me?" I whispered for only the two of us to hear.

"Raya, please," he said gruffly. Raising my eyebrows, I turned to him, my body language a warning for others to stay clear.

"I did not send the letter, Khol," I stated in a hushed whisper.

"Are we really going to do this now?" he countered, staring at the other people on the boat, all of them pretending not to be listening.

"I believe this is the only time we will have," I sighed. "Who knows what awaits us at the other end of the tunnel?" I paused.

I thought back to a sweet training session we had a few weeks prior. Khol was instructing me on throwing knifes and I was pretending not to know anything about it, pretending I hadn't learned to throw knifes before I'd learned to count to ten.

One slipped from his grasp as he looked upon me, a slash cut deep into his palm, a well of crimson forming. He cursed and I had laughed, taking his hand between my own and dabbing away the blood. Soon he began to laugh with me as I knitted his skin back together with my touch.

It had felt so natural, so lovely. Kind of like a habit, that we would get battered and bruised every day in training, but we would come together and heal together. Like something we'd do every day for the rest of our lives.

Khol's scoff brought me back to reality.

"So, again I say, I did not send the letter." My words were tired and frayed.

"But you wrote it," Khol argued, clearly not willing to yield.

"So that's it then? You can never forgive me?" I huffed, sick and tired of an argument that was going nowhere.

"Raya, you have given me no time to forgive you," his voice mirrored the exasperation of my own.

"Nothing is certain, Khol, nothing at all." My voice was barely a whimper. "And I don't want to die with this hate between us. So, know this, Khol, I am truly sorry," I whispered before turning away.

"Are you alright?" Rafael asked his brother, noticing the tension between us.

"How is everyone coping so easily?" He finally caved and whispered to his brother. "I feel like my insides are turning upside down. My supposed dead brother has come back to life," he gestured Rafael. "We just broke you out of jail, for Goddess's sake! I've left The Temple, my home, knowing I can never return, and now we've just decided we can trust these people we met only an hour ago?" His whispers were becoming louder as he became more vexed. "This is crazy!" He dragged his hands through his hair in the way he always does.

"Not to intrude on your… conversation," Jodie interrupted softly. "But this is a really small boat," she looked from Rafael to Khol, "and we can hear everything you're saying." She smiled awkwardly in the dark. "Just to let you know," she finished, looking down at her hands.

"If it makes you feel better," Jameson added. "I literally have no idea what's going on or who half the people in this boat are," he shrugged.

Laughter sprouted from Khol's mouth loudly, before he clamped a hand over his lips as though he was surprised the sound came from him.

Laughter erupted around the boat, all of us clutching our stomachs and the ridiculousness of what our lives had suddenly become.

Abruptly light spilled into the tunnel.

Finally, I thought to myself *finally we are in the light.*

But the tunnel didn't open, the light wasn't coming from the moon, it was coming from me. From my hands. Light bloomed in my palms softly, the brightness not daring to burn me.

Hello old friend.

Warmth laced through my entire body.

"You're a FireBringer," Rafael breathed. I looked up at him through the light, my eyes now a deep burnt orange.

"Yes," I stated, almost unsure how to explain the full scope of my power.

"And a MindWonderer, and a SkyChanger, and an EarthShaker," Khol said, running his fingers through the flames, absentmindedly, before pulling them away, remembering what was happening between us.

"It's beautiful," Joy whispered. "The Goddess has blessed you, Raya." Her eyes shone with awe. Once again, I felt something connecting us pulled tight.

The cave like tunnel surrounding us, lit up softly. Carvings and paintings marked all the walls. Bats hid their faces beneath their wings, and spiders slid back into the cracks.

With our heads tilted up to the ceiling we stared at the images on the walls.

"It's the Prophesy," Rafael spoke finally, after long minutes of silence. Khol nodded, before glancing quickly in my direction.

Paintings of two women, their hands clasped, covered the walls. Words in languages long dead told story after story. With their arms extended, the women changed the winds, broke the earth, and enflamed their enemies.

They became one and other.

"It's you, isn't it?" Joy whispered, staring at me. I swallowed against my dry throat.

Her words were so simple and clear, like they did not hold the future of every realm in their hands.

"If it is me," the light guttered slightly in my palms before reforming, "then I believe it is you too." My words were almost a whisper. Joy nodded slowly, absorbing the knowledge.

How was she coping so well?

"I think my mother knows; I think she has known all along." Khol spoke quietly. "I believe this is why she wanted you dead."

Silence filled the boat.

We did not speak as the tunnel ceiling finally became illuminated by the full moon.

"I hate the Northern Continent," Jodie mumbled under her breath as the rain began to fall. Drops stuck to eyelashes and soaked through cloaks as the truth settled around us.

I had known he was right, when Khol had mentioned The Prophesy all those months ago. I just hadn't wanted to believe it.

I still didn't.

Pressure fell onto my chest.

I was an orphan, a girl swept up in accidental missions and long slumbered power.

"When we touched earlier," Joy's now timid voice cracked through the silence, "I saw images, memories. Either yours or someone else's."

Silence found its home on our boat again.

"Or ours," my voice was hoarse, as though I had spent hours screaming. I rubbed my wrists instinctively.

"They can't be, the memories… I lived with my parents until they died, the memories couldn't have belonged to me. I'm not, I wasn't…"

"An orphan?" I whispered, glancing up at the crying sky.

"I saw the memories too, ones I had long forgotten." I picked at the split ends of my damp hair.

"My village burned, my mother murdered. I was slung into a carriage. Kept like a prisoner…" my words seemed to fail me.

"My memories are hazy, I don't really remember where I was or who had taken me or where I was going, but I remember the chains, and I remember the little girl who was taken with me. Her deep brown skin and braided hair." Grabbing Khol's hand instinctively, I searched for the words to tell my story. He stared at me momentarily, somehow knowing I needed his touch.

He did not pull away.

"The only memories I can truly recall are the ones I made at Matron's house. The rest," I looked up and met Joy's stare, "the ones from before, they feel like they've been dipped in water. The harder I try to reach them, the further away they feel." Wetness coated my cheeks as the rain fell harder.

"When we touched, it was the most I'd ever seen about

my past." I wiped the rain from my cheeks quickly. "I barely even remember my own mother." I laughed at the ugliness of life, at the unfairness at everything each of us have had to endure. Part of the truth had finally revealed itself, but so much was still veiled, so much was uncertain.

Land bumped itself against the edge of our canal boat, but none of us moved. We knew that we couldn't go back but we weren't quite ready to move forward, so we sat for a moment. Each of us trying to comprehend how we moved forward in a world that seemed to be moving in every direction.

41

JOY

YOU HAVE ALWAYS BEEN KNOWN

"He was bright and lively. Almost like a lightning storm."

- ERIN.

The moon was tired as we ascended land, using all its strength just to stay in the sky. It must've been close to midnight and fatigue weighed heavy upon us all. I couldn't remember the last time I had eaten a proper meal. All I wanted now was a place to rest my head, but we didn't have the time.

By now, The Temple would know Raya and Khol were missing, and that they had taken Rafael and Jameson with them.

Small huts were stacked around the river's edge, with bellowing gray smoke puffing from their chimneys. We stopped, staring at the houses ahead of us, pulling our cloaks tighter, attempting to beat the cold.

Rafael strode forward toward the closest house and rapped his knuckles on the wooden door.

"What are you doing?" Khol hissed. "Ezra has spies everywhere." He half stepped in front of Raya, as though to block her from the conversation. She tsked, moving out from behind him.

The door swung open, and a round woman stood with a quill in her hand, ink dripping down her wrist slowly.

"Yes?" she asked, ignoring the deep blue staining her dress. I looked down at my soft tunic and trousers and then over to Raya in her slightly dusty, but entirely beautiful, ball gown and wool cloak.

"Do you know where I can find Elian?" Raf cleared his throat, allowing a small smile to grace his face. The woman rolled her eyes.

"You're not bringing more trouble to him are ya?" she asked, wiping her dripping wrists against her thigh. Rafael shook his head. "Goddess knows he finds enough trouble on his own," she rolled her eyes.

"I just need his help." Rafael stared down at his shoes, before looking back at the woman. She smiled softly letting out a breath.

"His family home is two doors down, if he's not there, perhaps check the well." She smiled again sweetly, despite her maturity, she must have only been a few years older than us.

"May the Goddess bless you," she said softly before shutting the door.

We stared at Raf, unsure of what was going on inside his head.

"Care to explain?" Khol asked. Rafael began walking to the hut two doors down.

"Not really, no," he stated before hitting his knuckles against the wood.

The door swung open.

"Raf?" A tall, pale boy stood at the threshold. His golden hair swishing with his movements.

"Elian!" Rafael laughed before throwing his arms around the man.

"I see you finally escape from your wretched mother?" Elian teased as the men pulled out of their embrace.

"Yes, with no help from you!" Raf laughed, Khol cleared his throat. I watched him carefully, his brown skin stretched taut over his tense features.

"Elian?" Jameson chirped up, striding over to the door.

"Jameson?" Elian pulled both the boys into a hug. "What are you both doing here?"

I cleared my throat, my mouth a flatline. Jameson glanced at me, as though just remembering I was here.

"Elian was in the cell next to us, he managed to escape a week or two ago."

"Wow the security is seriously slack in The Church," I whispered under my breath.

"The Temple," Khol and Raya corrected at the same time.

Jameson looked back at Elian, ignoring the interruption.

"He tried to break us out, but he couldn't get our bars to shift," a cloud passed over Elian's face. "We didn't want him to waste his shot at freedom."

"He's a FireBringer, and so was his father," Rafael spoke, looking straight at Khol. I heard a delighted gasp from Jodie. Khol stared back in disbelief, his gaze shifting between his brother, Elian, and Raya.

"I've never heard of Sorcerers living outside of The Temple? Why would you live without the protection?" His voice was pained and soft.

"We learned long ago that The Temple did not protect us. Ezra, she was stealing our power, keeping it for herself," Elian spoke softly.

"We?" Jodie asked, looking at all the houses around us. Elian looked up and down the dusty road, from the river.

"You'd better come inside," he said quickly, ushering us all in. He ducked beneath the doorframe, ducking to avoid hitting his head on the low ceilings. A fire roared in the heath, casting a faint orange glow on the yellow walls. A single armchair sat in front of the flames; a bowl of half-eaten stew balancing on the arm. It was warm and cozy and homely, but also incredibly lonely.

"You live here, alone?" Raya asked, taking the thought from my mind. Elian turned to the fire, staring at the dancing flames. Moments stretched.

"Yes, I live alone." He strode over to the wonky cupboard, barely hanging on to the wall. "My mother died a few winters ago and I haven't seen my father since last summer, I believed him to be at The Temple but…" He grabbed mugs from the cupboard and set them on the small table next to the fire. "Well, we all know how that turned out." He choked on a fake laugh as he began pouring out the liquid warming above the fire.

"It's hot chocolate." He smiled.

"You're not the only Sorcerer here, are you?" Jodie asked, setting her mug down.

"No, I'm not."

"Where are the others?" Khol asked impatiently, confusion and frustration practically leaking from his pores.

"They're not here," Elian spoke softly. "But I can take you to them?"

Damp water dripped slowly as we descended a set of twisted stairs. I felt as though we must be close to the center of the earth, we had been walking for almost an hour in darkness, burning handfuls of fire from Jodie, Raya, and Elian our only light. Elian had taken us to a well an hour's walk away from his home, before leading us down a secret tunnel buried beneath the earth. My legs shook with fatigue. I still didn't understand where we were going, was there an underground cave or something? Did a handful of Sorcerer's live down there? Elian had not revealed anything.

"Elian?" Raf whispered. "Are we close?"

Light finally found us as Elian rolled a huge bolder to reveal a hole in the wall at the bottom of the staircase, the rising sound of voices and laughter filled the air. Light seeped through the cracks, all of us wincing at the brightness and the dust that surrounded us.

"Oh yeah, we're close." Elian flashed a grin before slipping through the hole in the stone. Nervous excitement thrummed through my body as each of us stepped through the gap in the wall. Color and light exploded in my vision.

"Welcome to The Circle," he heaved a deep breath, smudging dirt on his brow when wiping his sweat, his sculpted body moving swiftly beneath his white tunic. Erin coughed next to me.

"Careful, Joy, or you'll get drool on your shoes." She drifted by, a swing in her step.

"With my luck he'll probably end up dead or betraying me," I whispered after her, but she wasn't listening. No one was, they all stared ahead.

A cavernous room opened around us, it was as though they had carved a huge hole out of the earth and decided to call it home. All kinds of people milled around the space, some in balconies higher up in the stone and others deeper in the room. Big boulders lay in random spots and tunnels zigzagged in every direction; stone and people as far as the eye could see. Light from the moon filtered in through hundreds of small holes and cracks in the ceiling.

My gaze caught on what looked like a training ring, two fighters stalking each other, gaging when to attack.

"How many live here?" I asked softly.

"Around two thousand," Elian stated proudly, watching the fighter intensely. My eyes widened in the darkness.

"Two thousand people live here?" I asked, my mouth hanging open.

"No, Joy, two thousand Sorcerers live here." He winked at me quickly. Raya gasped next to me but I couldn't take my eyes off the Sorcerers that battled ruthlessly ahead of us.

"What are they training for?" Khol asked, following my gaze.

"They're preparing, readying for war," Elian spoke, his gaze hard, almost metallic.

My brain moved a hundred miles an hour. War?

In the Southern Continent we tended to shy away from the conflict in the Northern Continent, pretending it did not exist. The Southern Continent did not have an army, only pirates and thieves. We hid on our islands, kept our families safe and our livelihood protected.

We tried not to think of the war. Of Northerner against Northerner, villages against villages, family against family.

No one truly knew how the war began in Zetka, we were told a hundred different stories over the years. But most originated with one family.

A wealthy family living in the heart of Zetka. When the lands were plentiful and unmarred by war. But one day, sister turned on sister, the family split in two and a war began. First it was just the family and then the surrounding villages got involved, and now the Northern Continent is divided.

The Sage Guard fighting on one side and…

I wasn't sure who fought on the other.

"They're going to Zetka? To fight with the Sage Guard?" Raya stepped forward, waking me from my mind, something like pleading in her eyes. The Sage Guard were once her people, she had spoken of grueling training and then being taken from her home, she told stories of Alias, the mysterious man I had met at the night market.

"Zetka?" Elian asked, his head whipped around our entire group. When our confused faces met his, he softened.

For the first time he seemed unsure of himself.

He cleared his throat.

"Raya." His voice turned slow and tired, as though he was trying to calm a wild animal. "There is no war in Zetka."

42

RAYA

BURN IT TO THE GROUND

"Waiting for the prophesy, Raya."

- ELIAN'S CONFESSION

"What do you mean 'there is no war in Zetka'? I have travelled through the barren lands; I have trained my entire life to fight in the war." I stiffened my back and straightened my shoulders.

Elian rubbed his hands over his face, attempting to find the words to explain. Various pairs of eyes looked over to us from around the room, couples clasping hands stopped and stared, children playing paused their games. Unease clamped its teeth into my skin, my heart began to race, and my palms sweat.

"Raya," Elian stumbled over his words, "there was once a war in Zetka, but now it is no more than a distraction," he whispered into the damn air.

"Zetka is not at war, not anymore," his words were hushed and hurried.

"But I-I…" My words tumbled blindly. "I am a member of the Sage Guard," I whispered.

And the floor beneath us shook. Once.

"Raya," Elian looked around the room, raising a hand to stop the approach of other Circle members. "Raya, let me explain. Please." Elian began to step toward me, Khol stopped him with an outstretched arm.

I looked around at the crew circled around me, the friends I knew and the friends I didn't.

They had fear in their eyes. Fear and Betrayal.

Just like Alias had.

I glanced at Khol, he was staring at Elian, trying to uncover his secrets.

Look at me, Khol. I wanted to beg. *Show me you are not afraid of me.*

The ground shook again. The water from Jameson's open canteen lifted into the air. Bubbles swaying back and forth as though gravity did not exist. More water began to lift out of glasses and bottles, floating far above where we stood.

The fountain in the center stopped moving, all its water now up in the air.

"Raya," Khol put a hand on my shoulder, attempting to cut off the power. I heaved a deep breath and the ground shook again.

"They are afraid of me," I whispered for only his ears.

"Khol," Rafael whispered, "stop her." His face was a mixture of fear and confusion. Khol pressed his hand harder against my skin, bringing up his other hand to join it.

"I'm trying," his words were clipped and hard.

"Stop talking about me like I am not standing here." My fists flexed, my fingers turning white.

"Raya," Joy spoke, and her voice cut through everything.

Every head turned toward her. Her brown cheeks

pinking slightly. Anger began to coat my throat. No war in Zetka? A distraction? My friends, they had died for nothing. Had Captain Jala known about this? Had she sent my friends to die in an attempt to distract us, to distract us from what?

What were we really training for?

More water began to lift into the air, my own tears being plucked from my cheeks, until a small river floated above us. Cool air brushed against my neck as my hair began to lift. I faintly felt Khol's hands leave my body, but it felt although he was a hundred miles away.

My eyes fluttered closed, and a deep breath filled my lungs, my muscles relaxed, my constant headache eased.

Peace at last. The feeling of *home* seeped into my body as I was able to be one with my magic.

"The Prophesy?" A circle member whispered into silence.

And suddenly arms wrapped around me, pulling me into an embrace. It was Joy, I knew without opening my eyes.

She rested a hand against my blazing cheek.

"Raya." Her voice sounded as though she was underwater, or perhaps I was.

"Let it go." Her words whispered against my skin. "You don't need to hold the weight of the world in your hands. Let me help you, let me carry some of the weight."

Relief overcame me.

Water fell from above, splashing down and soaking everyone around us. Heavy, wet hair stuck to my back. I looked over at Khol, his tunic now plastered against the defined muscles beneath it.

I swallowed, my arms still wrapped around Joy, her braids dripping but still completely intact. Small rivers of water washed over our shoes.

Suddenly, hands rested against Joy and I, on our heads,

legs, arms, backs. Looking up, I saw the circle members, their heads bowed. Praying.

Fingers shook against my skin, lips moved as words were muttered.

Celestial Queens.

The words shot through me.

"You weren't kidding," Jameson whispered, daring to be the first one to break the silence. "I really don't want to get on the wrong side of you." He smirked, pushing the wet hair from his eyes.

"That's probably a good idea," Khol said, his eyes not moving from mine. The heat between us was ever present, despite the cold that lived there too. I slowly tore my gaze from Khol, turning to face the room. Every eye was on me, every breath held as the Circle members retreated away from Joy and me.

Turning to Elian, I smiled awkwardly.

"Sorry," I whispered.

"Don't be." He turned to the room. "Now you have seen it with your own eyes," he boomed, making sure no one could escape his voice. "You saw the connection between the two of them." He turned to Joy and me. "You saw what they are capable of."

"Elian," Jameson warned softly.

"We have been waiting for a sign, we have been waiting for the right moment to stake our claim, to attack." He clasped our hands together and lifted them into the air.

Unease scratched against my skin.

"And now our prayers have been answered. After hundreds of years, The Prophesy is fulfilled at last!" His last words echoed around the chamber as Joy and I snatched our hands back.

A beat of silence passed. And then another. And then another. And just when I wished the earth would swallow me whole, the cavern erupted into deafening applause. People began praying, crying, dancing, and singing. Friends embraced, lovers kissed, and I stood still, dumbfounded, and used. Again.

"Elian!" I spat through gritted teeth. He turned, a smiled plastered on his annoyingly perfect face.

"Get me out of here now! We need to talk." A flicker of fear flashed in his face so quickly I thought I might've imagined it. He nodded, leading us into one of the twisted stone tunnels, to what looked like a makeshift council chamber.

Circle members bowed as we exited into the tunnel. Jameson chuckled to himself.

"I could get used to this," he waggled an eyebrow at Rafael, who nudged his elbow and winked.

"Tell me about Zetka," I spat as soon as we walked into the room, shutting out the cheering and applause.

"Raya—" Elian began.

"Tell. Me. About. Zetka. Now." I seethed, barely able to keep a lid on my Sorcerer abilities. Staring at the fiery look on my face, Elian finally began speaking.

"There was a war in Zetka once, it started hundreds of years ago, when a family split in two. Just as we were told when we were younger." His voice was hurried.

"I've heard the stories, Elian, how about the truth?" I paced the room quickly. Elian nodded.

"But you don't know the whole story. A few decades before the war broke out, a Sorcerer was born into the family and its arrival woke the power in several other members of the family." I swallowed a gasp as Elian spoke.

"One half of the family was appalled, hating that it was

linked to Sorcerers. The Sorcerers hated how differently they were being treated and so a war was born."

All of us sat quietly, swimming in the information.

"After a few hundred years, the opposing sides called a truce."

He spoke again before heaving a sigh. We all leaned in closer, desperately clinging on his every word.

"But the humans, they didn't want a truce. They wanted every Sorcerer wiped from every universe. The war stopped but the humans continued murdering Sorcerers, they still wanted them to be the villains. They were filled with so much hate." He ran his hands over his face. "They kept the story the same. Telling everyone that the war raged on, the truth only passed down between certain individuals."

"But what of the festival of sacrifice? What of the children of nineteen that are offered up to war?" I couldn't help the words that fell out of my mouth as I choked on a sob lodged in my throat.

"Tell me, Raya, when you were in the Sage Guard, did you ever see the war? Did you fight on the battlefield?" he asked and I held my breath.

"No," I said, my voice barely audible.

"The humans still celebrate the festival of sacrifice, they still take the children of nineteen from training facilities, but they don't train them for war, they train them to hunt Sorcerers, they train them to hunt us." As the words let his mouth, I felt my knees go weak.

"The Sage Guard," I whispered, "are hunting Sorcerers?" Elian's silence pounded against my skin.

My mind immediately went to Alias, was he out hunting Sorcerers? Was he hunting me?

"Do they know?" I almost whispered, Elian stared at me softly.

"The soldiers, do they know they are hunting Sorcerers?" I asked, hope pawing at my skin.

"Not in the beginning, but yes, once basic training is over. They are told," Elian spoke, looking as though he wished to cram the words back in his mouth. I nodded slowly, sitting heavily on the velvet chair in front of me. I thought of all the Sorcerers had been slaughtered because they wished to be the most powerful beings in the world. Jagged memories filtered into my brain; my mother being slaughtered. Her empty eyes.

My mother being taken from me when I was only seven.

I pushed the memories away and heaved a shuddering breath.

"Okay," I nodded, trying to convince myself. "Okay, what do you want us to do?" I kept my voice as level as possible. "How can we put an end to this?" The seven of them stared at me. Khol nodded along with my words, Joy's gaze lit with fire, Jameson and Raf looked from me to each other, Erin and Jodie's hand clasped together.

I barely knew any of them, I had only known Khol for a few months and the others for a few days, but I knew they would stand with me. We were all Sorcerers or fighters.

We were all survivors.

"We need you to fight for the truth with us, to help us with the war against the humans. We need you to spark the match." Elian's voice was clear and crisp, his words soaked into my skin, seeping into my muscles, giving me strength. I nodded.

"We will burn them to the ground," I spoke softly, all my ancestors standing with me, pushing me to go on.

43

JOY

WHAT'S LOVE GOT TO DO WITH IT?

"Did you know this would happen?"

- JOY

Fists pounded on the door, all of us frozen from the iciness in Raya's words. *We will burn them to the ground.*

How could we burn the humans without burning ourselves in the process?

I heaved a sigh, clasping hands with Erin and Jodie, fear sitting plainly on their faces. Suddenly I felt like an imposter. Did they expect me fight against the humans? It was as though I had just remembered that I was a human. I was the enemy of these people. Everyone in the room was a Sorcerer. Everyone but me.

I was nothing but the supposed forgotten half of the Prophesy.

Celestial Queen. I scoffed at the ridiculous insinuation.

Fists pound against the door again, waking me up from my transfixion. Elian called a sweaty messenger inside.

"Someone is here," the messenger staggered into the room, swallowing a breath.

"What do you mean?" Elian asked, his patience wearing thin already.

"She must have followed you here," he stuttered over his words, heaving breaths in between them. "I don't know how it happened, but patrol found her next to the well, she was..." The messenger stopped for a moment, looking around at us. We all held a collective breath. Knowing prickled against my skin.

"Go on, Cretu!" Elian said sternly, unable to stand the silence any longer.

"She was trying to force her way in, shouting until her throat was hoarse."

The messenger doubled over to catch his breath; the air sizzled with anticipation.

"What was she shouting?" Erin whispered. The energy in the room died, no one dared to even take a breath.

I wiped the sweat from my palms onto my trousers.

"Just a name, over and over."

My stomach plummeted.

"What name?" I asked through gritted teeth.

Although I already knew.

The messenger looked up from the floor, meeting my gaze before looking over at Elian, asking for permission. A nod greeted him.

"Joy," he breathed and, as one, every single head spun in my direction. I saw Rafael reach for Jameson out the corner of my eye, their hands clasped tightly.

"Are you sure?" I whispered, my hands squeezing Erin's

and Jodie's. Elian's knuckles clenched white as he scrubbed his hands over his face. Guilt sat heavy in my stomach.

I had done this, I had brought danger to his door, to his family.

"Quite sure," the messenger spoke firmly, finally catching his breath. I nodded, swallowing hard as I unknotted my hands from the sisters', heading toward the door.

"Where are you going?" Jameson asked, fear of being separated again coating his voice.

"She's asked for me, has she not?" I forced a lifeless grin; I looked over to Khol and Raf.

"You should probably come with me." I winced at my words as though they had bitten me. The brothers exchanged looks before meeting my eyes.

"You go first," Raf spoke softly.

"We'll be right behind you," Khol's voice was no more than a rumble.

"Who is she?" Raya asked, I felt her energy shift softly as I left the room. Just as the door shut behind me, I heard Khol's voice again.

"I believe our sister has come to visit."

A Sorcerer stood over her in the small infirmary, assumably healing her hands, tending to any cuts or bruises. I couldn't see her face, but I knew it was her. I could feel it, deep in my soul, and I hated myself for it. For knowing her so well, for spending countless, sleepless nights worrying for her safety, even after she had betrayed us and left us behind. Left me behind. My steps slowed as I attempted to delay the inevitable.

She had awoken something within me, something I

thought dormant or even dead, since my Lolita passed. The iciness of guilt speared me again. When was the last time I had sent up a prayer for her? I shook off those feelings as I approached Florence, the healer stepping to the side.

A huge breath washed through me at the sight of her, it took me a moment to realize it was relief. Relief that she was safe, relief that she was here with me. The wave of the relief was edged with something else though, something hot and burning. Anger. Disappointment.

"Joy." Her eyes lit up before dimming quickly, her voice strained and soft. I tore my gaze from her, turning so that she faced my back, unable to stop the burning behind my eyes.

"Joy." This time her voice was closer, I could almost feel her warmth behind me before her hand brushed my waist. She swallowed loudly, tears threatening to spill from her eyes as I turned back to face her.

"I'm sorry," she stuttered, her voice barely a whisper. "I had no choice." Her voice clogged up softly. A purple bruise bloomed over her right eye, and without thinking I reached up my hand and brushed the skin softly. I pulled my hand away quickly, as if her skin had burned me.

"Why didn't you tell us?" My voice scratched against my throat. The healer scurried away, leaving us alone in the little infirmary.

"My mother wouldn't have understood," she struggled for the words. "I thought it wouldn't affect me. I thought I would be able to leave and never think of you again," her voice became quiet. "But I couldn't stop thinking about you, and losing you was killing me." Her eyes focused on my face.

"After losing my brother, I swore I'd never let myself be hurt like that again." Her words crashed into me, she still thought Rafael dead? Her mother had kept him from both Khol and Florence?

"Florence, I need to tell you something…" I started.

"No, me first," she interrupted. "When my mother first asked me to join Harlow's crew and learn his secrets, I thought it was an easy task, a steppingstone, something to wet my feet." She stepped closer to me, our shared height making our noses almost touch.

"But it wasn't, Harlow was dangerous, and I knew I had to leave as soon as I could, or I wouldn't have survived." I searched her eyes for deceit or lies but it seemed that everything she was saying was sincere.

"And when I saw you, sitting on that bar stool, watching Jameson dance. I knew you had a boat, and I knew you'd do anything for him, and I needed to get home." She placed her hand on my cheeks and sighed softly, the warm air hitting my skin.

"This was all before I knew you and before I truly got to know Erin and Jodie." Her breath caught at the mention of the names. "Are they safe?"

I nodded once.

"But as soon as I got home, this feeling of wrongness it flooded me. Drowned me."

My heart began to pound so loud I was sure she could hear it too. My traitor brain began conjuring up images of Florence and I together, happy. A ship of our own, the open ocean, the crew, and the sun. Perhaps a family of our own.

Stop.

What are you doing? She betrayed you; she left you behind.

I batted away the thoughts as though they were a bad smell.

"I don't need recognition from my mother or The Temple or anyone." Her bottom lip quivered as the words fell out, a tear streaming down her face.

"I just want you," she whispered, and it wasn't logical or brave or smart but I couldn't help myself.

I pushed my lips against hers. My lips parted immediately, her tongue sweeping through my mouth softly. A small moan sounded in the bottom of my throat. My hands reached up automatically to cup her face. As though this is where they belonged.

This was where they were always supposed to be.

She gripped my waist, pushing up the fabric of my tunic so that her hands were against my bare skin. Our lips and tongues danced together, finding a rhythm and pattern that we both loved. A gasp fell from Florence's lips as I dragged mine down her jaw and to her neck. Sucking and nibbling softly.

Her hands flew to my hair, and she pulled me back softly, her mouth eager to reach my skin. She licked from the base of my throat to my mouth, meeting me again for another earth-shattering kiss. When our lips finally parted, we rested our foreheads together, swallowing down deep mouthfuls of air, our swollen lips pulsing with desire.

"This is definitely not what I thought would happen when I saw you again," I whispered. "Did you?"

"Only in my wildest dreams," she breathed softly. And we lapped into a gentle silence, both of us trying to piece together what happened next. I didn't trust her, not as I had before, but I couldn't help wanting to be around her all the time. I couldn't help the half of me that now felt whole after days of feeling hollow. I thought of the journey we had taken together, of her leaving me to rescue Jameson and Raf—

Rafael. She still thought her brother was dead.

"Florence." She met my eyes immediately, something like nerves flitting across her face.

"I need to tell you something," I whispered, and she nodded.

"Your brother is here," I confessed, and her eyes narrowed.

"Khol is here? Mother said he had gone galivanting with the half human girl, but she was sure he would return." She pondered for a moment before meeting my gaze again. I mentally chided myself for forgetting she has two brothers.

"Khol is here but…" I swallowed against my dry throat. "But Rafael is here too." The words left my mouth in an odd choke.

"No, Rafael is dead." Her answer was automatic and cold, not one hint of emotion within it.

I shook my head. I knew this pain, the pain of not wanting to think of lost loved ones again. Not wanting to believe the impossible.

What would I have said, if the same was said to me? I would have laughed in their face.

"No, he isn't." I cupped her jaw, trying to be soft.

"He was imprisoned." Her face remained blank. "Let me take you to him and he can explain." She nodded slowly, her face portraying nothing. I grabbed her hand and led the way.

44

RAYA

CH-CH-CH-CHANGES

"It was what we all needed; it was like coming home."

- RAYA

The door to the council chamber swung open as Joy stepped through, another woman close behind her.

"Florence," Khol breathed, striding toward her. She turned to face him, her eyes shining brightly.

"Hey, Khol." She smiled, dirt and blood crusted around the edge of her face. They embraced fiercely.

"It feels as though much more than three years have passed; you've grown three feet!" She laughed softly, before catching her breath. "Is it true, Khol? Is Raf alive? Is he here?" she asked hurriedly, but before Khol could answer, Raf's voice sounded.

"Florence," he whispered and then their eyes met. Tears immediately sprung from Florence's eyes.

And mine, Jameson's, Erin's, Jodie's, and Joy's.

The siblings rushed toward each other, Rafael wrapping

his arms around his younger sister. The two soon began sobbing, beckoning a sniffling Khol to join their family reunion.

"How is this possible?" Florence whispered, her hands on Raf's cheeks.

The brothers launched into the story, Rafael telling his stories and Khol telling his and mine. Florence told her own in exchange. Her journey to Captain Harlow, her experience on the ship, Erin and Jodie often cutting in to share stories. Soon all of us were sitting in a huddle on the floor, sharing stories, attempting to create plans, and trying to decide what the hell came next. Elian was stubborn, adamant that now The Prophecy was fulfilled, we should be preparing for battle. But who were we really fighting? The Sage Guard? The Temple? The humans? Or were they all the same thing? How did we stop the rumors of 'war' in Zetka?

By the time the candles had burned all the way to the bottom, we still didn't have all the answers.

"I wish Ottie was here to share this moment with us," Khol murmured as he thought of his youngest sibling. Florence nodded softly.

"Who is Ottie?" Rafael asked and my heart broke again.

"Oh Rafael," Khol looked as though he had taken a knife to the heart.

"She is our youngest sister." Khol smiled.

"We have another sister?" Rafael's eyes were wide as saucers.

"Goddess, I missed her desperately. When I saw her at the ball, I barely recognized her. I didn't realize so much could change in three years," Florence sighed sadly. "I wanted to bring her with me, but she is just a child. It's not safe for her." Florence reached out to touch Raf's shoulder, and he nodded softly.

"I hope I get to meet her one day." He smiled softly.

"You need rest, all of you," Elian said firmly, breaking the sweet silence.

Jodie had fallen asleep in her sister's lap hours ago and Jameson was slumped on Raf's shoulder. We wouldn't be fighting anyone if we didn't rest soon. I nodded, jumping to my feet and exiting with only a smile at Joy.

The rest of them trickled off into groups. Jameson and Rafael heading to one room quickly. Erin and Jodie in another, Joy and Florence in the one next to it.

The cool water dripped from my chin as I washed the day away. Or attempted to. Staring into the cloudy mirror of the washroom, I gripped onto the carved stone basin, finding it hard to meet my own gaze. The girl I used to be, all those months ago, was gone, buried beneath scars and scrapes and magic. The woman that stared back at me now was hardened by the ugliness and the beauty of life.

Standing in only my undergarments, I cataloged my nearly naked body. The scorch marks, red and angry, still resided on both hands, travelling up my forearms too. Various deep, purple bruises and pale lines of scarring littered my body. Proof of my physical and mental training with Khol. I conjured a small flame between my thumb and forefinger, watching it flicker, remembering a time when I knew nothing of the power that lurked beneath my skin, a time before the Sage Guard, before The Temple, before Khol and Joy and sweet Elijah.

Floorboards creaked softly as someone entered the room. I winced, knowing who awaited me behind the bathing room door.

"Raya?" Khol's usual rumble was a soft whisper.

"In here," I whispered back, small thuds sounded as he made his way over to the washroom.

"We need to talk…" The door creaked open loudly. "Oh… um… I'll let you… sorry," Khol stuttered after taking in my almost nakedness, shutting the door behind him. I leaned against the wooden door, sliding down until I sat at the very bottom of it. The sound of sliding fabric and a small thud made me think Khol had done the same.

"I can't keep doing this," the whisper left my mouth quickly, barely making its way through the wooden door.

"I know," Khol replied, his tone equally as soft. "Me either."

"I can't keep telling you how sorry I am, or how much I regret the letter that lived in my top draw." A pained sounded came from Khol's throat at my words.

"But, Khol, I did not, and I would not have sent that letter." I spoke the words for the final time, I wouldn't allow myself to live within them any longer. "I had no choice, if I did not collect the information, my captain would have murdered me and those I care about deeply." An old anxiety flared to life within me, but now I knew Alias was safe; Joy explained her seeing him at the night market.

"Raya," Khol spoke softly.

"Please, just let me finish. If you cannot forgive me, then I understand but then we must draw a line beneath it, because I will not go on as if walking on broken glass. We have bigger enemies than each other."

A long silence slipped between us, after a moment I thought Khol had gotten up and left, but he cleared his throat softly.

"I'm sorry too, for spending so much time blaming you when you had no choice. I forgive you, Raya, and I hope you can forgive me too." His voice was slightly throaty for the last words.

Perhaps it was my feelings for Khol or the threat of impending confrontation and battle, but I swung the door open, immediately meeting Khol's iron stare. He was standing at the door, knuckles poised to knock, my lip trembled slightly as his eyes dropped down my body and then back up to meet my face.

I walked toward him hurried and wrapped my arms around his neck. Stunned, he paused for a moment before returning my embrace, wrapping his arms around my waist, burying his face in my neck. I breathed in his rich scent, rain and vanilla, clutching him tighter. All my feelings of sweetness and care finally coming to the surface. All his words from the night of the ball finally coming back to me.

I feel like my heart will burn a hole in my chest every time I look at you.

"I am so afraid," I whispered into his skin. He lifted me from the ground, and my legs wrapped around his waist instinctively. Forgiveness pulsed through me in waves. In reality, I don't think I would have survived losing him.

"I know. Me too," he replied softly. Leaning my head back, I admired his face. His pink, full lips and bright green eyes, his rich, brown skin folded into a frown.

"Khol," I began, resting a palm against his cheek. "The one thing I am not afraid of…" I took a deep breath and took a leap, "is my feelings for you." He let out a sigh in relief, I carried on.

"I want to be with you throughout…" I paused again, trying to figure out how to put our mess of a life into words, "all of this." I laughed. The frown between Khol's eyes smoothed.

"And after?" he asked quietly, as though afraid to say it out loud.

"And always," I said softly, pressing my lips to his gently, an almost chaste kiss.

He chased after my mouth as I pulled away, pushing his lips against mine as though he was dying of thirst, and I was the only water left on earth. My legs tightened around him, pulling him closer than I thought possible. A sigh escaped my mouth, breathy and quick, blood rushed to my cheeks in embarrassment, but the noise seemed to light a fire in Khol. Our kisses turn hungry, almost animalistic. Lips and tongues and teeth, working in unison to insight burning passion.

A deep sound grumbled in Khol's throat as I dragged my tongue up his ear. Heat pooled in my stomach, ferocious and wanting, as Khol walked us to the small bed in the corner. The feeling of smooth cotton against my back made my breath catch, and Khol's large body covered mine. His kisses turned slow, as though he was savoring every moment we shared.

Wet lips trailed across my jaw, down my neck and to my chest. I pushed up, flipping us over, now straddling Khol's broad chest. I held his cheeks within my hands, rubbing my thumb back and forth over the smooth skin. I leaned down, kissing his lips agonizingly slowly, sucking his bottom lip between my teeth. His hands began to slide around my waist, but I stopped him, pinning his arms to the sheets below us. He sat up to reach my lips before pulling my earlobe between his teeth.

My grip on his wrists loosened and he flip us over again.

"Tell me I'm the only one," he whispered into my ear, and shivers ran up and down my entire body. I swallowed against my dry mouth.

"You're the only one," I gasped, and our mouths clashed together once again.

Sunlight trickled through the small cracks in the ceiling and walls. I had almost forgot that we were underground. My naked body was splayed over Khol's like a blanket. Our legs entwined, our chests pressed together, the slow movements of his chest rocking me slowly. I stared up at his face.

Tell me I'm the only one.

His words from the night before sent shivers down my spine. His eyes fluttered open.

"Good morning," he drawled slowly, and my heart kicked up a notch.

"Good morning," I whispered, leaning down to kiss him softly. We stared at each other for a while, our unspoken language communicating how we felt about one and another. The pad of Khol's thumb drew lazy circles on my hip, my fingers brushing through his dark hair.

"Raya," he whispered after a short while, I nodded, although he seemed to struggle to find the words. I waited for the right ones to come to him.

"I have worshipped the Gods and Goddesses my entire life, and they are all you. In any form, in any shape, they are all you," he whispered, his eyes darting from mine. My lips parted as I took in a deep breath.

"I love you," he simply stated. Air whooshed from my lungs and everything in my body was pushing me to flee.

But I didn't want to, because I loved this stupid, behemoth, lovely, wicked man with my whole heart.

"I love you," I whispered back, wrapping him in a tight embrace.

45

JOY

READY. SET. GO!

"It's time to make a decision."

- ELIAN

By the time dawn broke through the cracks in the stone, I had only slept for what felt like an hour or less. When we arrived at the room Elian had given us, Florence and I washed, redressed, and climbed into the bed without speaking a word. Selfishly the kiss played on my mind, although I knew Florence's mind was far from it. She had just reunited with her brothers after years.

And all I could think about was her lips on mine.

We laid side by side, neither one of us daring to touch the other. As soon as the barely-there light hit the room, I lurched to my feet and into the bathing chamber. Cold water stung my face as I splashed handful after handful on my skin.

I just want you.

Her words burned into my skin.

Never in my wildest dreams.

I suddenly felt hot underneath my clothes. Sweat breaking out on my back. I dressed faster than I thought possible, bolting out the door to join Raya in the dining hall.

She shoveled eggs and burnt toast into her mouth. She lifted her eyebrows in a way 0f greeting.

"No Khol this morning?" I teased. "Is he too tired?" I wiggled my eyebrows at her. She choked on her breakfast.

"The walls may be made of stone, but they're not soundproof…" I said with a wink, flopping down next to her.

"Well, I never kiss and tell," she smirked, piling more eggs onto her plate.

Jodie and Erin slid onto the bench opposite us, creamed rice pudding in each of their bowls. Bags under their eyes.

"Raya and Khol keep you awake too?" I asked with a sneer. Jodie glanced at Raya, a smile hiding in the corner of her mouth.

"The walls aren't soundproof," Erin muttered into her rice pudding quietly. A laugh bolted through me.

"My sentiment exactly," I nudged Raya softly. "But enough about our new friends' scandalous antics, what's on the agenda today? Receiving some life altering news? Finding out someone else is trying to kill us? Perhaps our dead parents rising from their graves?" I said in a mock serious voice. All the girls laughed, earning stares from the other members of The Circle eating around us.

"Oh don't be ridiculous," Erin laughed. "Jodie can barely survive a walk in the dark, never mind our dear old dad returning from the underworld." She flicked some pudding at her sister.

"You are becoming more and more like Joy every day." Jodie crossed her arms, feigning anger.

"Jodie." I rested my hands on my chest. "That's the

kindest thing anyone has ever said to me!" I wiped away a fake tear.

"Speaking of being up all night," Raya said from out of the blue.

"No one was speaking of that," Erin spoke with eyebrows risen. "But go on." Jodie smirked before shoving a spoonful of rice pudding into her mouth.

"I am the queen of the subtle conversational maneuver," Raya boasted.

"You should let other people tell you that you're subtle," I chided with a smile. Raya nudged me, clicking her fingers, a flame appearing between her digits.

"Alright ladies, weapons down." Jodie rolled her eyes dramatically. "Back to being up all night." She pushed her empty bowl aside, leaning in for the gossip. The flame between Raya's fingers extinguished.

"I was going to ask Joy," she turned to me with a flourish, "what happened with Florence after we all went to bed?" The three of them leaned closer toward me, their ears ready to receive. I thrusted a piece of toast into my mouth, buying time to give an answer.

"What do you mean?" I said around my food. All three girls rolled their eyes.

"Do you want us to pretend we didn't notice the swollen lips, the longing glances, the 'oh please ravish me' looks to you and Florence were giving each other." Erin stared at me like a character from a romance novel, reaching her hand to touch my cheek. I batted her away, sticking my tongue out.

"Alright, alright!" I caved quickly, partly because I couldn't deny the looks between Florence and I, but mostly because I wanted to confide in my friends.

"We kissed."

"The understatement of the century!" Jodie bellowed, more heads turning our way as her sister 'shushed' her.

"We kissed… with passion?" My voice rose at the end of the sentence. We erupted into fits of laughter.

"Tell us!" Erin demanded.

"There's nothing to tell, we kissed. It was… nice," I promised, my hands raised in innocence.

"Details!" Jodie squealed. I reached for another piece of toast, but Raya stopped me.

She covered my hand with hers and closed her eyes.

Memories of the kiss ploughed through my head in a whirlwind. The feelings returning, heat creeping up my neck.

"Hey!" I slapped her hand. "Stay out of my head!" I couldn't help the smile on my face, the feeling of Florence's lips on my mine now fresh in my mind.

"Wow," Raya feigned a swoon, gulping her glass of water quickly. "Is it hot in here?" she asked, earning a shove that nearly pushed her from the bench. Our laughter filled the room.

"What are we laughing at?" Khol asked as he approached the table, a high-necked tunic trying to hide the mouth shaped bruises on his neck.

The four of us looked at each other, not sure what we were willing to share. Khol starred at us, his eyes narrowing.

"The walls are not soundproof," Raya said with a huff, Khol's face turned a bright shade of red.

"But we're impressed with your stamina," Jodie piped up, her attempt to diminish the awkwardness working in the exact opposite way.

We fell into laughter once again.

46

RAYA

MESSAGE IN A BOTTLE

"He's been trying to find me!"

- RAYA.

The same messenger that announced the arrival of Florence bounded into the council chamber again. We had been holed up in the room for three days, still no concrete plan. Elian had two thousand Circle members, all of them Sorcerers. With the nine of us added on, we didn't really make an intimidating army.

"What is it now, Cretu?" Elian said sternly, days of worrying shown in the bags under his eyes. The messenger held up his hand, a letter perched between his fingers.

"A messenger from..." Cretu struggled to catch his breath. Again. How far had he run? The entrance was only a tunnel away.

Elian's gaze sprang up, fire and ice mixed within it. Cretu looked between us all, a red blush creeping onto his face.

"Who?" Elian demanded. Cretu swallowed softly, unease coating his body like morning dew.

"A member of the Sage Guard," he spluttered.

I stood at his words, unable to stop my body from moving toward Elian.

"We found him scouting the Zlat above us. We have him detained, but he won't talk to us. He says he'll only talk to Raya…" the messenger trailed off, avoiding my eye line.

"Me? How is this possible?" I whispered. "The only people that know we're here… are here."

We all stared at each other, not daring to speak.

"It was easy to follow you," Florence whispered. "There are so many of you, and you were clumsy," her voice turned shy and embarrassed.

"But if someone followed us, why send a messenger? Why not talk to Raya in person?" Khol countered, throwing a hard gaze to his sister.

I took off from the council chamber, down the hall and into the main cavern. The Sage Guard solider sat tied to a chair, bruises and blood covering his face.

"Opal," I mused softly. "What in Goddess name are you doing here?" Footsteps behind me confirmed that Elian and Khol had followed me from the room.

"Raya," he smirked. "It's been too long." He wriggled in his ropes.

"What are you doing here?" I spoke again.

"Alias sent me," he stated, and the floor fell out from beneath me. "He scattered six of us around the Continents, the fastest in the Regiment to find you," he boasted. "I picked up your trail a few miles ago."

"Why?"

"Haven't you heard? You're the talk of the Continents.

The girl that escaped Captain Jala," he mocked slowly. My silence met him, urging him to carry on.

"He needed a message delivered to you." Opal's smug smile left his face slowly.

"And? What is that message?" Frustration hummed beneath my skin.

"He needs to see you. In person."

"And why not come look for me himself?" I countered.

"Captain Jala wouldn't let him. He's collateral, remember?" Opal seemed to enjoy the anger that rose within me.

"Why does he need to see me?"

"He didn't say." Opal catalogued the people behind me.

"What *did* he say?"

"He said he needs to speak with you, to tell you something that he couldn't risk sending in a letter." Opal leaned close so only I could hear his voice. "Meet him at your favorite place, where you promised to meet when your *service* was over." He scoffed at the word service, disinterest plain on his face. I turned from him, walking away so fast I thought the ground might shake beneath me.

"He'll be there when the moon is half full," Opal called after me as I entered the council chamber again, sitting with a sigh.

"What did he say, Raya?" Joy's voice was soft and quiet, as though she was helping a wounded animal.

"It's Alias," I breathed, and Khol was instantly beside me. "He wants to see me, he been trying to find me for a while, he's been sending messengers all over the continents," I breathed softly, looking up at the group of people that stared at me. "He's been trying to find me."

Warmth filled my chest. My oldest friend, my family had been trying to find me. I reached for Khol, grabbing his hand.

"Did he say why?" Elian asked, stepping closer to me. Looking up, I furrowed my brows.

"He needs to see me! To tell me something, too precious to risk sending in a letter." I grew defensive, flattening my hand to my chest. "Maybe this is the help we've been looking for?"

"Raya," Elian pushed up his sleeves. "Alias is a member of the Sage Guard, he knows you are a Sorcerer. He knows what is happening in Zetka." Elian approached me as though I was made of porcelain.

I looked up at the faces staring at me. The unease and pity flowing from them began to drown me.

"What are you suggesting? That he means to harm me?" My voice was accusatory as I swung my gaze to the entire group, my eyes at last falling on Khol.

"Khol," I whispered, tears burning behind my eyes.

"Raya, I know how you feel about him," he winced at his words. "But we… we cannot trust him, I'm sorry. You must understand why," he pleaded with me.

I stepped from him slowly.

"You don't know him." I struggled to control my quivering voice. "He has protected me my entire life, he wouldn't…" I tripped over my own feet. "He wouldn't hurt me."

Joy walked toward me, our strange bond soothing me. Her hands clasped my shoulders and she smiled.

"Where does he want to meet?" she asked, ignoring Elian's words of warning.

"The field of wildflowers near Matron's orphanage, we agreed to return there once our service in the Sage Guard had ended." I sighed. Would it have ever ended? Would we have been soldiers forever? Murdering Sorcerers until the end of our days?

"Where is this orphanage?" Elian asked.

"Two hours north of The Foothills." I finally met his gaze, my brows lifted.

"You want to go through Zetka? The Foothills?" Erin stammered. "We've heard stories of that place all the way in the Southern Continent." She stepped closer to her sister. "We'd never survive the journey."

"How far from here?" I asked Elian as he paced the room.

"Raya pl—" Khol started.

"How. Far?" I countered, my gaze burning into Elian's.

He huffed a sigh, dragging his hands through his hair.

"Two days ride, Northeast." He sat heavily into the chair, defeated. I nodded, staring at Khol. Turning over the options in my mind.

I recalled Opal's parting words.

When the moon is half full.

"When is the next half-moon?" I asked urgently.

"Three days' time," Elian whispered.

"Then we need to go. Now." My words were sharp and cold.

Elian nodded.

"Will you go with me?" I asked Khol, ignoring everyone but him.

"Do you think this is wise?" he asked softly, and I nodded.

"Yes," he nodded too. "I will go with you."

Warmth spread around me, filling every pore, every limb with sunlight.

"As will I," Elian spoke without looking up. "I can take you to The Foothills on the safest path I know." He heaved a breath before standing. "Less of a chance of you being brutally murdered." He shrugged.

"I'll come too." Joy squeezed my arm. "It's probably best

if we stay together, right?" she asked and I nodded. "I knew we'd receive some life changing news today," she whispered.

"Or find out someone new trying to kill us," Jodie said softly.

"The rest of you need to stay put," Elian claimed, before anyone else could volunteer. "We still need a plan, work with my people here, Lucile will be in charge in my absence. She knows what to do." He started putting a plan into action, collecting maps and candles from the room, and piling them onto the table. We all stared.

"If we go, we go tonight. We can't afford to waste any more time." He heaved the objects and left the room. "There are horses in a nearby barn up top we can use." He did not look up from packing. "The farmer trusts me."

"I've never seen him so serious," Jameson whispered from the corner of the room.

"Pack and be in the cavern before the sun sets." Elian's voice was bland for the first time ever as he walked away.

The messenger took Raf, Jameson, Erin, and Jodie to Lucile. Rafael and Khol embraced before he left.

Florence lingered behind, following Joy to her room to pack.

"Are you angry?" I whispered when Khol and I were alone.

"No," he whispered back. "I'm terrified."

He left the room swiftly.

The main cavern was packed as we readied to leave. Eager faces trying to a get a glimpse of us.

"What are they all doing here?" I asked Elian in a tense whisper. Some Circle members had hopeful expressions, others with furrowed brows filled with distrust. A voice called out before he could answer.

"They should not be leaving! Not both of them!" a broad woman shouted sternly, followed by various nods and hums of agreement.

"We cannot lose the Celestial Queens!" another voice shouted; this time a man with a long beard.

"Calm down," Elian raised his hands. "Please, everyone, calm down!" His voice rung out, and a quiet fell across the room.

"We are not going to lose anyone!" His voice was strong, like a leader.

Joy leaded toward me.

"Oh, don't worry about us," she whispered for my ears only. "Go ahead and talk about our impending death." I couldn't help but chuckle at her words.

Before another protest could take place, Elian whisked us out of the cavern into the endless, inky corridor from which we arrived almost a week ago. Only leaving a few seconds for somber goodbyes.

The walk seemed longer than before, no light to walk toward, no anticipation for what was to come. We had been underground for long enough that time began to ebb and flow around us. But it was enough time for Khol's mother and The Temple to know we were all missing, enough time for Ezra to alert the humans and the Sorcerers. We were being hunted, and there was no doubt about it.

It hung heavily and unspoken in the air around us.

"If Florence and Alias found us so easily, what makes you think that someone isn't waiting to kill us as soon as we step into the daylight?" Khol asked into the pitch-black tunnel around us. The sound of clothes shifting made we wonder if Elian was shrugging.

"I don't," Elian stated, leaving the space eerily quiet for a moment too long. "Maybe they're waiting to kill us, maybe they're not. There is only one way to find out." His was voice chipper and positive despite the content.

"In an odd way, you remind me of Captain Harlow," Joy said from behind me, and I narrowed my eyes.

"Who's Captain Harlow?" Khol and I asked at the same time.

"A ship captain that ruined my boat and tried to kill me. Several times. Very odd man. Funny." Her words came out in blocks as though she couldn't quite figure out how to describe the man.

"Oh well." I imagined Elian's brows furrowing. "What a compliment," he said through gritted teeth. "Harlow seems like a ray of sunshine." His footfalls became louder. Was he stomping around like a child?

"I said he was funny, did I not?" Joy said defensively. I smiled to myself.

The rest of the journey passed in rarely interrupted silence, our breaths becoming labored as the path inclined steeply.

Light broke into the tunnel a few hours later, sweat clinging to Elian's back from the exertion.

"Let's do this," Khol announced with a newfound energy.

47

JOY

BAT OUTTA HELL

"Once the snow melts, we need to be ready."

- ELIAN.

The mountains that surrounded the Zlat, the forest in which The Circle was hidden, were perilous. Ice and snow pelted against us and our borrowed horses for hours, slowly chipping away at our motivation. Elian guided us to a small cave on the side of a mountain, lighting a fire with his hands to chase away the cold.

Before that moment, I had completely forgotten he was a Sorcerer.

"We should be there by midday tomorrow." His words thawed the ice in my chest.

"Did we have to walk the mountains? I can't feel my feet." Raya shivered, moving closer to the fire.

"We did if we want to survive." Elian's usual spark had died out over the last thirty-six hours. I scooted next to him as

Raya produced more flames in her hands, attempting to keep us warm.

"Are you alright?" I whispered for only Elian's ears. He stared at me for a moment, I could almost see the cogs turning in his brain.

"Fine," his was voice clipped.

"I'm not going to pretend that I know you, but you don't seem… yourself," I pushed on, ignoring the warning burrowing into my chest.

"You're right, you don't know me." His words were harsh and emotionless, his gaze cutting. I stared at him, all the hope once living in his eyes, gone.

"Elian," my voice soon lost all its patience. "We're stuck together, whether you like it or not." He glanced over at me. "Talk. Now." Crossing my arms, I turned from Raya and Khol.

An internal war played out in Elian's head, his eyes flicking from me to Raya and then to Khol. He ran his fingers through his hair and huffed a sigh.

"I grew up outside Zetka, joined the Sage Guard just like Raya," he struggled over the next few words.

"I was in training, fighting another solider. He was getting the better of me, and I didn't want to lose, again." He angrily wiped a stray tear from his eye.

"All I was thinking was 'I can't lose again' over and over, and then suddenly there was fire everywhere. The solider barely made it out alive. I almost killed him, and I didn't know why." His voice cracked softly.

"They took me away, beat me, locked me in The Temple dungeons." His eyes finally met mine. "I haven't been back since." Elian's eyes glistened with unshed tears.

"I'm sorry." My voice was a whisper. It was all I could say, nothing could take away the pain he had felt. He nodded.

"We should get some sleep." He stood and walked toward Khol, Raya, and the fire, the former already fast asleep. He laid down, his body taught.

When the sun finally rose, ever so slightly thawing the cold and ice around us, my eyes stung, and my body ached. Raya and Elian were already up and repacking the bags, an unnamed animal twirling above the fire. I daren't ask.

Soon we were back on the mountain, the cold slightly less biting than the day before.

48

FLORENCE

FIGHT LIKE A GIRL

It was clear the people of The Circle did not trust us. Despite my brother's reassurance, I knew that he was the only reason I did not eat alone. No matter how often I tried, I couldn't get Erin and Jodie alone, I was never given the option to explain. Joy had forgiven me, hadn't she? Why wouldn't the sisters too? I knew Joy had told them my story, she had told me they understood, but weathering Erin's untrusting stare across the breakfast table suggested the opposite.

I missed Joy. More than I ever had before. Now that I knew she forgave me, it was harder to be away from her. Our hungry kiss played on repeat in my head and I wondered if she thought about it too.

My tongue sweeping through her mouth softly. A small moan sounding in the bottom of throat.

I swallowed, crossing one leg over the other.

Jameson and Rafael laughed loudly next to me; I ate a spoonful of porridge.

"We need to meet Lucille, she wants us to begin training

with the other Circle members," Raf announced to our table, noticing Erin's and Jodie's full breakfast plates, he nodded.

"Come when you're finished." He turned to me, winked, and kissed my forehead. Jameson stood ahead of him, smiling, waiting for him to catch up so they could walk together.

He had given me the chance to talk to them, to clear the air.

"We'll come with you," Erin stated, Jodie rolled her eyes.

"Sit down, Erin," Jodie said sternly. "For Goddess sake."

My eyes widened at the bite in her voice.

"Florence." She turned to me, and my heart hammered against my chest. "You hurt us when you left." She kept her voice steady. "We trusted you, we loved you." Her voice remained strong, never breaking. The unfeeling mask I had almost been taught to wear threatened to rise.

But I stopped, I wanted to feel this.

I had never had sisters, I had never had a female role model, never mind one that loved me.

"I know," I coughed away the cobwebs in my throat. "I'm sorry, I truly believed I did not have any other choice. I didn't know my mother was capable of all that she has done," I said, although it was a lie, I always knew she was a monster, I was just too scared to admit it.

"Nothing I can say will truly make up for it but, I'm sorry." I reached for their hands and they clung onto me. "It was the biggest mistake of my life, to leave people whom I love and who loved me." I smiled.

"Love," Erin corrected. "Present tense. We still love you." She smiled through shining eyes. I gripped their hands tighter, unused to the warmth provided by forgiveness. We finished our breakfast in a content silence. My food suddenly tasted better.

By the time we joined Rafael and Jameson in the main cavern, the three of us had eaten and shared stories of our time apart.

The main space, from which tunnels wormed off into different rooms, such as the dining hall we had just left, was bursting with life. The same training ring I had seen when I entered The Circle now teemed with life. This time Rafael and Jameson were involved. The two of them fighting against strangers with wooden staffs.

"You must be the others from above?" a women stated, walking across the pit toward us, fighting parting around her.

"She's a MindWonderer," Erin whispered to us.

"Well, how perceptive." Lucille's smile was sickly sweet. She looked at each of us in turn.

"Let me guess." She pointed to us. "Erin, Jodie..." Her gaze narrowed on me. "And Florence, daughter of The Temple."

"I'm glad you're not holding it against me." I smiled back, mirroring her honeyed gaze.

"Have you fought before?" she asked, ignoring me. Another person that distrusts me. We all nodded. She smiled widely.

"Josephine. Conrad. Ola," she shouted without her gaze leaving mine. Three figures glided toward us.

"My best fighters." Lucille smirked.

"For us? How kind," Erin said deadpan. Lucille assigned us each a partner. Conrad stood behind me, surprisingly taller than me.

"Sorcerers?" I asked.

"Aren't we all?" Lucille replied.

"Abilities?"

"Let's keep it basic, just combat."

"Weapons?" I spoke again, not leaving anything to chance.

Her eyebrows rose. "Let's keep it friendly, no weapons." I nodded, suddenly noticing that every head in the cavern had turned to us.

"You were raised in The Temple, weren't you, Florence?" Lucille purred, I nodded.

"Why don't you show everyone here how they teach fighting? Then we might gain the upper hand."

She turned to Conrad and nodded.

Before I even had a second to react, stars exploded in my vision and pain lanced through my skull.

49

RAYA

HERE'S RAYA!

"I saw her from the window! She had changed so much!"

- MATRON CLARA

The old battlefield in Zetka was barren and empty, further proof of the lies we had been fed our entire lives. How had no one stumbled across this land? How has no one wondered? Our horse cantered quickly across the cracked, desert ground. We had no choice; Elian had told us. There was no other way to get to the other side of Zetka, we had to cross the old battlefield.

Ghosts of the dead seemed to linger around us, warning us.

Go back, they seemed to say, *leave the battlefield, before it takes you too.*

I shuddered, pulling my horse closer to Khol's. At least we had left the snow behind on the mountain, warmth finally seeping into our skin.

"I know where we are now," the words slipped from my

mouth hours later, as the horses crested a hill covered in grass and wildflowers.

"Matron's house should be..." The words died in my mouth.

My childhood home. It stood like a mythical creature. I had only been away for less than a year, it felt like forever. The chipped red paint on the front door. The windows warped from the sun. It was battered and worn but it was home. My shoulders sunk, months of fear and anticipation and love and sadness slowly sinking away.

"This is where you grew up?" Joy asked from behind me. I nodded.

"This is the place." I breathed in the scent of home, pine and wildflowers and water from the stream behind the orphanage.

Memories of my childhood came rushing back to me faster than I thought possible. Helping Matron Clara wash clothes in the stream, Alias and I catching fireflies. The sun staying up all day and into the night in the summer months, eating dinner outside. Swimming in the water, skating in the winter. We had done all of it while training for the Sage Guard. It hit me then, that Matron Clara had created a beautiful life for us, with only the nurse Isla to help her. She made our training bearable, even when the work was hard and tiresome, we were still loved. I smiled to myself. Another memory surfacing; the last time Alias and I were in the field behind the orphanage.

"Finally," Alias whispered from behind me, as if greeting an old friend, as if he had waited years, rather than days, to be here. We stared in silence at the place we discovered when we were only children, the only place we called home.

"I'll miss it," Alias said. "Will you?"

"Of course, I will," I said looking back at him. "But we'll

see it again soon enough," I said, attempting to calm our combined nerves.

I clicked the horse onward, quickly pushing into a run.

"Raya, wait!" Joy shouted, but her words were lost in the wind, I was home. I would not wait another second to see Alias.

I pounded against the red paint of the front entrance, the door already opening before I could knock twice. I fell into Matron Clara's arms.

"Raya!" Her voice was so familiar I almost erupted into tears. She smothered me with her large body. Opening my eyes I saw the others behind her. I smiled at them softly.

"Matron," I breathed, hearing Khol, Elian, and Joy finally creak up the porch stairs behind me.

"Is he here?" I asked, pulling back hastily.

"Who?"

"Alias." I looked into the kitchen and back out the front door. "He told me to meet him here, he sent a letter."

"He isn't with you? You left for the Sage Guard together, did you not?" I nodded, only half listening to her words.

"They got…" Khol stepped through the doorway cautiously. "They got separated." He smiled warmly, Clara returned the gesture.

"I'm sorry." Clara followed my gaze. "He hasn't been here." She lifted a hand to cup my face, but I pulled back.

He must already be at the field. I took off, out of the door, around the house and up the hill. Soon the tall grass began to tickle my thighs through my loose trousers. I could feel Khol, Joy, and Elian behind me.

He clearly isn't here.

She's acting crazy.

How can I make this better?

I reached into their minds easily, prying out thoughts

without them knowing. I sighed. Stopping under the tree we had often sat beneath.

Where was he? Why ask to meet me and not show up?

I had just about given up on my oldest friend, until footsteps crunched behind me.

"Raya?" The familiarity of Alias's voice, mixed with the almost forgotten eastern continent accent almost brought tears to my eyes. I laughed to my feet and into his arms. Our embrace crushing.

"Where have you been?" I whispered, my arms still firmly wrapped around him.

"I guess I could ask you the same question." He smiled into my hair, before pulling me back to check my face. "I'm so sorry about Jala and the safehouse. I'm sorry I let them hurt you." I nodded.

"I told you we'd come back, I knew we would." I smiled and something odd flashed in his face, but it was gone before I could study it.

"How are you?" he asked, and we pulled apart softly.

"I'm okay. Really."

I looked back at Khol, he and the others were keeping their distance, giving us space to reunite. "You?"

"Fine." He smiled back.

It took me a moment to realize then neither of us had answered the first question. Where had he been? I couldn't tell him where I had been, it wasn't safe to tell him about The Circle, I would be putting thousands of lives at risk. He had figured out where I was, but he didn't yet know who I was protecting. I remember Elian's words.

Raya, he is a member of the Sage Guard, he knows you are a Sorcerer.

I steeled my breath.

"Where have you been?" I asked again. Alias's Adam's apple bobbed as he swallowed.

"Raya…" His voice caught in his throat. "Did you see Matron yet? She was so pleased to see me, I never really thought she liked me!" He laughed, the smiled not truly meeting his eyes.

But Matron Clara had not seen Alias. He had not stopped by to see her.

He was lying to me, why?

I thought back to my lessons with Khol, my training in The Temple. It felt like years ago, rather than a few weeks. I smiled.

"Yes, I saw her just a moment ago." My voice did not waver, his smiled slipped ever so slightly, not noticeable to anyone who didn't know him.

"Alias…" I walked toward him, resting a hand on his shoulder, and suddenly tears burned against my eyes and my heart began to sink.

"Why are you lying to me?" Once the words left my mouth, I knew they were the right thing to say. He glanced to Khol, Joy, and Elian, then over his shoulder, then back to me.

"What do you mean?" His words were rushed.

"Alias, I spent my whole life, almost twenty years, learning everything about you." A tear slipped from my eye. "I know when you're lying." I smiled softly. Alias looked over his shoulder again. Silver lining his eyes. He blinked and a tear fell from each eye. It felt like a punch in the gut.

Wrongness coated my entire body, my skin beginning to itch.

"Why am I here, Alias?" I asked, my voice breaking over his name.

"Raya," he whispered, shaking his head, reaching up to touch my face, and I stepped away.

"Alias," I repeated his name, softly. I could tell it was breaking his heart, whatever he was doing was breaking his heart.

He stepped back as thunder clapped overhead. It took me a moment to realize that I made it happen. Rain began to fall in small droplets, soon becoming big, fat ones.

"Something isn't right." I heard Khol's voice from across the field. "This is Raya's power," he whispered to the others as he moved toward me.

The rain soon soaked us and my hair plastered to my face, my scorch marks pulsing with power.

"Raya." Alias pushed his sopping hair from his face. "I'm sorry."

The air left my lungs. Fear now replacing the blood in my body.

"Why?" I forced myself to ask.

"I couldn't stop them," he stuttered. "And I had… I had to get you away, get you out." He rocked on the balls of his feet.

"I convinced them we needed you alive, but the others… I'm sorry, I'm so sorry." Tears fell fast and fat down his face.

"Alias," my voice cracked.

"What did you do?" Panic blossomed under my skin as Khol and the others arrived at my side.

"They're the enemy… but you're not like them, you're not a, a…"

"A Sorcerer?" I finished for him. He nodded solemnly.

"What did you do?" I repeated the question, and Khol tensed beside me. Wind thrashed against us, rain pelted us, but I felt none of it. Lightning struck only feet away from me, but I did flinch. I closed my eyes. Dipping into Alias's brain.

"Did you find her?" Captain Jala asked. I was seeing through Alias's eyes. *I felt him nod.*

"Good job." Captain Jala stood next to a giant metal contraption.

"Pass the coordinates onto Regiment 4 and we'll finish this. We don't need another outbreak of witches," she sneered.

"Sorcerers," Alias corrected her. She shrugged nonchalantly.

"Get the coordinates, drop the firebombs and we can wipe our hands of this whole ordeal."

I was sucked from his mind. A sweat breaking out on my back.

"Alias," I sobbed.

"What?" Elian asked. "What is it?"

I choked on another sob.

"They're dropping firebombs," my lip quivered as I spoke.

"What's a firebomb?" Joy asked at the same time as Elian said,

"Where? Where are they dropping it?" His voice became frantic, he already knew the answer.

"It's a Sorcerer made weapon," Khol muttered under his breath.

"They're dropping it on The Circle," I cried.

And Elian erupted in flames.

50

FLORENCE
GOODBYE

"The walls crumbled."

- FLORENCE

Sitting up with a start, I noticed Conrad looming above me, a fierce grin splitting his face. I spat a mouthful of blood onto the concrete ground.

"Cute." I grinned back, getting to my feet quickly.

"We fight fair at The Temple." Conrad began circling me as I spoke.

"The Temple is a lot of things, but fair isn't one of them," he sneered.

I rolled my eyes. Erin and Jodie were sparring with their partners, none of them in the same danger as me. Had they picked me out because of my history with The Temple? Did they think my staying here was all an elaborate plan to deceive them? I was glad Erin and Jodie were safe, but I couldn't help but think, why me?

Conrad feigned a punch, I flinched, feeling the

embarrassment flood through me when the others began to laugh.

"Scared?" Conrad was enjoying my embarrassment.

"Are you?" The ground began to rumble beneath our feet, small rocks falling from the ceiling.

"We said no powers!" Lucille called from the side of the make-shift ring.

"This isn't me!" I shouted over the sound of dirt turning over.

"Conrad?" she asked, he shook his head.

"Anyone?"

Silence met Lucille's words as the whole cavern began to shake, more and more rocks falling from above.

Erin and Jodie moved toward each other, determined to protect their sibling.

The truth rocketed through me.

If this wasn't Sorcerer magic, then we…

"We're under attack!" Lucille screamed. "CODE RED! GET ABOVE GROUND!" she shouted, her voice echoing loudly.

People began moving instantly, items dropped, conversations ended.

Moving toward the exit was the only thing to happen. People flooded from the network of tunnels. We ushered them toward the exit, people tripped up the stairs, their fellow Sorcerers lifting them back to their feet.

Several MindWonderers stopped large boulders of falling ceiling from crushing members of The Circle.

A screamed bounced around my skull, I turned and saw it happen. A boulder had fallen next to Erin and Jodie, crushing their sparring partners. The sisters glanced to me, nodded, and headed for the exit.

But more and more people were crushed and buried.

It was a massacre.

Hundreds flooded out of the exit.

But so many did not.

"Florence! You need to leave. Now," Lucille shouted over the falling stone. Heat began to fill the space, sweat licked my back. More and more people ran for the exit.

Another shout rang through the space. This one brought coldness with it, it touched every part of my body. My eyes searched the space as Lucille called out to me again, but I couldn't leave.

I knew Erin and Jodie had made it out safely, I knew they were already in the tunnel or possibly even in the fresh air.

A tunnel to my right collapsed, screams of the dying making the hairs on my arms stand on end.

They were too young, too young for such a disgusting death.

Cowards. The Sage Guard were cowards. Killing without even showing their faces.

Fire leaked into the stones around me, I didn't have long before the whole ceiling would collapse. The shouting sounded again, and I followed it, finding Jameson, shoving against a rock.

"Stop, Jameson, please. Just go."

It was Rafael. My breath choked me.

His legs were trapped beneath a huge boulder, completely crushed. My whole body froze. I couldn't move, I couldn't think. I couldn't breathe. A cough forced its way through my throat.

Jameson pushed and pushed at the huge rock, but it didn't budge.

No. No I wouldn't lose Rafael again, my sweet brother. He had only just got his life back; he had only just managed to break away from our wretched mother. I ran to his side, avoiding the blood staining his clothes. I heaved a breath, my lungs feeling as though they were filled with tiny shards of glass. Jameson tugged at the rock, pushing, and pulling until blood covered his hands and sweat dripped from his skin.

But the stone wouldn't move. I pushed at it with everything I had, trying to summon every last morsel of power I had within me to save my brother, to save Rafael.

The boulder wouldn't move, it wouldn't even budge.

A scream of frustration ripped from me as I punched the rock, and my knuckles crumpled against it.

I began to sob as the world fell apart around me, and I couldn't do anything to stop it.

Realization began to attack my heart and my breathing hitched.

"Hey," Rafael whispered. I looked down, and his eyes were already coated in a film of white. A drop of blood leaked out of the side of his mouth.

"No." I shook my head, pushing at the rock again, Jameson had stopped and laid down beside Raf.

Another tunnel collapsed, more screams echoing through the small space.

"Flo," Raf rasped, "Don't waste my last minutes by ignoring me." My eyes snapped to him instantly.

"I am not afraid." The words left his mouth softly and tears fell from his eyes. Running a hand through his soft, brown hair. I smiled weakly.

"You're not afraid?" I repeated back, my tears tasting salty on my tongue.

"I got to see the sky again, I got to breath fresh air," he choked softly. "I got to see you and Khol again, how could I be afraid? How could I be angry?" Despite his words, fear bloomed in his eyes.

"You need to go," he rasped, and I shook my head. He smiled.

"You need to go and tell Khol what happened to me." More tears leaked from his eyes, and he reached up with a weak hand and touched my cheek.

"You need to tell him I am gone, but that I love him so very much." He stared at me. "I love you so much, little sister." He smiled.

"I don't want you to go," I cried.

"I don't want to go either," he said quietly, Jameson still laid beside him. The room shook again.

"I wish I could've met our sister," his breath caught in his throat. "Will you tell her about me?" His voice was rushed and I nodded softly.

"I'll see you again, sister, in the next life. I'll find you again." His hand fell from my cheek and his face turned to Jameson.

He kissed him softly, trying to convey every emotion he had ever had, and every one wouldn't get the chance to have. Jameson wrapped his arms around Raf and sobbed quietly.

"My love, you must go," he said as rocks began falling close to us.

"I won't go without you," Jameson sobbed. Raf pulled back, starring at his love that no one knew about.

"You will never be without me." He smiled and laid his head back on the ground.

And then, moments later, my brother died in his beloved's arms.

51

RAYA

GODDESS DIVINE

"What did we have left?"

- RAYA.

Alias was thrown back against the tree we had spent most of our youth climbing. Elian's fire charring the trunk. Khol pulled him back, his hands damping down the fire that bloomed everywhere.

"Give it back!" Elian roared. "He has killed them! He has ruined my home and murdered my family. And now you defend him?" He turned to me. My body was numb and my chest aching. Joy mirrored my face and body language as the rain continued to fall around us.

Everyone Joy and Elian held dear had been in the cavern. Had they survived? Had anyone?

My body moved and I didn't know I had punched Alias until blood trickled from my knuckles.

"Thousands of people lived in the cavern!" I shouted,

thunder and lightning brewing at an accelerated pace. Alias staggered to his feet, blood dripping from his nose.

"*Sorcerers,*" he corrected me. I punched him again, a bruise already forming beneath his eye.

"They are people!" I turned to Joy, still slack and not moving, and then back to Alias.

"And you have murdered them." I turned from him, unable to deal with the betrayal, while my friends could be dying.

"We need to go, now," I motioned to the group.

"What's the point?" Joy finally spoke. "The firebombs have been dropped; the damage is done."

"There could be survivors," I countered.

"Do you hear yourself, Raya?" She narrowed her eyes. "*There could be survivors*?" She scoffed.

"He lured you here," she shouted, pointing at Alias, "because he knew! He knew you were the only one who would protect them! He knew that without you, this would happen!" She began to pace. "He doesn't care about you, he only cares about destroying Sorcerers." She stormed toward him, the rain seeming to part for her. "There were humans in the cavern, just like you and me," she spoke softly, her anger thrumming just beneath the surface. She walked back to me and nodded.

"We need to g—" she began but never finished, she disappeared.

Fear tugged at me as I turned in a circle fiercely. But she was gone, blown away with the wind.

"Where…?" Khol's word trailed off.

And then heavy breathing erupted from behind me and there she stood.

I stared at her, and she stared at me.

"Did she just jump?" Khol asked, moving forward.

Joy wobbled on her feet; Elian moved to steady her.

"I was near the cavern, The Circle," she heaved a breath. "I was thinking about it and suddenly I was there."

We all stood in shock.

"She jumped," Khol murmured. "But I've never known a Jumper to travel that far." He walked toward her, inspecting her from a distance.

"What did it look like?" Elian asked, almost scared to hear the answer. Joy trembled slightly, her lower lip quivering.

"It had collapsed completely," she began. "But there are survivors, and lots of them. They must've got out before the brunt of the explosions." She glanced up. "I wasn't close enough to see who had survived and who…" she stopped herself.

The rain slowed as I thought of the survivors. Elian seemed to ease slightly, but Joy shook softly.

"Do you think you can travel back?" Khol asked, still pacing around us, Joy nodded weakly. "Can you take us with you?"

I glanced up at Khol, my brows furrowing.

"It'll take us days to get back and by then there could be another attack, or the group will begin to scatter. We need to get to them as soon as possible. Before it's too late," he stated and Joy nodded, stronger now.

"I can do it." She stood firmly, no longer resting on Elian.

As she prepared to jump again, I turned to Alias. He stood watching us.

"I no longer recognize you," I spat. "You are a disgrace to Matron's family." Tears of anger bloomed in my eyes. "And I never, ever want you see your cowardly face again." He moved toward me; his hand extended.

"If you touch me one more time," I whispered between

gritted teeth. "I will kill you where you stand." My breathing was labored. I was so furious with the man that stood before me, but I mourned the boy I once knew. I mourned our friendship and our past together. The ride to The Foothills when we had our futures ahead of us.

Futures that will now never come to pass.

"Now go," my voice was cold. "Before I change my mind and kill you now."

Alias's eyes lingered on mine, but eventually turned and left.

Like the coward he was.

I turned to Khol, burying my head in his shoulder, his hands rubbing my back in small circles. I felt selfish for being soothed when so many people had lost their lives today.

"I'm ready," Joy looked up from her hands, a glow radiating from her skin. I nodded.

We decided she would ferry me first, and then Elian and then Khol.

"Be safe," Khol whispered, before planting a quick kiss on my lips. My hands joined with Joy's.

And then we disappeared.

Smoke clouded my lungs as we arrived around half a mile north of the entrance to The Circle. Or rather, what used to be the entrance to The Circle.

Joy wavered ever so slightly, sweat beading on her forehead.

"Are you sure you can do that again?" I asked, stepping from her grasp. I was met with a nod.

"Go," she rasped as she vanished with the breeze.

Sprinting toward the carnage, I couldn't help but pray to every Goddess that my friends had made it out alive. I pumped my arms, pushing my legs faster and harder than I ever had before. The clouds of smoke became thicker and thicker, until I could barely see my hand in front of my face. SkyChangers worked hastily to clear the air, but the smoke kept bellowing like dragons' breath.

I slowed at the first sign of life, a group of Circle members huddled together, blood dripping from various cuts and wounds. Healers ran from group to group attempting to fix the damage.

Finally, the air started to clear.

And then I saw the real destruction. The sheer massacre of land and life.

Bodies were strewn across the charred grass, some covered in white sheets, others not. I noticed Circle members scrambling their way back into the half collapsed underground cavern.

It took me a while to realize why they were making the journey.

But when I saw the lifeless girl held in another's arms, I knew they were collecting bodies. They wouldn't leave their family behind, not even if their family had not survived.

Bodies kept piling up, one after another and all I could do was watch.

I had all this power. But no power to reverse death, no power to ease grief. I jogged further into the chaos. Screams of the injured piercing my skull. My stomach plummeted as I kept moving without finding my friends. Were they were being carried from the rocks and rubble? Were they laid lifelessly in a stranger's arms?

A sob built inside my chest, tightness wrapping around me like a rope.

The hundreds of voices and screams around me blurred into a blank sound. My knees wobbled, threatening to drop me.

How had everything got so awful, so quickly? Only a few

months ago I was lying in a field covered in wildflowers, my best friend beside me.

And now?

I had just scorched that same field, ripped it apart like it was a scorned love letter. My best friend now dead to me.

My friends now possibly… dead.

"Raya!" a familiar voice shouted, and I locked gazes with Erin. Bloody and scared and dusty but very much alive.

"Erin!" I shouted back without thinking, running toward her, and crushing her into an embrace. A hiccup escaped my mouth and suddenly I was sobbing. Jodie hobbled toward us, her injured leg making her slower than her sister.

"Is she alright?"

Erin nodded. "She caught her leg on a shard of rock." I embraced her sister.

"How did you get here so fast? Where is Joy?" Jodie asked by way of greeting.

I told them swiftly, not bothering to include every little detail.

"Where are the others?" I asked once my story had ended. A shadow crossed the girls' faces, a loose tear slipped from Erin's eye.

"We don't know," she tried to get her words out, but they wouldn't move passed her lips.

"We escaped before the building collapsed on itself," Jodie finished.

Pressure, hard and heavy, fell on top of me.

I was the reason this had happened. I may not have pulled the trigger, but I killed these people. I killed my friends.

And suddenly I was seven years old, standing in the field of corpses, watching my mother die at my feet. I was the fire in the huts, the sword in the flesh, and the scream in their lungs. I was everywhere. A memory surfaced.

"They will come for her tonight," a male voice rung out, it was warm and soft and comforting. "We must leave, Raya."

Warmth filled my veins, remembering that I had been named after my mother, the leader of our village, of the Sorcerers in our village.

"We cannot leave the others," a female voice countered, it was my mother's. I knew it as clearly as I knew the sun rose in the day and the moon rose in the night. "They will come tonight whether we leave or stay, and I will not leave my people behind!"

"Raya! Listen to yourself, you're willing to sacrifice this..." my father had motioned between the two of them and then the rest of our home, "you're willing to sacrifice our daughter, for your people?" His voice became pleading. Silence followed his last words, the last words I would hear my father say. He left at my mother's silence, he would be killed in battle only hours later. As would my mother and everyone I had ever loved.

I was pulled back to reality. Erin and Jodie stared at me, their eyes wide as saucers.

"They're alive!" Jodie's voice boomed across the field, every head turned, hoping it was a loved one or friend.

Florence stumbled from the dusty wreckage, Jameson leaning heavily against her. Tears parted the dust and dirt on their cheeks as other Sorcerers helped them to safety.

I knew in that moment.

I knew that we had not all survived.

EPILOGUE
JOY

"They were stronger than us, and we knew it."

- JOY

From the look on Florence's face, I knew death now lived inside of her. When Khol and I finally joined the others, she was waiting for him, Raf's body lying limp in her arms, his head rested on her knees. They had found his body in the wreckage, SkyChangers, EarthShakers and MindWonderers working in unison to return each body home.

It was the least they deserved.

Two hundred dead and more injured.

"He told me," Florence choked on a sob, she was drowning in her tears, in her grief and mourning. "He told me to tell you, he loves you. He will always love you and he will always be with us," Florence spluttered; Rafael's final wish fulfilled.

Jameson sat beside Raf's body, his hand constantly gently

brushing through Raf's hair. Tears fell, never stopping, not even when he smiled briefly when I returned.

"I loved him," he whispered when I sat beside him. I nodded.

"I know," was all I managed to say. "I was waiting for you to tell me." I smiled through my tears. I had known Jameson loved Rafael since the moment I saw them together. I was so excited to share their future together, whenever they were ready to share it.

They would never have it now; their future was now buried under tons of rubble.

Khol had fallen to his knees before his brother's body.

"Don't leave us again," he rasped, his voice hoarse from crying. "I can't do this without you." Raya sobbed silently behind him; she lit a fire when day turned into night. Never once asking Khol and Florence to leave their brother's side.

We stayed together as the smoke cleared and The Circle scattered.

They were going to various hideouts and safe houses, Elian had explained. But he stayed with us. He burdened some of the grief we felt, he stood strong, helping us to stay upright.

As though her tears had finally dried, Florence looked up at me and smiled weakly.

"What do we do now?" she whispered, her brother's body cooling beneath her hands.

"I don't know," I whispered back. Our group remained quiet. The once busy forest, now only populated with our group. The eight of us still in the places we had met in earlier in the day. I passed a tin of water around to each person.

"What *do* we do now?" I looked to Raya this time, my voice louder for everyone to hear. "What do we do?" Although I was asking for the entire group, I hoped Raya understood what I truly wanted to know. What would we do now? Raya and me. We were a prophesied pair and yet all we had done was watch as chaos unfolded around us. We hadn't been able to save Rafael, or any of the hundreds of people that had perished that day.

How could we be their leaders? Their Celestial Queens?

Looking at each of us in turn, Raya stood from her sitting position, nodding to herself.

"I don't know what we do now, I don't know how we're going to stop the humans or The Temple or the Sage Guard. I don't know how to protect us." Her words were soft but mighty as she summoned a flame in her hand and watched it burn.

"But…" her voice picked up and blood pumped through my veins quickly, my heart hammered, and my new power sang. "I know that we are the grandchildren of the Sorcerers they could not burn." A lightning bolt stuck the earth behind Raya.

"And I know one more thing." She looked at us each in turn, her gaze snagging on Rafael for a moment longer.

"We Will Not Burn."

The adventure continues…
Get ready!

ACKNOWLEDGMENTS

First and foremost, I'd like to thank my parents… All four of you.

Dad and Alex, Mum, and Paul. This book would not have come to be without your encouragement, love and understanding. Thank you for always listening to me when I talk about books and encouraging me to 'do what I love', not many people get that, so thank you, thank you, thank you.

I would also like to take a moment to thank my two best friends, Erin and Jodie. Thank you for listening to me complain about writer's block and for helping me create my two favorite characters. This book is my love letter to female friendship, and you two are my biggest inspirations. Just like they did for Joy, you two brought my back to life when I was going through the toughest time. Thank you.

I want to thank all the women that came before me, the women that populate the stories we know and the women whose stories have been lost to time. All these women made it possible for me to write this book, to do something that sets my soul on fire. It's so important for us to take a moment to stop and look back at how far we've come.

A big thank you goes to Claire Monaghan, thank you for all your wisdom and support through this process. As a first-time writer this is so very daunting, but you have made this experience so much more enjoyable. Thank you.

This then leads me onto Hudson Indie Ink, thank you for

taking an interest in my story and the characters that inhabit it, you've changed my life!

Thank you especially to Claire Boyle and Libby Blandford for all your guidance and for answering my hundreds of questions about publishing. Thank you also to Catherine Sutton for designing this truly beautiful cover, you've brought my world to life!

Also, a huge thank you to Sarah for correcting all my spelling mistakes and gently letting me know when my writing made no sense at all.

And most all, thank you to the readers. This has been my dream for as long as I can remember, and I can't believe it's happening.

I hope you love my characters as much as I do.

ABOUT THE AUTHOR

Georgia Seren Mills received her undergrad degree in English and Drama in 2022, and later received her post graduate certificate in education in 2023.

Georgia currently lives in Abu Dhabi, where she is a primary school teacher. She spends her time writing, reading, rewatching Wes Anderson movies, and listening to Taylor Swift's Folklore album on repeat.

Georgia plans to keep writing until the stories in her head become real…You can follow along with her journey

Printed in Great Britain
by Amazon

52752598R00229